Traun

Sharilyn Skye

Copyright:

This novel is a work of fiction. All the names, characters, events, and incidents in this book are the product of the author's imagination. The businesses and places in this book were changed to meet the author's needs or are fictitious. Any resemblance to actual persons, living or dead, situations, places, hospitals, or actual events is purely coincidental. No portion of this book can be copied, distributed, or used without the publisher's consent.

#Countryroads

To Molly, whose story is nothing like this one and who is the antithesis of Elle Conroy. You are a beacon in the sea of darkness for more people than you know. And to Alex, who watches her shine from the stars.

And to FERNs everywhere. I see you, you crazy bitches

How can you just leave me standing?
Alone in a world that's so cold?
~Prince and The Revolution

I never meant to cause you any sorrow.
I never meant to cause you any pain.
~Prince and The Revolution

Glossary of medical terms:

Hospitals use different nomenclature to categorize traumas. Medical terminology is not standardized and may vary throughout the country based on location or institutional preference.

FERN: Fucking ER nurse

Priority One trauma (P1): For the purposes of this book, a P1 is the highest level of trauma. They are usually unstable or have to potential to become unstable and have a higher probability of death or severe disability. P1s must meet certain criteria to be labeled as such, including, for example, low blood, mechanism of injury, or whether or not they are intubated.

Priority Two trauma (P2): Injuries are significant enough to rate a trauma page. The trauma page gets the trauma response team to the bedside. Injuries could range from broken bones, internal bleeding, lacerations, or other usually non-life-threatening injuries. With that being said, a P2 can turn into a P1 or traumatic arrest in a literal heartbeat.

Traumatic Arrest: When a person's heart stops due to physical trauma. Sometimes these people can be fixed if the reason their heart stopped is corrected. For example, a chest tube can reopen the lung and allow the heart to beat on its own.

ET Tube: A tube placed into the patient's trachea so that their breathing can be controlled by a machine.

Ventilator: the machine that controls breathing and delivers oxygen to the lungs. Also known as life support.

Ambu-bag: a device that, when squeezed by hand, delivers oxygen to the lungs manually.

ECMO: Extracorporeal Membrane Oxygenation. This is a machine that pumps blood outside of the body and oxygenates it before putting it back in. Used when the heart and lungs are not working. Also known as a "heart-lung machine." Note: These people are very sick, and the long-term outcomes, if ECMO is needed, are not usually good.

IO: A needle drilled into a large bone such as the humerus or tibia with a special tool. An IO is used when an IV can't be obtained and is recommended for quick access to give drugs and fluids.

Non-accidental trauma: A term used with children and relates to abuse. Literally, the trauma was caused on purpose.

MVC: Motor vehicle accident (car wreck).

MCC: Motorcycle collision.

BCC: Bicycle collision.

GCS: Abbreviation for Glasgow Coma Scale. GCS measures neurological status based on criteria where 15 is perfect. A lower number is bad, and a three is the worst you can get and still be technically alive.

STEMI: ST-segment elevation MI is a serious type of heart attack usually caused by a blockage of one of the large vessels. It requires immediate intervention, or it will lead to death.

RSI: Drugs given rapidly to sedate and paralyze a person for intubation.

Forward:

The hospital in this novel could be anywhere. Accidents like the ones detailed in this book happen all the time, every day. None of the incidents in this book are real, although they could be. They are all the product of statistics, my imagination, and my imagination alone. Any resemblance to real people or real situations is coincidental and unintended. The other part of this novel that is a product of my imagination is the response Elle's friends have to her problem with drug diversion. I don't know a single nurse, doctor, clinical associate, EMS provider, or tech that would try and cover up for a peer struggling in the way Elle does. Also, in light of recent events, it would be incredibly difficult to obtain any type of medication the way Elle does as most institutions have tightened their process for medication removal. Most state nursing boards have very good recovery programs for nurses that find themselves in her situation, but just like any novel, the premise of this one is: What If?

What is real are the raw, gritty personalities and the lengths healthcare workers will go to cope with the devastation they see daily. There is nothing fictional about that.

Prologue

A dozen pagers sounded as I walked into the Emergency department for shift change, and my heart thrilled at the sound of it, beating like a war drum in my chest. The harshness of different tones meant another hour, another trauma, or ten, and I never grew tired of the response my body had to those pagers going off. My heart sped, my fingers tingled, and my eyes lit up with excitement. My breath caught in my throat, and the immediate adrenaline spike was a high I knew I'd never tire of. The smile on my face widened, reaching all the way to my eyes.

After sixteen years, I still loved the rush of a good trauma. It's a sickness; it really is. It's not that I wanted anyone to get hurt, but I didn't want to miss it when they did. Today was no exception. I was good at this, one of the best, if I was honest, and I usually was. Some nurses will lie for good reasons, thinking that they provide a sense of comfort in doing so, but I didn't operate that way. Honesty delivered with compassion provides the ultimate comfort, which is the mantra I lived by. Most Emergency nurses did. It's part of the culture embedded deep within those that are always ready and waiting to save or lose people at a moment's notice because trauma is like a coin toss, sometimes you win, and sometimes you lose.

A trauma nurse lives for those good saves when chest

tubes, rapid infusers, blood coolers, a cracked chest, and seven minutes or less to the CT scanner save lives, and as the symphony of different pager tones sounded, I grinned harder, practically dancing into the deceptively empty trauma bays, hoping they were set up and ready.

"What's coming, Doc-Cin?" I turned to ask the nearest trauma resident.

Dr. Cindy Branch was one of our third years and, all in all, a nice girl and a decent doctor. She wasn't overly cocky or difficult to deal with, making her a staff favorite. She listened to nurses when not everyone did, and that made her better because we all helped her out if she needed it. We called her Doc-Cin, which she thought was a cute play of words on her name, but we actually called her that because she looked quite a lot like an adorable dachshund puppy. It wasn't a bad thing, but we didn't tell her regardless, there's honesty, and then there's mean. None of us were mean-spirited at heart.

"Priority One trauma, someone took a motorcycle to a car fight."

"Yeah, that never works out," I half groaned, and half laughed. "Ugh, poor soul. Well, let's do it!"

Chapter 1

Breathing hard, I rolled over, snuggled under the soft down comforter, and reached for Keith before jarring awake. I realized for the millionth time that he was gone. And for the millionth time, I grabbed his pillow and fought to find his scent on it, sniffing so hard that I felt the beginnings of a headache long before I gave up trying to find a lingering piece of my husband.

The sob started before I could cut it off, as it always did. Keith was gone, and he was never coming back. Fighting through the hot tears on my lashes, I got up and stumbled into the shower. Turning it on full hot, I stepped in, praying the heat would burn the memories away. Only memories don't work like that.

Memories are insidious things that follow wherever you go. Like ivy on a foundation, the roots burrow deep until the blocks crack and crumble, and whenever you feel you can't look at them anymore, you find that you can't look away from them either. I often wonder if they follow you in death, and that fear makes me put one foot in front of the other and fight through another day, but it's often the only thing.

If my memories follow me to the afterlife, I won't survive it either.

Standing outside the employee entrance to the Emergency Department, I gathered myself. I'd been off for six weeks, and I'd been ready to come back to the only job I'd known as an adult and one of the few things I loved, or so I thought. Still, even from behind the safety of closed doors, I jumped at the muted noise of the pagers sounding and knew I'd been wrong.

I shuddered as pure fear swept through me, and my knees began to buckle. My heart raced in my chest, my breathing became shallow and quick, and I grabbed at the wall. My head swam as I fought to stay upright, and my vision narrowed while sweat beaded on my forehead, reminding me that there are some things that you can't come back from. How could I ever come back here? What was I thinking?

I suppose I thought that life had to go on, just like my employer-mandated therapist said it did. Emergency nursing was all I knew, and I had to come back to it eventually. You can't claim disability from a broken heart, or I would've tried. I could've done something else, but the fear of the unknown made me cling to what I knew best. My brain wasn't functioning, and it would be hard to train it in new ways. That's what I told myself as I tried to steady the tremor in my hand.

As I looked through the glass in the double doors, I saw nurses and residents, who were all my friends and colleagues, rushing to the bays to set up for whatever disaster was about to roll in right in time for shift change, just like Murphy's Law says it will. Taking a deep breath, I swiped my badge through the reader and stepped inside.

Immediately the sounds and smells of the Emergency Department hit me. Like a slap in the face, I was assaulted by the triple beeping of an ignored cardiac monitor, the smell of a drunk sleeping it off in the hallway, and the shouts from nurses and doctors trying to get the attention of each other over the noise. This place had once been as familiar as my face in the mirror, but now I didn't recognize it either, and it certainly didn't feel like the home I'd thought it would.

I froze where I stood, unable to make myself take another step toward the nurses' station, yet unable to turn and run. A few heads turned to me, and those people faltered before they hurried away. What do you say? How do you greet someone who lost everything? What do you say in the face of utter devastation?

I used to know. I used to be good at giving comfort with honest words, but I knew now that even honesty is a lie.

"Sixteen gauge in the left AC. Labs drawn."

"Sixteen in the right and warm normal saline up at wide open, the first unit of blood's up on the level one infuser."

"We have bilateral hemotympany, obvious skull, and cervical spine deformities. Positive step-offs. Obvious

deformities to bilateral femurs. Elle, get out of here."

"Elle!"

"Elle?"

"Ellie-Bo. Welcome back, sweetie. How are you holding up?"

I snapped from the scene I lived every night when I closed my eyes, and every day they were open to find one of the day shift charge nurses, Pam, had walked from the orthopedic supply room and caught my cold, damp hand in her warm one.

"How are you, really?" she asked. Pam Reed and I weren't friends, not even in the work sense. We had worked together for my entire sixteen years in this place, but we were cordial at best.

We deeply respected the skills the other possessed, and at any given time, one of us would be in charge of the department, and the other would be in the bays, but we were never really friends.

Pam used to run a rig with EMS and had balls bigger than any man I'd ever known, and she wasn't afraid to let you know it, either. She was a viper, but the ED ran like a clock when she was in charge. Still, she never called me anything but my given name, Elle or Conroy. Conroy was my maiden name, and I'd been known for it long before I met and married Keith Frazier. The 'Ellie-Bo' nickname coming from her and calling me sweetie didn't ring true, but I didn't call her on it; it was hard for my co-workers too. I understood that.

"I'm not sure, Pam. Okay, I guess."

"You could've taken more time."

"I know, but I'm not doing anything at home except dwelling." I looked away from her, scanning the people around me and taking note of the uncertainty on their faces. I didn't judge them for it because I felt the same way.

"Right, well, I put you on the non-E side in pod one. Okay?" she said, checking the time on her smartwatch before walking away.

My nerves settled a bit when I heard that like I might make it through the day, and I hoped it was true as I headed deeper into the heart of the place. Maybe the Trauma Gods would be kind, and I wouldn't get pulled into their bullshit.

The emergency department was split into two sides: the emergent side, which included the adult and children's trauma bays, plus all of the stroke and STEMI rooms. These were set up and used for the genuinely emergent cases that came in, usually by EMS or helicopter. Those rooms were larger and could handle any variety of disaster thrown into them.

The largest rooms could transform into operating rooms in the direst of situations. It was rarely done, but we'd once had a trauma so bad that we'd had to deliver a baby by C-section or risk losing it. The mother died, but the baby had been healthy. Still, the surgeons preferred to go to the main OR, but they would work in the ED if forced. The cardiac arrests went into those rooms too, if possible, but many an arrest had been run in the hallways on the busiest of days.

The other side of the department was theoretically reserved for the nonemergent stuff that is the bulk of what the ED sees daily. Colds, fevers, yeast infections, drunks, belly pains, and psychiatric evaluations were placed in those rooms. They were smaller and set up differently, but I'd run many a cardiac arrest on the noncritical side of the place, too. It wasn't ideal, but emergencies never are. Sometimes, a few nonemergent cases made it into the bays because it all depended on the flow of patients, and in the end, we did what we had to to make it all work.

Pod One was assured to be nothing but pelvic exams, psychiatric evaluations, and dental problems, seeing as how there were no cardiac monitors in those rooms. It also had the highest number of rooms per nurse, guaranteeing that I would be busy and hopefully unable to pay any attention to the department's emergent side.

Before coming in, I told myself I could do it, and I'd spent days gearing up to work. It was Sunday, and I had picked this day to come back because usually, they weren't that bad. I mean, you never know, but statistics were on my side. There'd been no sporting events or concerts the night before, and although I didn't want to be here, I'd planned it as best I could.

Pam took my elbow and walked me the last few steps before I could pull my arm back and make the rest of the trip on my own. I went past the trauma bays, ignoring the staff rushing to get ready for the shift's first trauma. Keeping my focus on the big flat screen that kept electronic tabs on every patient in the department, I ignored everything else. Pod One was already full, and I was glad for that.

I could do this.

I got report from some poor, overwhelmed floor nurse pulled from her unit to help. She was so cute with her little notepad containing an official label for every patient with a short, handwritten note next to it. She gave me details like no ED nurse ever would, and I fought to appreciate it. Our report usually sounded something like: "Room one is a drunk. Room two is a belly pain with an IV; labs were sent. Room three is suicidal and waiting on psych."

We give short, sweet, and to the point reports that usually take less than five minutes for an entire pod. Unlike the floor nurses, who talked about head-to-toe assessments and care plans, we keep it to the immediate problem and plan for disposition. In other words, we don't really care what your lungs sound like if you are sleeping it off from a frat party. Unless, of course, you were found drowning in your own vomit. Then we might worry about your lungs, at least a little anyway. We called it the down and dirty, and no other nurse liked EDstyle reports but our own.

I listened through half an hour of her report on my six patients, trying to be nice and maintain at least half of a fake smile, but the smell of fresh coffee kept pulling my attention away from her. Finally, I threw my hands up.

"Cool, cool. Good! Great job, I've got it from here," I said, walking away from her in mid-lecture about my drunk's last bowel movement so that I could get a cup.

She rose to leave, shaking her head and muttering something about damn FERNs that made me smile in a real way.

FERN was the not so affectionate term some of the floor nurses had given the ED nurses years ago that had stood the test of time. It stood for Fucking ER Nurse, and we loved it, adopting and wearing it like a badge of honor on our sleeves.

To call your work friend a FERN was a high compliment, and I'm sure the staff upstairs still scratched their heads as to how their disparaging comments turned into our love language.

ED nurses are a different animal, to be sure. To do what we do day in and day out, see all the horrible things we see, well, the chaplains say we are special, but I say we are a little crazy.

So, we make up for it by being brash pranksters with loud filthy mouths and no sense of personal space or shame. We sexually harass any and all of our peers at will and talk about any and everything at the nurse's station, often to the embarrassment of our younger, newer team members. We emblazon travel mugs and tee shirts with the FERN logo and wear them proudly.

Someday, if the newer nurses lasted, they would understand. They would understand why we weren't ashamed and were maybe a little bit proud to be called a fucking ER nurse. It's the hardest job you'll ever love but also the one discipline you might not last long in, so you cling to it while you can.

I grabbed my computer on wheels and tucked into the laundry alcove of pod one. Stealing a chair from the nurse's station, I made myself an office where I could keep my head down and mind away from the rest of the place.

The alcove was darker than the hall. With no light source, it relied on lighting from the hallway and was a little more peaceful because of it. I wasn't the only nurse who'd made this an office, and it was funny to see that someone had hung paper bats on the ceiling where they couldn't be seen from the hall.

The bat cave.

That added a little lightness to the moment that I was grateful for. You had to find humor in everything in a place like this, or it isn't sustainable. I steadied my breathing and closed my eyes for a moment to let it all wash over me.

Pod One was fast-paced in the morning and tended to log jam in the afternoon, but if I were lucky, I would stay plenty busy enough to avoid everyone, and time would fly.

Logging into the computer, I signed onto the tracking board and began catching up on nurses' notes in the relative quiet of my makeshift office.

"36-year-old male, helmeted MCC, head-on with a car at highway speeds. BP 60 palp, large bore IV infusing, intubated on scene with an 8-oh ET tube, heart rate 140's with peripheral pulses not palpable."

"Hey, Elle, are you awake in there?"

"Yeah, sure," I said, swinging my gaze up to meet Dr. Ross's.

"I, uh, I'm sorry you had to come back to this hell hole," he said, his eyes searching my face and not liking what they saw. I didn't judge him either because I knew what I looked like.

"Yeah, me too, thanks. What can I do for you?" I asked, steering the conversation away from anything personal.

"I need another alcohol level on the drunk guy. Maybe we can get him out of here. I'll put in the order. And it's good to see you back, even if it isn't where you should be." He lingered as if to talk, the look on his face sad and unsure. Daniel Ross and I had a long history, and I didn't want to look too closely at it. He was my best friend and had been for a long time, but I was struggling today, and the slightest kindness could make me lose it.

"Got it." I hopped up, not wanting any part of the help he

would offer, and went to draw the blood.

Chapter 2

As promised, the morning went fast, and, for the most part, I was left alone in my pod. Surprised at seeing my name on the staffing boards, some people would stop by and want to visit or talk. Some of them were even friends, but others were just curious. I neatly avoided them all by staying in my rooms and keeping up with orders much faster than I usually would. If there was any correlation between the number of bagged lunches handed out, my patient satisfaction scores would be through the roof. I was doing well keeping my mind off things, which was the goal. Just get through today, one step at a time, and until then, it wasn't going too badly.

"What is Elle doing in Pod One, Pam?" I felt Parker's voice sail across the nurse's station and cut through my gut like a knife. I sank in my seat, using the computer as a shield. Maybe if she couldn't see me, it would help, though I knew that wasn't true.

Melinda Parker was the nursing director for the emergency department, and she was not known for her tact or way with words. She was approximately one hundred and ten years old and built like a grey-haired Russian tank. Pam was one tough bitch, but Parker made her look like a soft cuddly puppy. It was Sunday, and she shouldn't be working. She should be home, cleaning her broomstick and sharpening her claws; I had counted on that. That had been the biggest part of my plan, and I couldn't believe she was here messing it all up.

"Parker, it's her first day back. She needs to get adjusted," Pam said, her voice lowered so that not everyone within ten miles could hear it, unlike Parker.

"Like hell she does; get her in the bays at three when the three to eleven crew comes in. It's a freaking waste to have her over there passing ice all day. One of you needs to always be in the bays, and since you're in charge, get her ass in there."

"Everyone needs a break, Parker. All the nurses cycle through the non-E side, and you know that," Pam argued, and I appreciated her at that moment more than I ever had. She was going to bat for me against a steel wall, but she was trying when no one else would have been brave enough to go against the old tank.

"Break time's over, Pam. She goes into the bays at three." I felt her walk away like a dark shadow passing over on a sunny day, and I fought the urge to cry.

I sat, not breathing. I wasn't ready. I wasn't ever going to be ready, but I certainly wasn't ready yet. Cold sweat broke out on my back, and my hands began to shake as the uneasy feeling in my stomach increased.

Many ED nurses at a level one trauma center never made it into the bays. There's nothing wrong with starting IVs in secondary triage or taking care of belly pains your entire career. Why couldn't I be one of them? At least for now. It didn't mean you were anything less, and I envied them more than I ever had.

Feeling sick, I got up and slipped unseen into the locker room at the end of the hall before going into the back bathroom, locking the door behind me. I fought the urge to vomit into the sink. Maybe I could sign out early; being sick certainly wasn't a stretch. My heart beat erratically in my chest, and I felt faint. Sweat ran down my back into the crack of my ass, soaking my underwear. I pulled my hair into a long black ponytail and ran cold water to splash on my face, refusing to look up.

Lately, I have avoided mirrors at all costs. I knew that the dark eyes set against the unhealthy, crisp-white linen of my skin would look empty, haunted, and scared if I looked into them. I was all those things, and I didn't think seeing proof of that would make me better. I hated to catch my reflection; it reminded me of how much I'd lost and the person I'd been. I didn't recognize myself anymore.

Sitting on the toilet, I put my head between my knees and tried to breathe as I stared at my royal blue pants legs. My dizziness increased, and my heart skipped beats in my chest. What had made me think I could ever come back? I should have gone to Labor and Delivery or Post Op. Post Op is where old

ED nurses went to die, and I should've transferred there. I couldn't imagine a department that wouldn't jump at the chance to get an experienced nurse, regardless of background.

"Elle, I know you're in there," Pam said from the door.

"No, I'm not. Go away," I whispered, my voice ragged. I sounded terrified. Even I could hear that, and I should because I was terrified; how could I not be?

"Look, it will be all right. We'll all help; maybe it won't be a bad four hours," she tried, knowing it didn't matter.

It was the room. Just the room was enough of a trigger. It didn't matter who helped or what came in; that room was going to end me. I couldn't handle it today. Maybe I wouldn't ever handle it.

"It's Sunday, and you have just taunted the Trauma Gods. You know how vicious they can be." I tried for humor, but my voice cracked and shook, coming out with the tint of abject fear.

"Elle, you are bigger than this. Come on, okay? Don't let Parker get to you. She gets off on it."

I shuddered at the thought of Parker getting off on anything.

"Why are you being nice to me?" I asked, grasping at anything to ground against the swirling emotions battering my soul. I wanted her to cuss me out and call me a bitch or tell me I was useless, not that she ever would, but anything else. Anything was better than kindness right now.

"I like you, Elle," she laughed.

"No, you don't. You don't like anyone," I argued, wanting her to fight me.

"Sure I do. Come on. Plus, I already ate that new med student for breakfast, so you're safe. He tasted like chicken, in case you were wondering," I heard a bit of laughter in her voice as she tried to ease my fears.

"Ha-ha," I said, smiling a little at the edges. I took some deep breaths, forcing myself to focus on the now in the way the therapist taught me. I am in the present. You are in the present. We are in the present.

I couldn't hide on the toilet forever, and there wasn't any way around that. Parker got what she wanted; she always did. Even if I went toe to toe with her, she'd win. She was the director of the largest department in the hospital, and if she wanted something, she got it.

"Right. Okay," I said, taking a big breath. I opened the door and brushed past Pam without meeting her eyes.

I circled back to the bat cave and tied up loose ends to get ready for four hours in the trauma bay. It was just four hours, and Pam was right. I could do it. Four hours was considered a princess shift, and anyone could do anything for that length of time. I'd been lucky, really. I could've come in and faced twelve hours in the bays. Instead, I had a little respite while I got used to the sights and sounds of the job again. It would be okay, I reminded myself.

Three o'clock came, and I handed my patients off to two other nurses. We added staff every four hours on the dayshift to better handle the increased traffic. Overall, things weren't bad from seven a.m. to eleven a.m. They started to pick up around lunchtime, and by four, the shit was typically hitting the fan at a high rate of speed. If we were lucky there were inpatient beds to admit patients into, and we didn't have to hold them forever waiting for a room.

If we were unlucky, we had to hang onto them for hours and still somehow manage the influx of new patients who came in the afternoon. If things were really, really bad, the hospital would fill up; the waiting room would fill up, the halls would fill up, and we would need to go on yellow diversion, which was supposed to mean that the incoming, non-emergent patients were taken to other hospitals. But as the only Level One trauma center in the region, yellow diversion meant a big fat load of nothing. The patients still came. They all came.

Red diversion was a different matter, but I'd never seen it and wasn't sure it actually existed. It meant the hospital was so overwhelmed that it was a hard no to anyone else wanting treatment. Even the sickest of the sick would be hard-pressed to get care and were diverted elsewhere.

According to the tracking board, there were plenty of inpatient beds for people of all acuities. It was also bright and sunny outside, meaning maybe people would wait until night shift to crack themselves against the mountains along the Appalachian interstates. Time would tell. That was the one constant in any emergency department; you never knew when the dam was going to break. You knew it would, though. It always did; it was just a matter of when.

I put on a fresh pot of coffee and tried not to think about it.

"Attending Physician to MedCom for flight request, Priority One trauma."

"What's coming, Doc-Cin?"

"Someone brought a motorcycle to a car fight."

"In the rain? What moron rides their bike on a day like this?" I said, glad that Keith would have enough sense to take the car in this weather and not his bike.

"Well, it's not raining anymore, so at least Lifenet can fly."

"That just means the party starts a little sooner."

I sipped my sixth coffee of the day and strolled through my empty trauma bays, mentally checking supplies to make sure everything we might possibly think to use was there.

Somewhere on the wall was a clipboard that listed these things, but I had done it so many times that it was by muscle memory alone that I worked now. I made sure my supplies were adequate, the equipment worked, and it was where it should be. With a glance, I could spot the smallest missing item, so I replaced a chest tube tray and a few bottles of saline before

24

calling the room ready.

The routine of coffee and checking the rooms settled my nerves somewhat, and my breathing evened. I no longer felt the urge to run, and my stomach eased into a steady nauseated feeling I could tolerate. It was almost four, so with nothing to do, I went to see if other nurses needed a hand.

It is easy to get caught up in the starting of IVs, drawing of blood, chest x-rays, EKGs, and STEMIs. I had gotten into a nice rhythm, getting my IVs on the first try and switching antibiotics on time. I passed ice and collected pee while the trauma bays remained blissfully silent and empty.

It wasn't often days like this came around, and nurses as a whole didn't look too hard or say too many things about it being slow when they did. A riot will ensue if a nurse hears the words "slow" or "quiet" uttered. Every health care professional knows precisely what's about to happen. Chaos. Saying fuck is fine. Saying any manner of cuss word is also okay, but never, ever, mutter the Q word; it just isn't done. New doctors and nurses come into the field thinking superstitions are trite and old-school. Give them a few full moons, and they come to understand what the rest of us accepted long ago- that shit is real.

I was checking in a patient with flu-like symptoms that had arrived by local EMS when a pager sounded. First one single alarm, then two, then ten until they all sang their different songs but signaled one event.

Trauma or stroke?

Trauma or stroke.

My gut seized, and I froze in mid-motion as my mind raced. Trauma or stroke. God, please be a stroke, I begged the Trauma Gods, knowing they didn't care now if they ever had. They'd turned their backs on me six weeks ago.

"Got a P1 coming. Forty-four-year-old female, vital signs unstable. Fall from twenty feet," Pam said above the sounds of the final few pagers dying off. They never started or stopped at the same time, and that last one echoed in my chest. "Going into Trauma One," she finished, glancing around.

That was the resuscitation room.

That was my room.

I caught Pam looking for me across the crowded nurses' station, and I thought about slipping away for a second. No one had caught my eye, and maybe I could make a quiet exit. I hadn't left for dinner, and the float nurse could cover the trauma. The ERT nurses would surely come. It would be okay, and it would have to be because I wasn't ready. Not yet, and maybe not ever.

"Elle, finish up with that patient and get your lead on. P1 ten minutes out." Parker came up behind me, and as if she could read my thoughts, she effectively blocked my exit. Why was she even here on a Sunday? Why? She should be home hanging from her ceiling by her clawed feet or out in the woods riding her broom, looking for small children to eat.

"Yeah, I heard. I'm on it." I faked bravado I didn't feel, knowing she wasn't fooled.

I felt the color drain from my face and the heartbeat skipping in my chest. A forty-four-year-old female. At least it was a female, and at least it was a fall. I could do this. I really could. I'd done it for so long that I shouldn't have to think about it. My mind would go into the trauma trance, and I would just do it like I always had.

I crossed the unit's emergent side and into Trauma One, not meeting the rest of the team's eyes. Pam was signing in to the computer, registering the patient as an emergent unknown because so many identifiers were used when registering someone into the system that it was easier to enter them as Jane or John Doe and fix the issue later.

Once the patient was registered, we could get the orders in and labels printed. It was much more efficient than waiting for a name that paramedics might not have. Still, it was expected that EMS in the field would appropriately tag the priority of a trauma patient, so the team had everything needed in place, and it was annoying to the registration people when a P1 came in sitting up and talking.

I pulled on a colorful lead apron and neck shield that made it unnecessary to step back from the patient while x-rays were taken. Not that you don't always prepare for the worst, but most of us don't wear lead for a priority two because it's bulky, heavy, and makes any task performed on the patient more difficult. Plus, trotting to CT scan in a lead suit is not something you want to do if the person is stable. Yes, we were always ready in case the priority level needed upgraded, but we were thankful for the most part that EMS got it right.

"36-year-old male, MCC at highway speeds. Car hydroplaned and crossed the median. He never saw it coming. Knocked him into the guardrail. No pressure and pulse is thready. Lots of deformities to the head, face, and neck. Helmet cracked in the back down the middle. We brought it so you can see it. Elle. Get the fuck out of here."

"Elle!"

"Yeah, what?" I startled to the present and the watchful gazes of twenty doctors, med students, nurses, clinical aides, and the chaplain, otherwise known as the trauma team.

"Sorry, Just reviewing the ABCs of trauma in my head," I mumbled as I went to pull the supplies I would need to start an IV while someone took a manual blood pressure and placed the patient on the heart monitor. There was a cadence of events and an order they needed to be done, it came like breathing, but I didn't care so much about that. Everything happened at once, and we all knew it. No one corrected me, though they could have called me a liar, but under the circumstances, how could they?

My husband of ten years died in this very room six weeks ago. He had taken his motorcycle to a car fight for what goddamned reason I will never know. He'd taken his motorcycle to a car fight in the rain and cracked himself against the mountainous interstates, and that never works out. I remembered laughing as I said that.

That never works out.

I took a deep breath and focused on today and right now. At this moment, a forty-four-year-old woman somehow managed to fall twenty feet and fuck herself up enough to land in my trauma bay. It was the worst day of her life, and even though it was also the worst time in mine, she needed help, and I would try to give it. While I fought to calm my nerves, EMS arrived, and the fluid motions of a well-run dance began.

"This is Cheri Phillips, a forty-four-year-old female who was hiking at Cooper's Rocks and fell about twenty feet down a rock face. Difficult extrication from scene. GCS is five of 15, failed intubation due to difficult airway, sats 92% while bagged, lowest blood pressure 70/palp but improved with fluids, and highest heart rate 125. Ready to move on three. One, two," EMS reported smoothly, and as one, we moved the backboard to the trauma stretcher and began working.

I tried to slow my breathing and focus on what I was doing, but it was hard with the sweat pouring into my eyes. My immediate job was to get a manual blood pressure since the CA wasn't on the correct side to grab it without getting in the way. I also needed to do a quick visual assessment that would give me an idea of what we were dealing with, so I could anticipate the next move.

I was to call all my findings to the scribe nurse responsible for documenting everything said and done. Medical students cut clothes off while radiology shot x-rays, and the residents assessed injuries. The ED resident would check her head and neck and place the breathing tube if needed. The trauma residents should do the hands-on head-to-toe assessment while the trauma and ED attending stood to the side, calmly ensuring we didn't screw up. A two-minute ultrasound called a FAST exam was done to check for internal bleeding, then the patient would be rolled off the backboard and checked for obvious fractures and other injuries to the back and spine.

This should all happen simultaneously, with each team member performing their assigned duties, usually without thinking about it. The goal was seven to ten minutes of elapsed time until the patient made it to the CT scanner, and we were not going to make that time today.

"She has a sixteen gauge in the left AC started prior to arrival. Multiple abrasions on her face, arms, and chest," I shouted as I tried to steady my hand and place another large bore IV needle into her arm so I could get labs. My eyes snagged on the blood pulsating from her nose, and my hand stilled above the skin of her arm. Sweat dripped into my eyes, and I could feel my heart skipping beats. My vision narrowed, and I saw black spots in my periphery.

"Crap, I blew the vein." I stepped back, wiping my face and looking to see who else was in the room. "Hey, Susan, will you look for me while I put her on the monitor?" I asked when I saw the float nurse trying to get the patient's big hiking boots off.

"Man, if you can't get it, I sure as hell can't," she said but took my place while I grabbed for wires and electrodes that would allow everyone in the room to see vital signs on the big screen mounted to the wall.

"Sixteen gauge in the left AC she shouted a moment later, then gave me a look from the corner of her eye.

"Here, that's a mess; let me get that," she said. "Why don't you run and get RSI drugs."

Grateful, I stepped out of the way and walked quickly to the medication room to grab the bag of Rapid Sequence Intubation drugs containing all the medicines we need when things go sideways. I should have grabbed it while trying to hide from this trauma. I should have had them ready and waiting in the room. I didn't. Neither the ERT nurse nor the pharmacist showed up, and I felt like I was fumbling in a situation I should have been in control of, with or without them.

While I waited for the Accudose to respond, I fought to pull it all together. I knew I was screwing it up. I was just rusty, that's all, and I tried to convince myself and still my shaking hands at the same time. I knew this job, and it was all I had left of my life before Keith died. If I couldn't do it, where would I be?

Bag in hand, I pushed into the trauma bay and began drawing up syringes of drugs and pushing them into Susan's IV line as the attending asked for them. The ED resident at the head of the bed tried to get an ET tube placed, and after several unsuccessful attempts, he gave up and let the attending do it with the fancy camera tool they used to intubate the really tough people.

I kept pushing drugs until the process was complete and the ventilator was in place. Susan continued to help, and the flow of the trauma smoothed out. Before going to scan, I filled my pockets with sedatives and drugs that would keep Cheri Phillips still while we checked for injuries.

"Susan, go ahead to CT scan; I want to talk to Elle," Ms. Parker said, catching us in the hall.

Susan kept going, and I was stuck with the director holding on to my shirt sleeve.

"Elle," she started.

"I know I was slow in there, okay. You don't need to tell me," I interrupted, trying not to let my temper rise.

"It was more than just slow," she said. "That was a cluster

fuck. You weren't the only one off their game, but you tried to put the IV in before you took a blood pressure. That's first week stuff. You know better. Get your head in the game," she finished and walked off, leaving me alone to seethe over her words.

How dare she? How dare she judge me?

I tried to keep the tears back as I walked back into the bay to begin the task of cleaning up, but a few slipped silently down my cheeks. I ran to a trashcan, lifted the lid, and vomited my morning coffee into it since that's all I'd had. My hands shook as I stood there, waiting for the nausea to pass before straightening and looking around the room, ignoring what just happened.

For some reason, no one even tried to hit a trash can when they were working a trauma, and you had to wade through a huge mess to enter the room once the patient was gone. The worse the trauma, the bigger the mess, and the room was a giant mess.

People took great pleasure in going wild and throwing trash wherever they wished, and today was no exception. Empty packages and shredded clothes covered the floor. Blood coagulated where it had dripped from the stretcher, and I threw the shredded jeans over it, scrubbing it with my foot as I scooped up trash and threw it in the large cans sitting in every corner of the room. I mean, throwing trash on the floor does save steps, which saves seconds, which in turn saves lives, but still.

Parker was right. I had screwed up and made rookie mistakes. Monitors and vital signs came before IVs, and I had been slow and distracted into forgetting the basics by the visuals I'd learned not to see years ago. I took a deep breath and let it go.

"Don't beat yourself up, Elle," Daniel spoke softly from the doors of the bay. His green eyes held mine, and I wanted to sink into them. I was drowning, and he was a life preserver.

"I'm not," I lied as I swiped at my eyes and turned my back to him to pick up trash.

"Yeah, you are. I know you. You re-run these things in your head and wonder what you could have done differently," he offered, coming deeper into the room.

"I've been off for six weeks. I'm just out of rhythm," I lied again. Maybe that was partly true, and maybe there was more to it.

"No one had a rhythm in this one. It happens."

"Yeah, it does. It just didn't click." I stood, straightening the sore muscles in my lower back, and flicked the long black ponytail over my shoulder.

"For what it's worth, Elle, you are a great nurse, and you wouldn't believe the number of out-of-sync traumas we ran while you were out. I speak for all of us when I say the physicians are glad you're back," he traced my movements around the room, his concentration never wavering.

I watched Dr. Ross as he tried so hard to find something to say to soothe me, and I did appreciate him. Our history was long and complicated. We had dated when I was a new grad, and he was a third-year medical student. It had been serious at the time but never gotten beyond long sighs, heavy petting, words of love, and plans for the future.

He was busy with school, and I didn't want to get a reputation for doctor chasing, so we called it off. I'd really liked him, though, and we had remained best friends through our years together. I'd often thought that he was the one and that we'd get back together after the dust settled, only we hadn't. I met Keith and moved quickly into marriage. I'm not sure how that happened, but it did. Regardless, Daniel was the second most important person in my life, and I hated for him to see me like this.

He was older than me by two years and already starting to go softly gray in temples. This place would do it to you, but he still looked terrific with his dark green eyes, dimples, and easy smile. He had sandy-blonde stubble that matched his tousled hair and a jawline that could cut steel. A deep sense of loss filled my soul as I looked at him.

"Thanks a lot, Daniel. I do appreciate it," I said, giving up the pretense of being okay. "I'm trying; I am. I think maybe this was a mistake," I added, looking around the room, knowing he was the only person I would ever admit that to.

"No, it wasn't, Ellie Bell," he said, dusting off another old nickname. Only coming from him, it sounded natural. "Don't think that way. You're brilliant in here; you really are. Give it time." He turned and left, leaving me alone for a few more minutes before the housekeepers came in and finished the room.

In a few short minutes, Susan was back with an empty stretcher. She'd called the ICU and given report while the CT scans were being finished, then taken Cheri Phillips to her room.

"Thanks for helping, Susan; I'm off my game."

"Don't thank me. Girl, you've saved my ass more times than I can count," she said, smiling over her shoulder.

"Well, thanks all the same," I said, meaning it.

An emergency department relies on having a solid team, and any Level One trauma center should boast the strongest team possible. Most days, it takes everyone to make it flow. Poor teamwork can make a good day bad, and great teamwork can make the worst days survivable. The saying you're only as good as your weakest link applies to the ED more than any other unit in the hospital.

And today, the weakest link was me.

"A few of us are going to grab drinks. Would you like to come along?" Susan asked as she walked with me to the breakroom.

I glanced at the clock above the line of now empty stretchers. The day was finally over, and I hadn't realized it was almost seven.

"No, thanks, I don't think so. I have to be back in the morning, and I'm too old to hang with you young things anyway. Have fun, though," I chuckled at the thought of drinking with the twenty-somethings.

"Old? You?" she asked, quirking an eyebrow my way.

"Let's just say I can't do an all-nighter and show up bright-eyed and bushy-tailed like you will. Once upon a time, I could. I think those days are gone," I sighed.

"Well, I'm off tomorrow," she laughed. "So I can stay and drink all night."

"Even more reason to take my tired self home. Be safe." I grabbed the dinner I hadn't eaten from the breakroom I never sat in and headed for the door.

Chapter 3

Elle was not okay, Daniel thought as he watched her walk away. Her eyes were wide and dark, showing white edges caused by terror. Despite what he'd said, he agreed that she was probably right and that this was no place for her. She'd been teetering on the edge of burnout for a while, though she'd never admit it. That, combined with Keith's death, made him wonder if she could come back from it. If he was honest with himself, he wasn't sad that Keith was gone. Daniel had never liked the man who had eventually won Elle's heart away from him, and he didn't think he had deserved her. He certainly hadn't been good for her. But he'd never wish her suffering on anyone and would take it from her if he could.

Daniel knew Elle was the one from the beginning. He'd screwed around building a career, thinking that their friendship would be enough for him, but he'd been wrong. She hadn't waited for him to be ready, and he'd lost the best thing in his life to another man. Now that man was gone.

Keith left behind the shattered pieces of the wife Daniel had always wanted for himself, and he didn't know what to do about that. He'd do anything to put those pieces back together again, and what he wouldn't give to see the once bright smile she gave him whenever they were together. It was gone now, replaced by shadows and haunted glances. She was a wraith of the person she had been, and Daniel blamed Keith for that too.

She would avoid Daniel if she could; he knew that. He hadn't let her and had refused to allow her to put distance between them during her grieving process. As much as he loved her, she had always been his best friend, and he wouldn't let that go.

He watched as she ghosted through her rooms, tidying them using rote memory and mechanical muscle movements. Gone was her witty chatter, quick step, and playful jabs at interns and residents. Elle Conroy was the best nurse he'd ever met, and watching her now was a painful reminder of just how quickly things change. It was heartbreaking, and he hoped that somehow she'd come back from this. Not only had she lost her husband, but she'd been there, desperately trying to save him. She'd seen it all.

Trauma is kind to no one, and not even survivors walk away unscathed. It would've been a mercy to Elle and Keith both if EMS had just waited a few seconds before bringing the man in. Dying on the side of the road was better than dying with someone's hand squeezing your heart through a hole in your ribs. Daniel would know; he'd been in the room too.

As much as he wanted Elle to himself, he had wanted Keith to live more because he knew that winning her from a dead man would be impossible. He knew Elle. Now the only choice he had was to wait for her to pick up the pieces and want to move on or, if she didn't, to let her go.

Chapter 4

With empty stretchers in the bays and the mess cleaned up, I didn't stick around to give report to the night shift, and I clocked out a little early, not caring about losing the time.

I didn't want to get tangled up in the shift change and the well-rested faces of those coming in and seeing me for the first time since Keith's death. I'd go before anyone could ask me how I was doing or give me the standard platitudes grief elicits. I'd shown up and done the best I could, but it wasn't enough, and it seldom was. No matter how hard I pushed or what rabbit I tried to pull kicking and screaming out of the hat, it might never be enough.

I'd go home and think about what came next because deep inside, I could admit that I had to. I left without telling anyone, and as the doors closed behind me, I heard the pagers sound again, making my stomach drop. It was three minutes before the night shift could clock in, but they should be ready in plenty of time for whatever tragedy the pagers signaled unless it was right outside the door. I couldn't do it, not today. Today, I was done.

I ducked down the stairs and clocked out on the first floor, beating the rush of bodies across the parking lot to my truck. I slid onto smooth leather seats, closing the door and surrounding myself in near darkness made deeper by window tinting. I breathed in the scent of leather and air freshener, letting it soothe me.

Two years ago, I had gotten stuck in a massive snowstorm driving a Subaru they claimed could go anywhere. I had not been at all happy about the situation, and when the snow cleared, I took myself to the Ford dealership and bought a giant four-wheel-drive truck. I'd liked the sexiness of it and the deep throaty purr of the diesel engine. It was lifted just enough to be noticeable but not too much as to be obnoxious.

Keith said I didn't need it and that deep snows were a rare thing, but I bought it anyway. It hadn't taken me long to fall in love with the thing and the feeling of independence it gave. I sank into the seats, letting the size and feel of it block the outside world.

Hands on the steering wheel, I watched in silence as the blue and white bird of Lifenet circled in front of the football stadium the hospital shared a parking lot with. The sun had almost set as it approached the roof where the helicopters landed, and its last rays struck the helicopter beautifully.

Even after all these years, that sight would have thrilled me six weeks ago. I used to love watching them land and take off. It had been a thrill to work at a place the helicopters flew toward and not away. Turning the ignition to the big Ford's diesel engine, I listened to it growl to life and left before I could catch another glimpse of sunlight on the helicopter.

I drove out of town, taking the long way, which passed my favorite bar, Crockett's Lodge. It was one of the few places in town that didn't attract students, and the parking lot was full because of that. I thought about stopping but couldn't bring myself to run into people I might know, and I would, so I crossed the bridge and wound my way down Route 19 to the turnoff that led to my house. I only lived six miles from the hospital, but those six miles brought you to another world in this part of the country.

Traffic gave way to a narrow gravel road and downtown's brighter lights to the country's growing dusk. The sound of helicopter blades faded to the last songs of crickets and frogs.

Appalachia is one of those areas where the disparity between classes is glaring. To get to my large, expensive home, I had to drive through what the locals called a Country Ghetto. Yet, we shared not only the same zip code but the same street.

I passed ramshackle mobile homes and falling shacks with people sitting on their porches, enjoying the evening cool down. When I first moved here, I would wave as I drove by. In the south where I grew up, you waved at everyone whether you knew them or not. No one had ever waved back here, and I eventually broke the old habit. It had been an adjustment, and sometimes I still missed the friendliness of the deep south.

Fifteen minutes after leaving the hospital, I pulled into my driveway and stared up at the dark house greeting me. I didn't want to be here. Grief rolled over me in such a heavy wave I thought I might drown, and it was too much. There was no place I fit anymore. Home wasn't a refuge from a long day, and the hospital wasn't respite from a fight. I didn't want to be there, but I didn't want to be here either. I drifted in the never-ending fog of uncertainty, wanting nothing and everything at the same time. I was too old not to know where I belonged, and seeing the massive house was another reminder of how much my life had changed.

Clutching the wheel, I stared at the place that had once been my dream home. It was a cape cod with a broad, wraparound porch, allowing three hundred sixty-degree views of the surrounding hills to the left and the rolling pastures to the right. Rocking chairs and chaise lounges spread along the expanse of the porch, offering plenty of comfort from which to take in the scenery. Outdoor ceiling fans whirred unforgotten and lazily, beckoning us to sit and enjoy the night, only there wasn't an us anymore. I'd gone from an 'us' to an 'I,' and it wasn't a transition I thought I could make.

My once cherished raised stone flower beds were filled with weeds and showed their neglect. Dead rose blooms adorned the shaggy, uncared for plants, and I found the sight of them depressing. The house, like the hospital, was overwhelming to me.

I thought about killing myself.

Again.

But I had been hard-wired to believe that suicide was never an option, so I was stuck. Here, but not here, dead inside but not gone. It was the limbo that was worse than anything.

The garage caught my eye. Keith's domain, not mine. My truck wouldn't fit with his stuff, so he used it for his car and the bike, and I hadn't been in it since his death.

Opening the truck door, I slid to the ground and walked away without bothering to shut it, leaving like I might need to run back in a hurry. I took a deep breath and headed to the garage door. I flipped the switch, shedding soft light on the mess.

Scattered about in organized, chaotic fashion were pieces of Keith's bike: hundreds of pieces of Keith's bike. My hand fluttered to my mouth before I could stop it, and a strangled sound came from my throat because I had forgotten that I demanded the bike be brought here.

Keith's friends had scoured the road for a mile looking for all the pieces. And here they were. Parts large and small. Shattered. Like Keith. Missing was his helmet, which came to the Emergency Department with him, but pretty much everything else was there. For the thousandth time, I wondered...why?

Why had he taken the bike on a rainy day? He loved that bike. He called it Penny. Referred to it as a "her." As a trauma nurse, I had hated her instinctually, but she had not been a cheap toy, and it made no sense to me that he would have driven it in anything but perfect weather. Keith wasn't the kind of man to take chances, and the whole thing was odd to me. Maybe if I understood, I could move on.

My eyes skimmed over the pieces of the bike, then moved to his car. The neat little Mercedes had cost him a fortune, but then he earned one. He always joked that he liked to collect beautiful things, like me, and then he would laugh and ruffle my hair with a smile. Keith had been an investment broker and had done very well for himself. I hadn't bothered with any of that yet. Going through his affairs would take more energy than I had, so I put it off.

I picked my way through the wreckage of the bike and over to the Mercedes covered in a thin layer of dust that made me feel guilty because Keith kept the little sportster spotless. Steeling myself, I lifted the handle soundlessly and opened the door.

Keith's smell wafted out, overwhelming me. I'd been prepared for the feel of the car and the memories that it brought, but I hadn't been prepared for that. It was heaven and hell at the same time, and I couldn't stop myself from shaking. I slumped in the seat and found my hand resting on his keys still in the ignition that were supposed to be on a hook by the door. I hadn't noticed they'd been missing, but then I hadn't noticed much lately.

I turned the key over, and the battery clicked a few times lifelessly before going silent. Had the battery been dead that day? Is that why he took the bike? That might explain why he'd taken the bike. It could have died over the last month, but something in me settled as I realized what had probably happened. Keith, in a hurry, had taken the bike when the car wouldn't start. He hadn't bothered with the battery charger in the corner. He was running late. He should've been at work when the accident occurred. That tiny bit of insight helped. It did. Maybe now I knew why. Maybe that would give me some closure.

I left the garage and went inside, not bothering with the lights. I dumped my pockets' contents on the granite countertop in the bathroom before stepping into the shower. With the water as hot as I could make it, I washed my day away, running my hands over the body that I knew was too thin. Gaunt. Empty.

As I brushed my teeth, three little glass vials caught my eye as they peeked out from under the stray dollar bills and wads of paper shoved into my pockets over the long day, making my stomach sink. I hadn't returned or wasted any of the drugs we used on Cheri Phillips.

I was in such a hurry to leave that the one critical step that could cause me trouble had slipped my mind. I dressed in my nightclothes and placed the drugs next to my toothbrush so that I'd remember to take and waste them tomorrow. I checked the thermostat, wandered around the too silent house for a few minutes, then climbed into bed, pulling the covers high while praying for sleep to take me.

An hour later, still wide awake and restless, I got up from the bed. I was to the point that I was so worried about not being able to sleep that I would never fall asleep or else fall asleep right before my alarm went off. I had already tried taking a Benadryl and was still wide awake. My anxiety about working the next day grew with each minute that passed. My heart raced, and I couldn't breathe. Cold sweat formed under my arms, making me shiver, so I got up, needing to do something other than lay there and obsess about work.

After wandering the house again, straightening throw pillows and old photos, I found myself in the bathroom in a state of total panic, rummaging through our medicine cabinet until I found a bottle of Percocet with Keith's name on it. It had expired and was probably from when they took his appendix out, but I would sleep if I took one. I knew that. Just one night's sleep would make a huge difference. It was what I needed, and just one would be enough.

I rarely took a Tylenol, so one Percocet and the Benadryl I

had already taken would do it, I convinced myself as I popped it in my mouth, washing it down with tap water. Not long after, I tucked myself back into bed, feeling sleep sneak up and take me away.

Chapter 5

My alarm went off, and I instinctively hit snooze before stretching out in bed. I felt pretty good. I had finally slept. Keith's absence hit me like it always did, but it was a distant ache. Of course, it was there, but for the first time, there were no tears the minute my eyes opened.

I showered again and blew my hair out before putting on just a touch of makeup. My reflection looked less terrified. I was still pale, but the circles making my dark eyes black were better. Other than being too thin, my face wasn't unrecognizable, and I considered that a win.

I grabbed a to-go cup of coffee and went out to the truck. The early morning air was crisp, but the day promised to be a scorcher, as early fall days often are. I hadn't closed the truck door last night, and dew covered the dash and dampened the leather. Hopping in, I settled into the wet seat and turned the key, loving the sound of the jet engine under the hood when it started with a high-pitched whine before settling into a low rumble.

My drive to work was quick, even with the students back in town. I chose to live close enough to be able to get there in bad weather and flying, I could make the drive in about seven minutes, but only if I risked the police force's wrath. They sat at the bottom of the hill into town, waiting on people rushing to work and handing out tickets like candy on Halloween. That's how they afforded the fancy new baseball field on the hill, but I'd been pulled over so many times that they knew my truck and often left me alone regardless of my speed because they understood that they might need me later.

Inside, the ED was already on overload. Stretchers lined the hallways, and the tracking board showed we were holding twenty-one admissions with no available beds. The waiting room was at capacity, and the assignment board was one nurse short. My name was next to pod six, trauma, like I knew it would be. Parker would have her way because that's who she was.

I sighed, peeking my head into the big resuscitation bay to check it out, only to find it demolished. An intubated patient lay alone in the center of the room, and the floor was buried in trash. Blood had dripped off the stretcher and dried on the rubber tiles, and shredded clothes lay where they'd been thrown. My other room was no different, except that patient was female instead of male, but it had been a rough night for them, and looking at their rooms, I could tell tomorrow wasn't going to be much better.

Backboards were stacked against the wall by the ambulance entrance, and used equipment lay on every surface.

It had been a long night.

Pam was in charge again, and she popped her head over the desk and then ducked quickly when she saw me. I knew it wasn't her fault. Friends or not, she'd have never done this on her own, but it would be okay. We were a team, and somehow we would get through it.

Staff gathered around the desk for our morning huddle, similar to a pep rally but without the pep. Sometimes we would even make one of those moves where everyone put their hands in and brought them back out with a yay team, but today was not that day.

The mood was subdued as we listened to the two charge nurses, one day and one night shift, review the plan.

"Okay, everyone," Pam started, "Any patient that doesn't need a monitor, get them out and into the hall or the results waiting room. Any patient that doesn't need to stay, push your docs for discharge orders. Push your docs to call their consults. Push your docs for anything that will help. We've got to get this place moving. Any orders not finished, get them done ASAP. It's Monday, and everyone knows what that means," she finished and sat down to get report on every patient in the department because, as charge, she was responsible for all of them.

Over her head Daniel caught my eye and rolled his, making a face behind Pam's back. I smiled despite myself, then scurried away when Pam looked up and glared.

Monday is traditionally the busiest day in our emergency department and probably every other. For some reason, we had more of everything, and overall, the patients were sicker. Statistically, you are more likely to suffer a heart attack or stroke sometime in the late hours of Sunday and into the wee hours of Monday morning. Maybe the looming work week affected everyone because Mondays were a special kind of hell.

The heart attack patient that had waited until the weekend was over because the weather was nice and their chest pain 'wasn't too bad' came in. That grandma who had a stroke on Sunday, but she looked so peaceful 'sleeping' that no one wanted to bother her; she came in. Then there were all the folks who were sick and needed their doctor's notes because they called out of work, and oh, can you write it for Friday too? They came in. Rain on a Monday? You can forget it because all those late commuters racing on the interstate led to trauma after trauma.

Mondays are a beast.

I grabbed Susan on the way to her assignment. She was next to me in one of the stroke rooms and pediatric major trauma bay, not that those designations meant anything; we'd get what we got in them, but they did contain special equipment. She'd be a good buddy to have because she was quick and efficient. We'd help each other through the worst of it if we could. "Hey, can you witness a return and a waste with me from the trauma yesterday, Phillips?"

"Sure," she answered, and we entered the medicine room together, watching as I used my fingerprint to log into the Accudose machine.

"I'm wasting fifty mics of Fentanyl and returning some Versed that we didn't use. I kind of skated last night and forgot all about it," I explained, feeling suddenly sheepish. In all my years, I'd never left early. Not once. I often stayed late to work a trauma to its completion so that continuity of care was maintained.

"Yeah, I saw you running for the hills; I don't blame you. It was a tough day," she replied, putting her finger on the print scanner to witness my waste after I drew up the drug and emptied it into the waste container.

"Yeah, thanks," I said, appreciating her empathy. We finished up and headed to get report from the night shift, both of us hoping that today would be better than yesterday and maybe we'd defy the odds of Monday. We wouldn't, but then I knew that when I saw the tracking board.

My two ICU patients had rooms in the Surgical Intensive Care Unit, but they were not clean and ready yet. The guy on the backboard outside my bay had fallen off a ladder and complained of back pain, so he'd gotten a ride with EMS. He had a history of chronic back pain and had not had any testing.

I had a tech take him to CT scan while he waited on the trauma docs to clear him. He could come back and go into one of the remaining hallway spaces, but the priority was getting him out of in front of the ambulance bay doors and my trauma bay.

I started by restocking the drawers with the supplies I would need to get through a twelve-hour shift. I checked ET tubes and ventilator settings, ensuring my SICU patients were clean and in gowns rather than sending them to their rooms naked and bloody the way FERNs usually did. Housekeeping came and started clearing the mess off the floors while I zeroed timers and set up the Level-One.

The rooms were beginning to look like the trauma bays should when the first pager sounded, and I held my breath, waiting the heartbeat it took for multiple pagers to start their songs.

Trauma or stroke, I wondered as my heart sank. I could have stayed in the bays all day taking care of my two intubated patients. I would have been perfectly happy to tip back foley catheters and measure urine output every hour. I might have even charted a little bit. I didn't want to do trauma, but I liked ICU; maybe I could transfer there. Peace could be found in the meticulous labeling of lines and managing patients long term. I could grow to love it. I might need an extensive orientation on how to be anal-retentive, but I would eventually get it.

I felt my heart race and took a few deep breaths to calm myself. My palms began to sweat, and my vision narrowed like I might pass out, but this was my job, and I had no choice but to do it; I knew that. I forced my breathing to slow and clenched my fists until they stopped shaking.

Doc-Cin came rushing in, stopping with a visible step backward when she saw me. The ghost of my dead husband flashed before her eyes, and I watched it happen, wondering if any of us would move past it.

"Oh wow, Elle, good to see you," she said, trying to cover up her surprise.

"What's coming, Doc-Cin?"

"Someone took a motorcycle to a car fight."

"That never works."

I turned from her as quickly as I could.

"What's coming." I didn't make it a question.

"Priority One. Eleven-month-old fall from a shopping cart. Unresponsive at the scene and needs tubed. Five minutes out. Peds trauma is already full. Someone is taking this guy upstairs," she said, waving to the patient I already had.

"Okay. Thanks." Inside I relaxed a bit. I didn't like sick kids, no one did, but I was damn good with them. I didn't have children, so detaching myself was easier than for the nurses who were moms.

One of the ERT nurses came in and grabbed the ICU

patient, wheeling him away while the tech brought an empty stretcher in. I readied it for a pediatric patient by setting up smaller-sized blood pressure cuffs, IV catheters, and intubation equipment. Respiratory Therapy brought in a ventilator, and everyone started putting on the lead aprons to protect them from radiation while x-rays were taken. No one would step out, not even for a second. All traumas are serious matters, but kids brought your game to another level; it's just how it is.

The pharmacist came in with a long tray filled with colorful boxes of medications that might be needed for intubation or resuscitation, simply called the 'tray,' and began to set it up.

The trauma team waited, talking among themselves, until Monongalia County EMS rolled through the doors, then the room fell silent.

"This is Michael, eleven-month-old male, fell from a buggy at the Kroger," The paramedic started, pausing next to our stretcher as he gave a brief report. "Stood up in the front seat, then fell onto the top of his head. Vomited immediately but seemed okay at first.

"Mom grabbed him up, and he went limp and is now unresponsive." Dale, the paramedic giving report, made eye contact with the trauma surgeon as he spoke, and everyone listened without interrupting as he removed safety straps and wires, not once looking at his hands.

He caught my eye and faltered for a second. I couldn't

remember if he was on scene for Keith or not. How long would those little glances and skipped beats last? Months? Years? Forever? I didn't know and hated that my tragedy slowed this trauma even one second.

"Lowest blood pressure 76/40, highest heart rate 152, bagging for respers," he said, continuing to unpack the kid and get him ready to be moved. "Had apnea and snoring breaths on scene. Couldn't get him tubed, so we scooped and ran. Ready on three. One, two." We moved Michael to our trauma stretcher and stood clear for a quick weight.

"12.6 kilos." The Clinal Associate said before getting a manual blood pressure while medical students began cutting off clothes.

"Twenty gauge in the right AC," I said as I drew blood and prepared to hook up IV fluids.

"Twenty-four gauge left AC," said Pam. "Nice job," she added under her breath to me as she shook her head.

A twenty gauge is an adult-sized needle. The smaller the number, the bigger the catheter. Go big or go home was my motto. A large-bore IV could save a life, and it didn't matter to me if it was a kid. If he had big veins, he got a big IV. Period.

Around Michael, everyone worked like a well-tuned piano. Ten different people did ten different things, and in seconds, the child had a complete assessment, two IV lines, lab work running, and all monitoring devices in place and displayed on the big screen.

Chest and pelvis x-rays were being taken and transmitted wirelessly to a large monitor at the head of the bed for the attending doctors to review. Anything found on assessment was spoken out loud in the general direction of the scribe nurse, who wrote it all down.

"Left pupil 4mm and sluggish, right pupil blown," Doc-Cin said.

I sighed inwardly, knowing that was not good. I took in his bruised and swollen shut eyes. His skull was misshapen and probably fractured. His skin was pale and his arms lifeless as we traumatized him in ways a healthy child would never allow. Little tufts of downy hair blew in the breeze made from our movements, and dried blood trailed down his ear canal to his neck. He was so small on the big bed that we had to reach over one another to work on him.

"RSI drugs ready," offered our pharmacist.

"25 milligrams Succinylcholine and 12.5 mics Fentanyl," Daniel ordered.

"Hey, Doc, how about Etomidate instead?" I asked without looking up from placing a catheter in the child's bladder.

Etomidate was another drug we used to sedate someone for intubation, and recent research found it was better for children with head injuries. I wasn't sure where I read the article, and more than that, I couldn't believe I remembered reading it.

"Great idea, Elle, 3 milligrams Etomidate. Check my dose, Kelley."

The dose is correct, I thought as the pharmacist handed me the syringes and agreed with Daniel's order. "Dose verified, Etomidate in," I said.

"4.5 uncuffed ET tube 14 centimeters at the lip."

"Nice job, Dr. Branch. First try. Let's roll to CT scan," Daniel said, but I was already packing Michael up and moving that way. I glanced at the timer on the wall above the bed space as we rolled out the door. Seven minutes and thirty-five seconds, and that was a good time for a P1.

The CT scan showed a significant subdural bleed. We called neurosurgery and took him straight to the operating room from the scanner. Kids can do amazing things. I'd seen it before, and I'd see it again. Even kids with serious injuries had something adults rarely did- a chance. They bounced where adults broke, and that's why I didn't mind caring for them. You can't count a kid out, and I hoped and prayed Michael was one of those who recovered.

I wheeled my empty stretcher back into the bay and began cleaning up the mess. Someone had checked on my other patient and charted some vital signs for me, but I did a quick assessment on her and checked my vent settings anyway. I was almost done setting up my empty room when the pagers sounded again.

Pam stuck her head in, "Gotta stroke coming, and Susan's room is still full. Two minutes out."

"Nothing like a little warning," I muttered as she popped back out of the room.

The stroke team arrived, and with the exception of the nurse practitioner, they were not my favorites in general. I hated that three neurologists would yell at a stroke patient to follow directions when most of the time, they couldn't be understood anyway.

Older Appalachians have difficulty with foreign accents, and neurology ran long on those. Not only were they having a stroke, but they also got mixed and confusing commands from three different people.

It also never failed that the more confused the patient became, the louder the doctors would yell, thinking maybe that was the problem. Our stroke center had extraordinary treatment times compared to other stroke centers in the country. We were undoubtedly one of the best, but the patients' lost a little dignity in their treatment, and I hated that.

EMS came through the door as the team waited. The ERT nurses hadn't arrived yet and were probably on the other end of the hospital doing something non-critical, and with a two-minute warning, I hadn't expected them to make it.

"Sarah Gorman, 76-year-old female, last seen normal at 0700. Husband says she woke up and made breakfast just fine.

Found her in the shower with right-sided paralysis and aphasia. BPs have been 150s over 90s. I put a 20 gauge in her left AC. On three. One, two." We moved Mrs. Gorman over, and, as predicted, several doctors got into her face and began yelling.

"Raise your left arm."

"Raise your arm and hold it."

"Raise your arms like you're holding a pizza."

"Raise your right leg." There were a dozen stroke scale questions, so this would take a while if they were allowed to continue on their current path. I didn't say anything because I knew that they needed a chance to know how severe the stroke was, and I would give them a few minutes to figure it out.

In the meantime, I put in a second IV line, drew labs, packed up monitors, and stood tapping my toes, waiting to go to the CT scan. With a stroke, every second counts. Medicines can sometimes reverse the effects of a blockage, but time is of the essence. There was a window for all interventions, and it was fast approaching for this lady. I started pushing the stretcher toward the door. "Going to the scanner now," I said, nearly running over the resident's toes.

"But I'm not done," they complained.

"Your time is up. You've got to learn to be faster; you can finish when we get back. Your score doesn't matter if the patient isn't in the window." I bumped into him on the way out.

It was part of my job to push residents to be better, smarter, faster and I took it seriously. These baby docs would be turned loose in the world someday, and doctors didn't always teach other doctors the best way to do things, and that's where old nurses fill the gap. Residents learned early to make friends, and if not, they missed a lot. But it was also my job to make sure every patient got the best care promptly, and it's a fine line to walk sometimes.

The complaining resident tried to trot beside the stretcher yelling at Mrs. Gorman, "What's going on in this picture?" he said, waving his little stroke handbook in front of her face. Sadly, the hallways were so full that he smacked into another stretcher with a patient on it and got left behind.

"Nice move, Elle. I was getting ready to cut him off when you saved me the trouble." The ERT nurse rushed around me to open the doors to CT scan. You would think they would be automatic to make our life easier, but they weren't. "Sorry I'm late."

"No problem. Interns get more annoying every year," I said. They also seemed to get younger, I thought, feeling old.

"No kidding," she answered. "You know I will take her, right? You can go back to the ED," she added.

"I know, but it's faster with two. This won't take long."

It was hard for one nurse to make the goal times for stroke intervention, and we were already a little behind. Just like everything else, strokes were tracked and dissected by some committee, and it wasn't the doctors who'd be judged if the times weren't met.

The CT scan showed that Mrs. Gorman had a large blood clot in a vessel that had cut off the circulation to part of her brain. With twenty minutes to spare, the attending neurologist pushed a clot-busting drug through her IV line, and within the hour, Mrs. Gorman was talking to us. Fifteen minutes later, she was moving her right side, although some weakness remained. It was a good save.

With her parked in my trauma bay, waiting for admission, my pod was now full. I stuck my head out to see where things stood and wished I hadn't. It wasn't even eleven, and we were above capacity.

EMS stretchers filled with patients lined the hallways on all sides. Nurses and residents rushed through the halls, and patients called for attention. It looked like a war zone to anyone who hadn't seen it before, but, to me, it was just another Monday.

It was around noon when I sneaked out of the bay and onto a computer in the break room. I worked up the nerve to apply for a position on the same-day surgery unit after deciding I couldn't do emergency medicine anymore and didn't want to try. It hadn't taken long, but maybe longer than it should have. Change is hard, and the familiarity of the Emergency Department was difficult to walk away from.

My good night's sleep had worn off, and when the pagers sounded again and again, my hands started shaking. This was no way to live. I would be happier starting IVs for same-day procedures and giving out discharge instructions, and I would have to be. As I applied, I crammed half a sandwich down my throat before sliding back into the Monday chaos.

Parker found me somewhere between the drug overdose, STEMI, cardiac arrest, and another trauma. I could tell by the look on her face that she was not happy. "My office. Now," she said, not giving me a chance before turning her back and walking away.

"Pam, you've got Elle's pod. Make it work." A look of fear flew across Pam's face, and that alone terrified me. I'd never seen her worried, let alone afraid. I shrugged at her encouragingly, then scuttled down the hall to Parker's office.

She sat behind her desk with hands steepled and eyes closed. "Sit down," she said without opening them.

I sat.

"I'm not letting you go," she said, opening her eyes and pinning me with them.

"I'm not sure you have a choice. It's in Human Resource's hands now," I replied quietly.

"I'm writing you up," she responded, "For clocking in late and out early." She sat, waiting for me to get it.

"You can't do that," I said when it sank in.

I wouldn't be eligible for a transfer from the emergency department if disciplinary actions were taken against me. It would hold me right where I was for three months. "You can't," I repeated. "It's only two occurrences, and you need three to write me up."

"You clocked in late today, too. There's three." She watched me, her face emotionless.

I felt my anger rise and blood pound in my ears. "You have got to be fucking kidding me." I jumped up, coming across the desk at her.

She rose to meet me, "I'm not going to fire you either, Elle. I'm not, but watch your mouth anyway," she threatened. Smoothing her pantsuit, she sat back down, glaring at me until I did the same. "I know this is hard, Elle. I know."

"That's the problem, Parker, you don't know," I said, not yelling this time. "You can't hold me hostage; you don't know what it's like. I can't do it. It's not fair to make me. This is total bullshit."

"You think you're the only one who has lost a loved one?" her voice rose from its perfect calm. "You work in the only Level One trauma center in this region, and you see patients from Eastern Ohio, Southern Pennsylvania, Western Maryland, and West Virginia. Do you really think you are the only staffer who has lost someone? Absolutely not. Everyone does," she nearly hissed at me before she shook herself and regained her composure. "Everyone who stays for any length of time loses someone they love here. It's the nature of the beast."

"It isn't for you to decide, Parker. I'm telling you that I can't do it anymore. You gotta let me go."

"No. I don't," she paused, lowering her eyes to her desk.

We sat in silence a few minutes before she continued, "Not long before you started, my daughter came in as a P1 from a skiing accident at Wisp in Maryland. She skied around a corner on a double black diamond and lost it into a tree. It took ski patrol forty- five minutes to get her off the mountain and another half an hour for Maryland Trooper Five to get her here by air. I was a hotshot then, just like you, Elle. A hell of a nurse. I knew trauma like I knew my face in the mirror.

"Nothing I did could save my baby girl. Nothing anyone could have done would've, but we all tried anyway. I walked away and never came back, not really. Like you, I was a trauma nurse to my soul, and I walked away. When I returned from leave, I took this position, and I came to regret that. I lost more than my daughter that day, and I won't let you make the same mistake. This is what you were born to do."

"You don't get to decide that."

"Then quit. Right now, that's your only choice. Three months, Elle. After that, if you still want to transfer, I won't stop you." She sat, meeting my gaze in the worst game of stare-off ever.

And I blinked.

"Get back to work," she said, dismissing me.

I sat for a minute, stunned, staring, and trying to figure out where I went wrong. Then, without another word, I got up and left with tears sliding down my face.

In the department, things had gotten worse. Pam wrote for a trauma in my room while a nurse worked it with a few new residents and no actual doctors. Across the hall, Neurology huddled outside of a room while another nurse worked a stroke page by herself.

Nurses and CAs hustled from room to room, trying to manage what must've been a busload of patients that got dumped off in the few minutes I was gone. My intubated patient lay, still ignored, but the monitor was quiet, and I had no idea where my stroke was. Pam finished writing on the trauma sheet, looking up when she saw me. "How'd it go?" she asked.

"Not well. I put in for a transfer, and Parker wrote me up. Yelled. Dismissed me. The end," I said, leaning against the wall and watching the trauma progress with a critical eye.

"That bitch," Pam said, not looking up from what she was doing on the computer. She worked efficiently and without thought.

"Yeah, so, what can I do?" I asked, steadfastly ignoring the trauma in my room.

"Take over writing for this one, then let the float nurse

travel with it to the scanner. After, get that ICU patient out of here. Their bed's ready. We'll clean this mess up and talk about it later." She finished something on the paper and logged out of the computer, stomping out of the room in irritation.

Hours later, we sat slumped in chairs we had arranged around a fake potted plant and an old payphone in an area we unaffectionately called the office.

The day never got better and, if anything, became worse. When we signed out of the tracking board, forty-nine patients were in the waiting room, most of whom had been there for hours. The hallways remained lined with stretchers, and the board we used to keep track of incoming transfers had no spaces left. The place was on yellow diversion, not that it mattered, and it was going to be a hell of a night. I was glad to be leaving.

"You could quit," Pam whispered, keeping her voice down so the others couldn't hear.

"And start over where?" I asked with a sigh.

"Anywhere. You could go across the road and work their ER. They'd love to have you. Fairmont is close. Waynesburg is a band-aid station. Get a nice easy ER job there," she chuckled when I caught her reference.

We had an older doctor that came from a smaller hospital with a three bed ER. He would get offended when you called our monstrous ED an ER, and he'd say it's a department, not a room if he caught you. He was so proud to be in a bigger ED than the one he came from, that long ago, he made sure the term ED caught on, and it had.

"There are no easy ED jobs. I mean, they may be easier than this, but there is always that *one* day. No ED gets away from it. I don't think I can do it anymore. Plus, I'd have to start over. I'd lose my seniority and maybe have to rotate shifts, weekends, holidays, my retirement. I would lose too much if I left the system entirely." I slumped deeper into my chair and pulled my jacket tight around my middle. "I just need to get out of the ED," I said, keeping my voice down and looking at her from the corner of my eye.

"You could file a complaint with HR, a grievance, or whatever," she suggested.

"And say what? She's right; I did clock in late twice and out early once," I said, glancing at the time clock to see how much longer we had.

"And so does half the staff every day. When we are done, we leave. Parker's never written any of them up," Pam growled, looking to make sure she didn't appear in a puff of smoke when she heard her name like the demon she was.

"No, but she could have. I'm screwed. I know it. I've just got to get through three months." We rose as a group when our phones told us it was a minute until clock out time and lined up in front of the device that kept us here twenty-three minutes longer than necessary. We didn't talk anymore, just swiped our badges and walked out, going our separate ways.

Chapter 6

I cruised through Star City proper at the requisite twenty-five
miles per hour because anything over that gets you a ticket. I
didn't want to go home, but I didn't have any friends I could pop
in on.

I wasn't ready to walk into that silent tomb of a house, so at
the last minute, I took a quick left and pulled behind Crockett's
Lodge. I would go in, have a quick drink out on the deck,
nothing crazy, but it would help unwind after a shitshow of a
day. Crockett's is one of those local holes in the wall that most
overlook, preferring downtown's bright lights and crowds.

I stepped out of my truck and glanced around the lot,
finding it full for a Monday. Maybe I wasn't the only one
having a bad day, I thought as I walked toward the bar. The
early fall night was cool, and the smell of leaves beginning to
change was in the air, and it was already almost full dark. God,
where had the summer gone?

I dreaded winter with a passion.

I walked up the stairs to the back deck and picked a table in
the rear, knowing the wait staff would find me eventually. I sat
with my back to the deck wall and listened to the laughter
floating out from the bar. The waitress popped by, and I ordered

a double Grey Goose on the rocks as I watched through the windows while the few twenty-somethings racked pool balls and joked with their dates.

I sipped my vodka and let the stress of the day go with each breath, and I felt almost good.

"Hey Elle, can I join you?"

"Daniel," I said, surprised to see him, but then again, I shouldn't have been. Crockett's had always been his favorite place too. And after how bad today was, I should've known he'd be here. "Of course you can," I added. This is what I had wanted, right? I could drink alone at home.

"How are you? Really," he asked before settling into his seat with a Yuengling hanging from his fingers. He watched my face for the truth when I answered.

I sighed and signaled the waitress for another drink and downed the rest of the one in my hand. "I put in for a transfer out of the ED and Parker wrote me up. I'm stuck there for three more months, and I'm not sure I will make it, if I'm honest." And I knew I couldn't lie to Dan. "I thought I could do it, but I was wrong. I shouldn't have come back," I finished, not telling him anything he didn't already know.

"You're a hell of an emergency nurse, Elle. There is none better. Even on your worst day, you know more and do more than all those new kids put together." He covered his hand with mine looking at me with bright green eyes. His face had lines on it that it shouldn't, and I was sure that mine did too.

"Maybe. Maybe not. I feel like I'm dying on the inside, and I don't know how to fix it," I said, dropping my eyes to his hand in mine.

"Time?" he asked, his voice soft.

"That's what everyone keeps saying, but it isn't getting better," I said, finally looking up at him.

"Ah, Ellie," he sighed and reached over and grabbed my hands in both his. "It will get better. It will. Don't do anything rash; you love your job. You've still got so much to give. I'm rooting for you. It hasn't been that long. But you know what? If you hate it, quit. Screw that place. You don't owe them anything after giving so much." His smile broke the lines of his face, reminding me of the boy he'd been so long ago.

"Thanks, Dannie Boy." I smiled at him, a smile that I felt all the way to my core. It was the first one in a long time, and it shattered something deep inside of me.

The waitress brought my drink, and I sipped it while I watched him. He sat relaxed, eyes closed, and sipping his beer, his long legs stretched out and his bare feet peeking out from the hem of his jeans. He had kicked off his flip flops, and I thought the hair on his toes was adorable.

The way his soft gray tee-shirt clung to his chest was the perfect mix of hard abs and soft flesh. I remembered how once, in what felt like another lifetime, I loved him. God, what kids we had been then.

"Do you want to come home with me?" I whispered, keeping my eyes glued to his face.

"What?" his eyes snapped open and found me staring.

"We aren't twenty-two anymore, Daniel," I whispered, tears forming in my eyes.

"No. I mean yes," he stammered. "Fuck. No, we aren't twenty-two, Elle," he finished, recovering from his moment of surprise. He leaned over and grabbed my hands, looking me in the eyes. "God, yes, Elle, I want to go home with you. You can't imagine how much I would love to go home with you. You know that," he said, the hesitation in his voice catching me off guard.

"I hear a but," I said, feeling my heart break a little more.

"But I don't think now is the time; you're not ready, and I don't want to be just a distraction or a bandaid. You know how I feel about you, Ellie. It's not right for you, and it's not fair to me.

"I've seen you at work; I know you're still raw. This is something you have to come through before you can move forward. I want to be there and help, but I know you. You're stubborn and independent; you'll resent me if I let you use me as a crutch now, and I want forever, not just today." His face showed so much concern that I had to look away, catching some of the younger guys staring.

I was still in my royal blue scrubs, my hair a mess. My eyes were probably red and puffy with mascara down to my cheeks. Simply put, I was wrecked.

Hot embarrassed tears filled my eyes, and I dropped them to the table, pulling my hands from his. "You're right," I said, anger taking the place of embarrassment. "It wouldn't be right." I downed my drink and rose to leave.

"Elle, please, that isn't what I meant. I meant," he tried, backpedaling.

"I know what you meant," I interrupted. "I get it." I got up, paid my bill at the bar, and walked out, wiping angry tears off my face.

"Conroy, wait up."

I tracked the voice back to the door and found one of the second-year ortho residents rushing to catch me. "Where are you heading off to? It's early yet," he said, his blue eyes twinkling.

I struggled for a minute, trying to remember his name. I don't usually get them down until they are third or fourth years, but it came to me before the moment became awkward.

"Tim, right? Tim Franks." I said, smiling at him.

"I'm flattered you know that," he laughed, running his eyes down my body.

"Don't be," I laughed, "I had to chase you down to sign my trauma sheet yesterday, remember?" I said, earning a deep belly laugh from him.

"And you caught me." His bright-white smile dazzled, showing perfectly straight teeth.

"And now you've caught me. Do you need me to sign something?" I gave a little chuckle and cocked my hip. I could feel that last double Goose settling in, making me warm from my toes up.

I glanced over Tim's shoulder and saw Dan taking in the scene from the deck. He frowned when I looked up at the resident and smiled.

Ortho residents are known to work out. They have to muscle joints and bones into place, and sometimes it takes effort. They are the buffest of all the specialties; some border on looking like they use steroids, and Tim was no exception. At over six feet tall, he dwarfed me, his muscular body taut and ready to spring. Strong hands held my upper arm in a near bruising grip.

"I don't need you to sign something," he chuckled, letting my arm drop.

I gave him my best nurse look, the one that withered more doctors than not.

"I mean," he amended. "I guess I do have something you could sign," he laughed, leaning low to my ear. "With your lips," he whispered. "You're so beautiful."

"Doctor Franks," I chuckled, grinning up at him. "I'm old

enough to be your mother," I whispered, leaning toward him.

"Hardly. Besides, I've been called a mother fucker enough to make good on it if you're okay with that."

I barked a laugh, and it might have been the first genuine laugh I'd given since Keith died. With that thought, I felt my smile drop.

"Come on, Conroy," he said, stepping closer to me. The heat of his body sent shock waves to my core.

I looked around his shoulder, watching Daniel start to rise and walk our way.

"Sure. Okay," I said, walking toward the door with Tim. "What did you have in mind?" I asked, flipping my hair over my shoulder and casting a glare at Daniel, stopping him in his tracks.

He'd refused me. Tim hadn't, and Daniel lost the right to tell me how to live my life a long time ago.

"Well," Tim said, drawing the word out. "My place is right there, Conroy. I'm pretty sure I signed that trauma sheet; you should come and get it."

Smiling, I shook my head, following Tim into the dark alley behind Crockett's. "You're incorrigible," I laughed. "I'll grab my truck and follow you."

"I've been told that before, Conroy." He gave me a dark look adding, "My place is literally right there." He raised his finger, pointing at the long row of townhomes a short walk away.

"Oh," I said, feeling my heart trip. What was I doing? I tried to pull away, but he held my hand tightly, making my heart race faster.

"I mean it, Conroy. You're the most beautiful woman I've ever seen. Fuck Ross. On second thought, fuck me instead," he laughed, tugging me along.

He was right, I thought as I tripped over a loose stone, only to have his strong arm right me again. He'd seen Daniel reject me and stepped in. I'd wanted something when I stopped at Crockett's; I just needed to calm down and remember that.

As soon as the door to his townhouse was open, he had me against the wall. He kicked the door closed as his lips crashed into mine. Stunned, I tried to push him away and catch my breath, but he wasn't having it.

"I haven't showered; I'm a mess," I tried, thinking to slow him down.

"Fuck if I care. I like it dirty," he groaned into my mouth, his tongue finding mine. I couldn't keep up with the force of his kiss and felt my breath catch in my throat.

He pulled my bra down, cupping one breast in his hand. My heart pounded in my chest as he pushed my scrub top up, latching onto my nipple and sucking it into his mouth. I gasped at the feel of it, and he groaned, grinding his hips into mine.

"Fuck, Conroy," he said, spinning me around and sliding

my pants over my hips.

"Wait," I said, panting from the speed of it. But before I could finish the word, he was inside of me. I gasped again, clutching at the wall for support.

"Damn, you feel good. So fucking tight," he growled, setting a punishing pace. His hips slapped against mine before I got over the shock of the stretch. My eyes wide and my mouth frozen in a wide O, I struggled to breathe as he slammed into me.

One of Tim's hands grabbed my ponytail, pulling me against his chest while the other reached between my legs and sought my clit, rubbing it furiously.

I came violently, crying out against the onslaught of his hips and hands. After one final thrust, he pulled out, releasing his cum across my back with an obscene moan. His hand found my nipple, and he pinched it to the point of pain.

"That was so fucking good," he sighed, leaning down to kiss my jaw.

I was stunned, unable to say anything. It happened so fast. Confusion narrowed my eyebrows, and I blinked, trying to clear my head. It had felt good; I couldn't deny that. I mean, I came.

"Let me get a towel." He slapped my ass before walking toward the bathroom.

I was still standing with my hand braced against the wall when he returned and wiped his cooling cum from my back. He kissed my cheek, tossing the towel behind him. "You want a beer?" he asked, walking through his townhouse to the kitchen.

"I, uh. I need to head home," I said, straightening my clothes.

"Suit yourself, babe," he said, flashing me a megawatt smile. "When are you working?" he asked, turning on the TV.

"Um, Friday," I said, reaching for the door. The need to leave was so great that my heart seemed to stutter and stop.

"See you then," he said, his attention on the football game displayed on the TV screen.

Without answering, I closed the door and scurried across the parking lot to my truck. I didn't feel better until I sank into my soft leather seats, but even then, the cold trickle of cum down my side was sobering. I was already sore from how roughly he'd fucked me, and my core felt raw where my underwear rubbed.

My hands shook as I put them on the wheel. It was then that I looked up and caught Daniel standing on the deck of Crockett's watching. I'd been out of the bar for less than five minutes, but I was wrecked, and I knew it. Jamming the Ford into gear, I spun gravel and headed home.

Chapter 7

Daniel watched from the balcony of Crockett's as Elle stumbled out of Tim Franks's door. Haunted eyes darted right and left, and her black hair flew wildly about her face as she hurried to her truck and climbed in. She'd only been in the door a few minutes, but something had happened to upset her enough to send stones flying as she peeled out of the parking lot.

Dr. Franks had some personal issues that had landed him in human resources more than once already, and when Elle walked out of the bar with him, Daniel almost chased her down and grabbed her away, but Elle was hurting and had to make her own decisions. When she stumbled out of the townhouse door a few minutes later, clutching at her scrub top and scowling fiercely, Daniel assumed that Franks had gotten a hard slap on the cheek for his efforts and breathed a sigh of relief.

It's not that Daniel hadn't wanted to go home with Elle. In fact, he'd have given up his medical license to do so, but it wasn't the right time. She needed to heal, and sometimes healing was bloody, painful, and complex. Healing left scars, and Daniel wanted to be with her beyond the wound's closure and not be left in the scar tissue. Once, they'd had dreams and plans, and she needed to get to the place where she remembered that. And even if it wasn't him that she moved on with, she deserved to move beyond Keith.

Death does crazy things to people. It makes those left behind see the past through rose-colored glasses and not in the bright light of reality. Nurses talk, and ED nurses talk about everything. Nothing is off-limits or too taboo for them, and he and his peers had sat at the same desk and heard every conversation they'd had about boyfriends, girlfriends, and husbands for years. It's a coping mechanism that almost all of them employ. As bad as ED doctors have it, the nurses have it worse. And to a one, they use sarcasm, anger, and honesty to balance the scales.

Daniel knew things that Elle might not realize he knew. But this was the river that she had to wade through to come to the other side, and she would. She was the strongest person Daniel knew and she would recover. Until then, he would maintain his status as her closest friend and staunchest ally, even if it was the hardest thing he'd ever done.

Elle was struggling to find her footing in a new world, and as much as he would be there for her, he knew that it was time for him to move on too. He just hoped that she would see the situation for what it was and move on with him, not away from him.

In the meantime, he sent her a text, asking if she was doing okay and reminding her that he was there for her. Turning from the railing, he went back to his table and ordered another beer.

Chapter 8

When I pulled up, the house was dark, reminding me that I needed to start leaving a light on to chase the ghosts away. My driveway was long, and I had a lot of time to note how haunted that place looked. Parking outside the garage, I shut the door and walked inside, flipping on every light as I went.

I stopped at the thermostat, turning it up to eighty, before walking into the kitchen to pour myself a shot of vodka to warm my soul. My breathing had evened out, and I chided myself for being such a baby.

I stripped off my scrubs, tossing them into the hamper on the way to the bathroom. I turned the shower on, leaning over so that the water would run down my back and soothe the soreness between my legs. My black hair hung like a curtain around my face, protecting me from my surroundings, and shrouded in that privacy, I let the tears come.

What the fuck had happened? I wasn't sure I understood, and my emotions were raw and conflicted. I'd had enough vodka to make the situation fuzzy when I looked at it directly. I wanted to understand, but I didn't. Sighing, I washed everywhere twice before standing under the spray until the water started to cool.

I'd never cheated on Keith, but although he was dead, I felt like I had done exactly that. I toweled off, downing the rest of my vodka and taking another of Keith's Percocets. I needed sleep badly. It made everything better and the mind clearer. Maybe in the morning, this situation would make sense, and I could laugh about it.

Leaving the bathroom light on, I slipped between the sheets, reaching for Keith for the thousandth time. Drained of everything, I slipped into the darkness of my mind and let go.

I slept in. For the first time in weeks, I woke up well after sunrise. I slid from bed with a groan, feeling the pull between my thighs. After another hot shower, I went to the kitchen to put on coffee, checking my phone while it brewed.

Daniel had texted me several times and called once without leaving a message. I ignored him, choosing instead to take my coffee to the porch and sit in the sun. I'd thought the light of day would bring clarity, but it hadn't. If anything, I felt worse.

Stress over my job mingled with the thought in the back of my mind that maybe I'd been raped. Had I? Shaking my head, I tried to lighten the heaviness in my soul to no avail. Looking across fields next to me, my breathing came faster as I was unable to reconcile my feelings.

I hated my job, but I hated my days off more since they gave me nothing but time to think. I chased thoughts of work and Tim while my coffee went cold in my hand. It was noon when I finally gave up, changed clothes, and climbed into my truck.

Not wanting to run into Daniel or Tim, I avoided town, heading to The Mason Jar instead. I loved their wings, and their food, in general, was the best in town, regardless of the bar's appearance. It was a dank hole in the wall near an overgrown cemetery, and I loved that about it. At first, I'd been terrified of going there until I realized that the crowd wasn't nearly as rough as I'd thought.

In the beginning, they'd sold no top-shelf vodka, but they'd added a few over the years, looking to draw a more varied crowd. I sat at the bar, ordering wings and a Cîroc on ice. It was Tuesday, and the place was filled with a rowdy lunch crowd, and I wasn't surprised since The Jar was close to downtown businesses without being in the middle of them, it was big small town, and everyone knows someone who knows someone else. It's like playing six degrees anytime you go out, and I was no exception. I may not have grown up here, but I knew just about everyone, mostly because of my job.

"Hey, Elle," the bartender greeted, setting my drink down. "How're you holding up?" she asked.

"I'm holding up, Jill. How's the hubby and kids?" I asked, following the required social rules.

"Good, good," she said, moving down the bar as she passed

out drinks. "Hey, uh, if you need anything," she trailed off.

I knew what she meant.

People mean well. No one knows what to say or offer to someone who's struggling with a significant loss. I understood that. Jill was great, and we'd shared a beer on occasion at the bar after her shift. I liked her, but as much as I appreciated her sentiment, there was nothing she could do to help me. I wasn't sure anyone could.

I ate in silence, tuning out the noise of the place. Jill kept the drinks coming, and I let her, never bothering to decline. Back when I'd had a life, I would've cut her off after two. Three was my max, but I glanced at the pile of straws on the counter and knew I was deep into double that.

The day wore on, and I ordered an appetizer to soak up some of the alcohol before I headed home, knowing I didn't want to be the reason the pagers sounded.

"Hey, gorgeous."

I looked up from my drink and into eyes the color of topaz. Straightening my spine a little, I felt the rush of alcohol to my head. Somehow, despite the appetizer, I'd was more intoxicated than I thought, and there were more straws on top of the ones I'd had sitting next to the empty basket of mozzarella sticks, even though I swore I'd stop accepting those drinks.

I'd learned in college to keep my straws from finished drinks on the table. As a woman, I needed to know my limit, and keeping my straws helped with that- except for today. Today the straws had piled up unnoticed and uncared about. I blinked, looking into the face of the stranger who talked to me.

I'd never seen him before, and he was cute in a rugged, mountain-man kind of way. Sandy-blond hair with a tinge of red touched his collar, and cinnamon freckles dotted his nose. He had a trimmed, red beard and full lips tilted up in the corners in a smile.

"Hey," I answered, hearing the slur in my voice. My southern accent was thick, as it always was when I drank too much, and I kicked myself for letting it get this far.

"Is this seat taken?" he asked, his eyes roaming my face for permission.

"Uh. No," I said, breathing deeply to chase the fog from my mind.

A quick glance at the clock told me I'd sat in the same spot all day and would need to leave soon if I wanted to get out of bed at all in the morning.

"Can I get you something?" the man asked, sliding into the seat next to mine.

"I think I've had enough," I laughed, feeling my head spin as I turned to him. "I'm Elle," I finished.

"Charlie," he said, reaching to shake my hand.

Smiling, I took it. "Well, Charlie. I was getting ready to head out. I may or may not work tomorrow, but even if I don't,

Jill is going to charge me rent for this bar stool if I stay another minute."

"Nah. Jill lets the pretty girls sit as long as they want to. Now, if you were ugly," he stopped, shaking his head with a laugh. "Maybe not."

I reached over, punching his arm lightly. "Uh-huh. I really do have to go. I didn't realize how late it was." My head spun as I went to stand, and I steadied myself on his arm."

"Darlin'," he started, holding my elbow. "Pretty sure you shouldn't be driving."

His face blurred for a second when I looked up at him, and I knew he was right.

"It's backroads. I've got to have my truck; I'll be okay," I said, handing Jill my debit card. She watched me, her eyebrows narrowed, and a frown pinched her lips like maybe we'd both lost track of how much I'd drank.

Charlie slid my debit card back to me and put a hundred dollar bill on the bar, giving Jill a nod. "In that case, I'll follow you to make sure you get there."

I should've been worried about that, but I wasn't. If Charlie knew Jill, then he was okay. Jill wouldn't let a woman leave the bar with someone she didn't know or think was safe. She was very good about that. Then again, safe was relative, and Charlie was a stranger.

"Make sure she gets there, Charlie. She doesn't live far,"

Jill said, making me feel better about swaying on his arm.

Why do people follow a drunk person home? What's the point? Because, if the drunk person is in a car by themselves, there is no point. The person following them is just a witness to the destruction they cause, if not an active participant. Still, Charlie guided me out of the bar, and I let him.

When the cold air hit my face, I felt better and breathed deep, straightening my spine. I blinked and cleared my eyes, walking to my truck under my own power. "That's better," I said, smiling at the man next to me. "I actually think I'll be fine. I just needed to get some fresh air," I added, only swaying a little when I stepped into the truck.

Charlie shook his head, "I already told Jill I'd see you home. If I don't, she won't serve me for a month, and I like their wings too much for that," he said. His eyes smiled into mine, and he stepped on the running board, reached over, and buckled me in. "Back roads only," he said.

I made my face serious and saluted him. "Aye, aye, Captain." I put the truck in reverse, easing out onto the main road. It was a tricky spot, and because of a blind curve, there were a lot of accidents. I made the turn safely and headed into the night with Charlie's headlights behind mine.

I hadn't driven drunk since college, and even though one thinks they are good at it, they never are. I missed gears, stripped gears, and popped my clutch one too many times, but I made it. I wasn't proud, but alcohol is the great encourager, and I cheered as I eased into my driveway with my heart pounding and my throat dry. I needed a gallon of water and my bed.

Opening my door, I went to step on my running board only to miss and nearly fall. Charlie caught me under the armpits, steadying me. "I'm never drinking again," I murmured as my head spun.

"Sure. Come on; let's get you inside."

With one hand on my arm and the other arm around my waist, he helped me up the steps, used my keys to unlock the already unlocked door, and ushered me inside.

"You want a drink?" I asked, grabbing the tallest glass I owned and filling it with water. "Vodka, Bourbon, or water? That's all I've got," I added, downing the water with a chuckle.

"I'll take a bourbon," he said, looking around the house.

I knew what he must have thought. It's a lovely house, even if it felt like a crypt on a good day. It's neat and tidy, almost like no one lived in it. The finishings were high-end and obviously expensive. I'd worked hard to make it look like a showpiece. I'd once been proud of my home, even if all I felt looking at it now was empty.

I poured myself a vodka on ice and Charlie a bourbon, and we stood sipping as we assessed each other. He leaned in, keeping his eyes open, and his lips tasted like spice when he kissed me. The bourbon was Keith's, and the scent made me think of him. I opened my mouth, loving the way it tasted. If I kept my eyes closed, I could almost pretend.

I broke the kiss and finished my vodka, thrilling in the heady rush of it through my veins. I didn't look at Charlie but felt his eyes on me as I sipped another, sliding the bourbon toward him. The hands on the bottle were strong and calloused, and he poured himself a second glass. They were the hands of a worker, of someone who used them hard and daily. I wondered how they would feel on my skin. Keith had smooth hands, almost silky. Charlie's would feel the opposite, and I shivered at the thought.

He raised his arm, brushing the hair from my face and draping it across my back. Leaning in, he kissed up my neck to the shell of my ear. His hot breath smelled like heaven, and I closed my eyes, sinking into him. I knew he wasn't Keith; I knew. But it felt so good to think for a moment that he was.

Cupping my chin, he turned me to him and kissed my lips gently. For a man with hands as hard as his, it was one of the most gentle kisses I'd ever experienced. His other hand skimmed my arm, and I sank into him before grabbing it and leading him to my bedroom, where wedding pictures taunted me as I slipped off my shirt.

My eyes watered as I reached to untuck the tee from Charlie's jeans, but I refused to look too closely at why. I felt like I was watching through a window as he lay me on the bed, stripping me of the rest of my clothes. Almost reverently, he kissed my lips, caressing my tongue with his, and in that way, he was nothing like Keith.

He made his way down my body, planting himself between my thighs. I tried to move away, but I was boneless and unable to rally for that fight. His tongue found my core, and I arched into him, sinking my fingers into his long hair with a low moan. He took his time, tracing the pieces and parts of me expertly. His hands smoothed over my breasts, rolling my nipples until I was ready for him.

The first orgasm swept over me like waves at low tide crashing onto the sand. It was delicate and soft but no less powerful than if it had been pounded out of me. A guttural moan that seemed to come from my soul escaped my lips as he moved up my body, placing kisses on my bare flesh and exposing me further.

He slid between my legs and into my body in one careful push, and the smell of bourbon made me pliant and happy. He was big, bigger than anyone I'd had before, and the burn of the stretch was fantastic, lighting fires as he went to parts that had never been opened. I arched into him, taking what he offered.

His lips found mine, and the taste of him nearly sent me over the edge. I trembled as he slid in again, his lips never leaving mine as he made love to me. A stranger. It finally broke me, and I came around him, clenching as he grunted against the pressure of my walls. My orgasm was bone-deep and soul-shattering, but not in a violent way. It was one of those orgasms that satisfy you for days after and leave your pussy clenching at the thought of it.

When my body relaxed, he rolled me to my stomach, keeping my legs together and pinned between his. He used his strong hands to rub the knots from my shoulders, and I wondered what he was doing. I'd never been made love to like this. He didn't know me, yet he gave so much; it was confusing despite feeling incredible.

Wedging himself between my legs, he entered me again. The feel of him between my unparted thighs was exquisite as they served to increase the pressure on my core. Bracing himself above me, he increased his pace until I cried out with each thrust, coming again. I moved limply from the pressure of his hips pistoning into me while stars swam behind closed eyes, and I knew I was passing out.

I was gone when I felt him let go deep inside of me. His tense muscles and deep grunt signaled his pleasure, and he held the position until his violent spasms stopped.

For a long time afterward, I felt him caress my back and move my hair to kiss it as I lay dazed and unmoving on my stomach with his cum dripping from my core. I could feel his presence, and I sank into it, the smell of sex and bourbon taking me to another time and another man.

I barely roused when he kissed my shoulder, and the bed dipped as he left.

Chapter 9

I awoke to the sound of my phone ringing, then going silent. My mouth felt like a squirrel had crawled into it and died. I lay spread eagle on my bed, boneless. The semen on my thighs was barely dry and still dripped when I rolled to the side of the bed.

No one but Keith had ever cum inside of me. I felt the tears start only to dry when the phone started ringing again. It lay on the nightstand by a tall glass of water that I had not placed there.

If not for that and the obvious evidence left from the night before, I could chalk it all up to a dream. I could tell myself that Keith had been the one making such tender love to me, even though I knew he was never that gentle. Keith had liked it rough and had rarely touched me the way I'd been touched during the wee hours of the morning.

The phone silenced only to start right back up with its annoying brand of get the fuck up, bitch. I went to answer it, my head still spinning from vodka.

"Conroy, where the hell are you?" Parker growled. "You're twenty minutes late," she said.

"Fuck. I thought I was off today." I groaned, feeling light-headed when I moved to stand.

"Get here by eight, or I'll add a shift to your week," she said, ending the call.

I tried to stand, only to find my legs wouldn't hold me. I dropped to my knees, bracing on the carpet before managing to rise and stumble into the bathroom. I showered as quickly as I could, unwilling to go to work the way I was.

I was still drunk, at least technically. I knew that, but I didn't want to make the day up, and Parker had absolute dominion over the nurses in the ED. Maybe she'd fire me and solve all of my problems, but somehow, she'd just make me more miserable than I already was. I had to get through this so I would still be eligible for that cushy job on same-day surgery. I had to play her game and win.

I grabbed a cup of coffee and ran to my truck, slamming it into gear and going sixty through town. My head was clear enough, but my heart raced from alcohol and dehydration. I felt like shit, but there was no way around it. Maybe someone could give me a bag of fluids so that I could make it through the day.

When I was a new nurse and partied too much after work, we would sneak into an empty room and start IVs on each other the next day. It was once a running joke that we needed to keep banana bags on hand, not for the drunks that came in needing the electrolytes and vitamins in the fluid, but for the staff.

The ED had always prided itself on being a close-knit unit that was more family than coworkers, but that was before the department's size tripled. Now, you were lucky to know the nurse's name in the pod next to yours. Though some stayed close and still went out, most moved on to other friends and interests.

Emergency department nurses tend to have short careers, with burnout and PTSD limiting their lifespan. You can only see so much before you start to slip into despair, and most new nurses won't make it more than two years. How many failed resuscitations does it take? How many lost traumas? How many abused children and dispassionate parents? It's different for everyone, but there is most definitely a limit.

The ones who stay turn into uncompromising, battle-hardened witches. We've had a few nurses literally die on the job, but that wouldn't be me. I needed to leave. I'd done more time than most managed and wasn't too proud to say I was through. I just needed to survive Ms. Parker, and then I could move on.

I clocked in with five minutes to spare, hurrying to get my assignment from the charge nurse's desk. I wasn't surprised to be in the trauma bays; I knew I would be. Not only because of Parker but because it was the best place to put a nurse when they were late.

Usually, the bays are empty when the day starts, making it easier to absorb into another assignment. I sipped my coffee, checking my rooms with a glance. I was still pleasantly tipsy, and my anxiety was a low hum instead of a scream.

"You smell like a Russian prostitute," Kat laughed when she passed me on her way to the med room.

"Long night," I said, chuckling back at her. "I thought vodka didn't have a smell," I added, sniffing my arm.

"Maybe in small quantities, but it's coming from your hair follicles. I think that makes a difference."

"Fuck you." I smiled at her, and she smiled back, flipping me the bird.

Kat was one of the younger nurses that I thought might survive long enough to be good at the job. You can always tell the ones that won't make it. They come in bright-eyed, friendly, and without a trace of sarcasm. Those folks belong on the floors and not in a place that eats happiness alive. The first time one of them gets called a cunt by a drunk, they break down instead of telling the asshole that they'd rather be a cunt than smell like one. It's just the way it is.

That being said, ED nurses struggle to thrive on other units. Their dark sense of humor, foul language, and direct communication styles don't lend themselves to being on a med-surg floor. An ED nurse develops protective layers of coping skills that aren't appreciated outside of that department. Most retire to units that turn patients over quickly, like pre or post-op. That way, they don't have a patient long enough to offend them into emailing the manager.

Think of a large emergency department as a city and the nurses low-level, street smart thugs just trying to survive the brutality the streets offer. If an accountant gets groped, slapped, stalked, or punched in the face, it's assault. Nurses are just asked what they could have done differently to deescalate the situation. It's our fault; it always is.

The funny thing is, despite the violence and cynicism inherent in the emergency department, I still loved it until the day Keith came in shattered like a dropped lightbulb. And I think he got the better end of the deal as I was left trying to put myself together again while he'd moved on to something else, maybe something better.

"Hey, Ellie. You okay?" Daniel said from the bay door where I checked the intubation bags to make sure they had the correct size tubes.

"I'm good. No worries," I added, keeping my back turned. I'd hoped he would walk away and leave well enough alone, but he came up behind me instead.

"Long night?" he asked, inhaling deeply.

"I thought I was off today," I said, defending myself even though I knew I shouldn't. I was too embarrassed to look at him. He'd rejected me, and even though a part of me understood why, it still hurt.

"You're losing weight," he added, leaning against the wall and watching my fingers fly over the endotracheal tubes and rearranging them into ascending order by size.

Intensive care nurses think they have the corner on OCD behavior because their IV lines and pumps are labeled in perfect script and spaced exactly one point three inches apart on the pole. Still, ED nurses have their own neurosis that are no less invasive to the species. I arranged the color-coded oral airways in descending order based on size while I struggled not to look at the man I'd loved before Keith.

"I'm okay; it's been a long week. Thanks for asking. I'll be sure to get a good lunch. Maybe the Eloquis reps will bring Chinese." I tried to push past him and leave, but he grabbed my arm.

"Please, Elle," he whispered, and I made the mistake of looking at him. His eyes were filled with pain and longing that I didn't understand or deserve. I'd offered myself, and he'd refused. I pulled away, my wet hair smacking against his chest as I went.

"There's gum on the charge nurse's desk. Grab a piece. I'm running to Starbucks and will get you something," he said, implying I smelled like alcohol and was probably at least still a little drunk. He wasn't wrong, but I didn't care. I was beyond caring about some things. I watched as he walked away, heading for the doors to the atrium.

A few years ago, the hospital had renovated the lobby and turned it into something you saw in five-star hotels. There was marble everywhere and a wide, curving staircase leading to the upper levels. The atrium, they called it, was five stories high with stunning views and balconies where staff took breaks and the med students studied. Sometimes music students would take advantage of the acoustics and play their instruments, lending a sense of peace to the air.

A giant gas fireplace with glass stones twinkling below the flames sat to one side. Chairs surrounded it, and families would sit there to wait for news of their loved ones. On the other side of the atrium was the one thing that kept every professional in the building alive: Starbucks.

One stroke of engineering and planning genius had brought the mecca of caffeine to the people needing it most. That green and glass storefront was the one bright spot in the hospital, and it was packed at all hours.

I was checking my last room when Daniel put a hot, black Grande Americano with two extra shots in my hand, placing a piece of gum in my pocket for afterward.

"Medcom called for a flight request. There's a P1 coming," he said as the first pager sounded, making me jump into him. The next fifteen that went off made my heart stop, and a cold, vodka-laced sweat bead on my upper lip.

"Thanks," I said, holding the coffee up as I slipped past him, unable to meet his eyes as the sound of pagers faded to nothing.

"Elle," Susan said from the charge nurse's perch. "P1. Forty-seven-year-old male. MVC. Vitals unstable. Intubated. Five minutes out."

I nodded, accepting it. My room was ready, and I put my lead apron on and covered it with a fluid impervious gown so it wouldn't be ruined when the life bled out of someone. I flicked my long, black hair over my shoulder and used an elastic to tie it back. It sucks starting an IV and having the ends of your hair trail through puddles of someone else's blood. It was one of the first lessons I'd learned as an ED nurse with long hair. It may be pretty, but it collects all manner of bodily fluids if left down. I sipped my coffee, waiting. I took a minute to let the remnants of the vodka calm my nerves as my head drifted to a place where this wasn't killing me.

Soon the room filled with the trauma team, and I put my coffee on the rail along the wall as roles were assigned. The team let one of the first-year surgery residents give the rest of the staff jobs, and I chuckled to myself when he assigned me to do the blood pressure and the tech to do the IV. While the tech was perfectly capable of doing the line and I the blood pressure, we knew what we'd do once the patient got here, but it was an exercise the resident needed to practice. Still, once the patient arrived, the plan would fall apart as it usually did. They say that battle plans only survive until the first contact with the enemy, and traumas are much the same.

The tech looked at me and winked, forcing me to give him a small smile. Nerves calmed with caffeine and a slight buzz, I readied myself.

Lifenet came in hot, starting the man's story before they were in the room. The patient was an unrestrained driver in a single car rollover at interstate speeds and had been ejected from his vehicle, landing down an embankment. As they unbuckled the straps holding him onto their gurney, I leaned across the stretcher with my hands on the backboard, waiting patiently for the paramedic to finish report.

The man had been intubated on the scene, and his blood-smeared face stopped my heart.

"Sixteen gauge in the left AC. Labs drawn."

"Sixteen in the right and warm normal saline up at wide open, the first unit of blood's up on the level one infuser."

"We have bilateral hemotympany, obvious skull, and cervical spine deformities with positive step-offs. Obvious deformities to bilateral femurs. Elle, get out of here."

"Move on my count: one, two." On three, we moved the backboard to the stretcher, and our initial assessment began.

On instinct, I ducked under the tech as he reached over me to put the manual blood pressure cuff on the patient's right arm.

"Sixteen-gauge in the right AC," I said, pulling blood from the line and handing it to another nurse who appeared out of nowhere to take it and put it in lab tubes.

I hooked saline to the line and flipped the Level One rapid infuser on, listening to the sound of it humming in readiness.

"80/palp," the tech said, calmly tossing his stethoscope around his shoulders while attaching the last cardiac lead to the patient's chest. "Heart rate 120, Sat 93, end-tidal 39," he finished reciting vital signs as I opened the blood cooler and chanted off the donor number of the first unit with the nurse next to me.

Behind me, medical students used razor-sharp scissors to cut the clothes from the patient. "Obvious deformities to bilateral femurs," one said, tossing the clothes to the side as my heart stuttered in my chest, causing a backup of blood to my brain.

Ortho swept in and got to work on the man's lower legs. They twisted in ways that no leg should and had more movement than was natural. His thighs were huge, one larger than the other, and his skin was paperwhite.

"Two units on the Level-One," the chief resident ordered, and I spiked the first bag, making the rapid infuser sing.

I looked from my shaking hands, catching Tim Franks watching me over the shattered leg of the patient. I looked away quickly, not meeting his eyes as I switched from one bag of blood to the next seamlessly.

I loved running the machine that pumped a pint of blood into a patient in two minutes or less, and I was good at it. There was a certain peace in chanting donor numbers from blood bags and gliding between the two pressurized chambers that forced the blood to run faster.

"Repeat pressure 74/46," someone said.

"Two more units."

I flipped the release button on one side, slipping the third bag into it before switching sides and repeating the process for the fourth.

"Fast exam is positive."

One of the jobs a resident has during a trauma is to do a rapid ultrasound of four points on the patient's torso to check for bleeding. It's called a fast exam because it should be completed in two minutes or less. The fantastic thing about a well run trauma is that ten things are happening simultaneously. It's a well-choreographed dance that, when done right, is beautiful to watch.

"Call the OR and get a room ready." The trauma attending pushed off from the wall where he'd been watching. "Pack 'em up."

The pagers sounded again, first one and then many, bringing coffee-laced bile to the back of my throat.

"P2 coming. I heard there's three more behind it," Susan said from behind the computer where she'd been taking notes on everything said and done in the last few minutes.

Pulling the monitor down, I sat it at the foot of the

stretcher, spiked a bag of saline onto the rapid infuser to make sure every drop of blood went into the patient, and unlocked the stretcher.

"I'll take him." One of the ERT nurses stepped into the room. "I saw you were in the zone and didn't want to step on your toes," she said with a smile.

A small group of nurses worked as the in-hospital oh-shit squad called the ERT. They went to all the strokes, traumas, cardiac arrests, and did the unstable transports, hence their title of Emergency Response Team. Most ED nurses loved having them because they were highly skilled and knowledgeable. Still, they'd been accused of stepping on toes during the biggest traumas and taking all the fun for themselves.

I knew she meant well, but I wished she'd have come into the room at the beginning. She could have my thunder- all of it. But with over eight hundred patients in the hospital and just three ERT nurses dealing with them, I understood why she hadn't. She'd probably been late to the party.

"Thanks, Rach," I said, stepping aside and letting her guide the stretcher down the crowded halls.

I looked over my shoulder, gauging the mess left behind. Blood pooled on the floor where it dripped from the stretcher, and a carpet of trash spread into the corners. The only clear spot was where the stretcher had been.

I glanced at the clock on the wall. Six minutes fifty-seven

seconds. The trauma was in my bay for seven minutes, then gone to the operating room. It was a good time, I thought, even as I felt the tremors start. Running to the sink, I threw up Starbucks and the last dregs of vodka until my stomach was empty.

Wiping my mouth with the back of my hand, I grabbed my cooling Americano, stripped the bloody gown from my lead apron, and went to the next room where the P2 was already unloading.

Three hours later, I leaned against the brick wall of the ambulance bay, struggling to keep my mind from going any further down the rabbit hole. My hands shook as I finished the coffee that had long ago gone cold. Tipping my head to the fall sun, I let it warm places nothing else could reach.

My portable phone rang, and I fumbled through my pocket, spilling the contents as I pulled it out. "Conroy," I answered, hating that my voice shook.

"Stroke in ten minutes. Last seen normal 2 hours ago," Susan started, pausing for a minute. "Are you at lunch?"

"Yeah," I lied. "I'll be right there."

Merc, one of the medics who had brought the most recent trauma, went by me to load his ambulance and leave. A cigarette dangled between his lips, taunting the security guard that kept random people from wandering in the ED's back door.

"Can I get a drag of that, Merc?" I asked.

"Since when do you smoke, Conroy?" he asked, slanting his eyes at me.

"Since today," I answered, reaching toward him. He slipped the cigarette into my fingers, and I breathed it so deep that I felt it in my toes.

I'd smoked in college when I was drinking but had quit as soon as I'd graduated, so I wasn't a complete noob at it. The nicotine hit my system, recharging me and making my head swim pleasantly. I took another drag before handing it back to him.

"Thanks, man," I said.

"You dropped some stuff." He walked away, shutting the door to his bus and driving off.

Sighing, I bent, scooping up the detritus of a busy day. My eyes snagged on the packet of medication lying next to the stick of gum Daniel had given me hours ago.

One of the traumas had been a young woman. She'd had a panic attack after being told that her boyfriend was rushed to surgery. The doc had ordered her a Klonopin, and Kat and I had both pulled one from the Accudose dispensing machine. She'd given hers, and I'd forgotten to return mine.

I grabbed the pill, looking to see if anyone watched me before opening the package, breaking the pill in half, and dry swallowing it.

Fuck it. It was a shit day, and I needed something to slow

the spiral. My shrink had prescribed the same medicine after Keith died, and I'd blown through it in the weeks following. I needed to call for a refill.

"What's coming, Doc-Cin?"

"Someone brought a motorcycle to a car fight."

"In the rain? What moron rides their bike on a day like this?"

Chapter 10

The stroke came and went. The ERT nurse, Rachel, helped give the clot-busting medicine that might reverse some of the damage while I restocked the trauma bay and grabbed a sandwich from the vending machine in the waiting room. She didn't need me, and I appreciated that endlessly.

I hadn't seen Daniel all day and figured he must have been relegated to the department's non-E side, and I was glad for him. After a relatively peaceful half an hour, the pagers sounded again. I heard them, waiting for my skin to crawl, only it didn't. I watched through a haze of calm as people rushed into my room, donning lead, gowns, and gloves. The Klonopin had taken the edge off of my panic, steadying my hand as I grabbed lead of my own. I slid it over my shoulders, flipping my ponytail from beneath Velcro straps. "What's coming?" I asked, the words burning my throat like acid.

"65-year-old female. Fall from standing. On blood thinners. Vitals unstable," Susan said, not even finishing before the medics swept through the bay doors with Merc doing one-armed chest compressions.

"Lost a pulse under the canopy," he said, giving every medic's excuse for not calling ahead and alerting us that the patient was in cardiac arrest.

Sighing, I climbed onto the stretcher, reaching to the EMS cart to continue CPR while medics unbuckled the straps holding her down.

"One, Two." On three, I scrambled backward, continuing CPR until my feet hit the ground and someone else took over so that I could put in an IV. The tech didn't bother with the blood pressure and simply slapped on the EKG leads. My hands didn't shake as I slid the needle into the vein at the crook of her arm while the resident placed a breathing tube into her lungs. Her vellum-thin skin was a deep purple from bruising wrist to shoulder, and I had to feel for the vein and stick blindly.

"Sixteen-gauge in the right AC," I said, drawing blood and handing it to the waiting nurse.

"Epinephrine in," someone called, and CPR continued for two more minutes.

"Pulse check," the attending ordered.

"We have a pulse."

"Call neurosurgery and get to scan."

I threw the monitor on the bed and unlocked it, steering through the crowd of people on the way to CT scan as I pressed the bag that would deliver oxygen through the breathing tube.

In radiology, the patient was moved onto the table and the ventilator set up. I went to the control room, leaning against the wall and enjoying the layer of padding that separated me from the world.

I listened to the beeping of the patient's heart monitor, letting it lull me into the Klonopin-induced cloud. Monitors are like babies; each cry means something different. I've never met a nurse who can't ignore any but the most critical alarms a heart monitor makes, and I was no exception. I listened to the beeps and chirps, hearing them but not. An arm banded around me, pulling me into the vacant scanning room on the other side of the control area.

"Hey, baby," Tim said, roughly shoving his hand into my scrub bottoms.

"What the fuck, Tim. I have a patient on the table," I said, pushing at him to dislodge the fingers that tried to pry their way inside of me.

"Doesn't matter," he said. "Someone else will watch them. Come give me my pussy. I'll be quick," he chuckled, and I knew he was right. A minute or less was all he'd needed the last time.

"Fucking no," I said, my voice rising. I pushed at him harder, and the door to the room swung open, and a stretcher wheeled inside. Daniel trailed behind, his eyes pinned to the resident hovering over me.

"What the fuck, Dan. Why you gotta be a cock block on my pussy?" Tim laughed, causing my cheeks to flame red.

"Thirty seconds against a wall doesn't make it yours, asshole," I whispered, glaring at him. I pushed hard, finally escaping the much larger man.

He laughed, bringing his fingers to his nose. "Smells like someone else has been in it anyway." The look he gave me warned of violence and pain. I'd embarrassed him. Maybe Daniel didn't know what we were talking about, but Tim did. I didn't care about the baby doctor's feelings; he had no right to touch me like that. One of his buddies sniggered from the hallway, alerting me that we had even more company.

"Fuck you, Tim," I said, banging through the door into the control room. My head was spinning and heart pounding as the radiology staff looked up from their screens, missing the incident entirely. I caught my breath against the wall, trying to calm my slamming heart.

Dehydration added to lack of food and sleep made me twitchy. The Klonopin whispered that everything was fine and I only needed to breathe, so I did. False peace settled my nerves, dissipating the anxiety that started to build as I waited through the last of the scans.

My patient had bleeding on the brain that caused a significant shift of the structures inside. That was what probably led to her cardiac arrest, and her outcome wasn't going to be good. Neurosurgery came and wheeled the patient to the operating room, where they would try to relieve the pressure and save her life. With her age and condition, it wouldn't work, but we get paid to try, so we do.

Back in the department, I found a bathroom and splashed my face with cold water before taking large gulps of it from my hands. Avoiding the mirror, I watched the water circle the drain, noticing the similarity to my life. A knock at the door pulled me from my thoughts.

"Elle, let me in," Daniel said, his voice soft and filled with the sadness regret leaves.

I flushed the toilet, scrubbing my hands down my face before opening the door.

"Are you okay," he asked, pulling me into a tight hug.

"I'm fine, Dan," I said, enjoying the scent of apples and cinnamon that lingered in the depths of his cologne.

"You could have his license for that. What happened?"

Daniel had always been my best friend. Even when we'd dated, he'd been the only person I turned to with my problems. I'd always been the type of person to keep my thoughts to myself, not sharing them with anyone, but somehow Dan had gotten past that. When we broke up, the only thing that changed was that we weren't planning a life on the same trajectory because we'd remained the best of friends.

"I made out with him the other night," I said, hating the lie that flowed like water down the drain. "I was upset, and I guess he's the possessive type." I stopped, shaking my head and avoiding the storm of his eyes.

I wasn't going to say anything else; I couldn't.

He sighed, tipping his head back but not loosening his arms from around me. "God, Elle," he started, and I heard the pain in his voice. It struck me harder than the sound of pagers going off. "I love you. I've loved you from the beginning. The dumbest thing I ever did was let you go, but you know what?" he paused, ruffling my hair with his nose and breathing me in. "Do you remember that night we laid in the grass on that hill outside of town and watched the stars?" he asked, changing directions from what he originally intended to say. "You told me then how much you loved astronomy and that if there was money in it, that's what you would've done." He pulled me tighter, resting his chin on the top of my head as I leaned into him, breathing deeper still.

"I remember." My voice caught in my throat, and my eyes burned with unshed tears.

"We are celestial bodies in orbit around each other, Elle. And just like them, we will inevitably collide. It's just not our time, but when we do? It's going to be extraordinary. It's going to be something that neither one of us will be willing to let go of again, and it's going to be forever unchangeable. I promise you that, Elle." He kissed the top of my hair, and I shuddered a breath into my lungs, swaying at the force of it.

"Are you okay?" he asked.

"I'm fine."

"Elle, I know that's a lie, but you will be okay. I swear. Eat more, worry less," he said, trying to laugh. Still, the gravity of the situation wasn't lost on him.

I nodded my head in agreement, even though that was a lie too.

After wiping my nose on the back of my arm, I pulled from him, missing the heat of his chest instantly. Dan was right; I knew that. I wasn't ready for a relationship. I couldn't get through the night without seeing Keith's bloody, shattered face in my dreams or hearing the sounds of those damn pagers going off. I might never be ready to move on, and I sure as hell wasn't ready now.

They say it gets easier, but I don't believe that. How do you move on after the loss of a limb? Obviously, people do, but they miss that limb, and the phantom pain from it never goes away. Keith was a part of me I couldn't see beyond, and I questioned whether or not I'd survive his loss. Maybe he was my heart, and my body just didn't realize it was dead yet.

But I'd loved Daniel, too. He'd been my first love as a woman and not the crush of a girl. If it had been Dan that died in my trauma bay, would I be this adrift? Yes. Yes, I could admit that I would be, but Keith would've been there to guide me through it, whereas Daniel was waiting for me to get my shit together mostly on my own. Obviously, he had more faith in me than I did.

I walked away from him, feeling the weight of the day

press in on me. In the kitchen, I grabbed water and swallowed the other half of the Klonopin on a whim. My day was almost done, and if I played my cards right, I would be in bed soon. I hoped the pill would give me what I needed most: a good night's sleep.

The rest of the shift was uneventful and went by in relative peace. For some reason, Parker was still there when I clocked out. "Good job today, Conroy," she said as I passed her open office door.

"Fuck you," I answered, just low enough for her to hear me but not loud enough that anyone else could; I never missed a step as I escaped out the door.

I left the parking lot, shadowed by three helicopters circling the roof like vultures. Once upon a time, I would have loved seeing them, and I might have taken a picture to post on social media because the way the moon rose behind them as the sun set was beautiful. Now I ducked my head and steered the truck toward home.

I passed Crockett's, ignoring the pull of alcohol and hot wings. I was in charge the next day and hadn't slept more than a few hours in days. Like the gears of a woodchipper, that place would rip through me if I wasn't careful, so I needed to be the best I could, even if I knew that it wasn't good for me.

Parking my truck outside the garage, I went for the stairs, changing my mind at the last minute and walking into the garage instead. I took in the devastation of the last remaining parts of Keith's life, understanding that I needed to start making decisions about this stuff. I couldn't keep the bike's wreckage forever because knowing it was there was a deterrent to healing, or so my shrink said.

Inside, I stripped off my scrubs, leaving a trail behind me. I stood at the island in the kitchen in nothing but a bra and panties and poured a shot of Grey Goose. I tipped my head back, letting the clear liquid burn the last edges of my day away. I took another shot for good measure and walked into the bedroom feeling light on my feet.

I sat on the bench in the shower while hot water rinsed my mind. There was bone-weary tiredness settling over me that's weight made it difficult to focus, yet my mind raced from thought to thought and vision to vision, letting me know sleep would be difficult, despite my chemical efforts to ensure it.

I stripped the sheets from my bed, picked up my scrubs, and walked into the laundry room. Glass clattered against the metal of the drum when I dumped the laundry in, making me dig through to see what had fallen from my pockets. After scooping out trauma shears, pens, and empty glass vials, I started the laundry and padded to my room. I tossed the scissors and pen on the counter, pausing at the glass vials. The vial of Versed on my palm was empty, but the Fentanyl vial was not. I'd planned on taking one of the last Percocet pills left in the bottle, but the Fentanyl would work better and not leave me as groggy in the morning. I clutched the vial as the thought of a good night's sleep weighed on me.

Grabbing the trauma shears, I used their edge to pop off the vial's top then dumped the remaining fentanyl in my mouth, holding it under my tongue until my soul started to float away. A smile came to my face unbidden, and I learned the appeal of the drug as it reached into my mind, vanishing the dark spots and leaving everything around me soft and shrouded in sunshine and cotton.

I made the two steps to my bed on shaky legs, laughing at what a lightweight I was. I had the presence of mind to check my alarm before my phone fell from my fingers with a clatter, and my brain went blessedly silent.

Chapter 11

The pagers finished their song as I walked through the ED doors the following day, making me groan. I woke up feeling better than I had in weeks. I'd slept so hard that I hadn't moved and awoke with my arm still hanging over the side of the bed. I sipped the hot Americano as I waded through the sea of staff donning lead and fluid impervious gowns.

"It's too early for this shit," I grumbled at Kayla, the night shift charge nurse. Her eyes were bloodshot and heavy-lidded as she took in my perky appearance with a sigh.

"You smell good," she said, stifling a yawn with her hand. "I can't wait to smell good and go to sleep. This place sucks. It's sucked all night, and it will continue to suck into the foreseeable future. PS, you're two nurses short at eleven," she added, handing me the list of nurses and their assignments.

"Thanks for the report; sleep well," I said, taking the staffing sheets and watching her walk away. I would look at the tracking board and figure the rest of it out. I grabbed the pager from the counter, checking the last entry to find out what the others were prepping for.

Just as I figured when I heard the racket, a P1 was coming. A seventy-year-old man had wrecked his ATV and was being transferred from a smaller hospital in the southern part of the state. He was intubated and had a head bleed. He was being sent because he needed a higher level of care than the local hospital could provide, and a large portion of our traumas came for this reason. Unless the helicopter could scoop them up from the accident scene, they first went to the closest place to stabilize and await transport. We joked and called these traumas 'used' since they were typically wrapped up and tied with a bow when they came to us, leaving nothing to do but find them a bed on one of the units.

ATVs are an interesting facet of Appalachian life, and the area has the highest rate of ATV-related trauma in the country because of it. We've seen toddlers in the emergency department that have wrecked an ATV. For some reason, they are endemic to the population starting from birth. One of our clinical preceptors had presented ATV-related statistics at a conference only to learn that most people there didn't even know what ATVs were. She laughed about it for months afterward.

I grabbed a trauma sheet and walked into the bay to see if they needed help checking in the patient, only to find the room full.

"Only hands-on staff in the room, please," I said, making eye contact with several students and residents. "Spectators out. You can watch from behind the line."

The trauma bays had sliding glass door fronts and taped

lines at their thresholds. It was a sad attempt in crowd control on my part, but my scowl and reputation had people moving out of the way. Not everyone enforced the rules, but traumas were more efficient if the staff wasn't tripping over gawking med students, so I did. Yes, they needed to learn but learning to stay out of the way was also important. The room cleared effectively, and as the crew rolled through the door, I left, giving myself a chance to check the pulse in the rest of the department and let the nurses in the room do their job.

We may have been short-staffed, but what staff we had was experienced and efficient. The attending physicians on duty were quick, and enough beds were available above our heads that we shouldn't get bogged down with admissions before the end of the day.

The non-E side was quiet as most of the rooms were closed until another provider came in at nine, but a few rooms were open, and nurses quickly walked in and out of them.

"Are we good over here?" I asked, knowing that once the department's emergent side exploded, I might not check on the non-E side as much as I should. I'd always thought they should have a separate charge nurse, but god forbid anyone agree with me.

"We're good, Conroy," someone answered. "Paige is floating."

"Perfect," I replied, knowing Paige was a heck of a float

nurse and would make sure that both sides of the ED flowed as smoothly as possible.

I walked through the breakroom and into the administration offices to ensure no one was hiding in the clinical preceptor's office before rounding back into the ED proper.

The pager on my hip sounded, then sounded again before the first one died away. Two priority-two traumas were coming from an MVC. With a sigh, I headed toward the charge nurses's desk, wondering how I could make it eleven more hours without cracking.

"Conroy." Ms. Parker's voice called to me from the depth of her office as I walked by.

"Yeah," I said, continuing on my way.

"Come in," she said, leaving no doubt that it was a command and not an invitation.

My shoulders slumped, and I backed a few steps before walking into the well-lit room

"Sit," she said, nodding to the straight-backed chair in front of her desk.

"There's a P1 in the bay and two P2s five minutes out," I said, ignoring her request and standing in the doorway.

She stared at me expectantly for what seemed like a minute, saying nothing. I walked deeper into the room, sinking into the chair with an aggravated groan. Ms. Parker had a way of making you feel like an unruly teenager instead of a busy adult.

"How are things going?" she asked, steepling her fingers on the desk between us.

"Fine," I spit, meeting her stare and wondering why she picked this moment to pull me into her office.

"Things seem to be going better?" she asked rather than stated.

"Right. Sure," I said, rising from the chair. "We're short, and I need to write for one of these traumas," I added as I headed through her office door.

"Oh, and, Conroy?" she barked, stopping my progression. "Keep it together. No more coming in drunk," she warned, looking at me over the rim of her glasses. I wanted to punch her in her sanctimonious face because, how dare she? She was the reason I was in this situation. I fumed inside but forced my face to remain blank.

I met her glare with an expression devoid of any emotion at all. I didn't blink, didn't smile, didn't nod my head. After a second, I turned on my heel and left without another word; she didn't deserve one. I wouldn't be drinking if I'd been allowed to transfer out of the ED. She'd kept me in an untenable situation for her purposes. She didn't get to tell me how to cope with it. I understood that she thought she'd made a mistake not returning to the bedside after her daughter died, but she didn't get to make that choice for me. Her concern wasn't appreciated, and her directive wasn't fair. At the end of the day, it was my career, and if I wanted to flush it, I could. I would.

The first trauma was already being settled, so I grabbed a trauma sheet and stalked into an empty room, and logged into the computer to begin the process of checking in the second.

"Twenty-Six-year-old restrained driver was in the right lane at The Split and was clipped by the driver of another vehicle. Moderate damage, but the car was driveable. Complained of neck, back, and shoulder pain on scene. No LOC. On three: one, two." the patient was moved onto the stretcher. Then, nurses and residents began their careful dance around the woman, shouting their findings to me.

The Split is a hot spot for accidents locally. Also, affectionately known by EMS as the Bermuda Triangle, it is the place where Interstate 68 merges with 79 and splits north to south. It forms a triangle that can be seen from the air, and as it had no actual merge lanes, accidents happen there almost daily.

Because of its winding S-turns and dramatic elevation changes, I-79 is one of the country's top fifteen most dangerous interstates. It doesn't help that the state's insufficient funding for road maintenance left portions of the roadway unpainted and riddled with potholes. Unwary travelers don't stand a chance and often find themselves scattered in pieces amid the beautiful mountain scenery. The Split only adds to the statistics involving I-79, and better lighting and signage would do nothing to help that.

The two drivers today were lucky. The worst trauma I'd seen before Keith had come from The Split, but these people would go home without much more than a few scrapes to show for it. I finished writing the last of the details on the trauma sheet and handed it to the nurse taking the patient to the CT scanner as she passed me.

An hour later, I picked at yet another breakfast bought from the cafeteria and stared at the assignment sheets. A nurse had called off at eleven, and at three nurses short, I was paddling upstream. I'd lose my float nurse and my flow coordinator that acted as the second triage nurse. With over eighty beds, the shortage was devastating. Assignments would have to be expanded, leaving fewer nurses to do more work. While other units could put the charge nurse into staffing, due to the nature of the beast, the ED could not. Though the supplemental pool had nurses trained for the ED, they had no one to give me today, and the staff crunch would be painful for all.

I drank my second Americano as I directed ambulances to empty rooms. Belly issues, Alcohol withdrawal, and chest pains began to clog the arteries of the department, threatening larger problems. The traumas kept coming, and though none had been serious, a few awaited admission to one of the many trauma step-down units.

The smooth feeling leftover from the Fentanyl the night

before faded, leaving me tired and edgy. Someone dropped off about fifteen patients at the front door, and the triage nurse called for help. I left instructions for the next three ambulances and dashed out to check in as many of them as I could in the shortest amount of time. Upon return to my desk, I paged the ERT nurse to transport patients to their rooms upstairs in hopes it would decompress the department. We were hovering dangerously close to needing to go on diversion, which required approval from the hospital's administration, who had likely never set foot in a busy emergency department in their life.

On top of having to explain why we were backed up in the first place, diversion didn't help much. All it accomplished was sending a few ambulances to the smaller hospital across the street that probably dreaded when we couldn't manage on our own. Still, if a patient requested to come to our ED, EMS brought them. The department couldn't refuse traumas, strokes, or walk-ins, so diversion was often a band-aid on an arterial bleed, and I was hoping to avoid it. The ERT nurses came as a group and moved anyone with a ready bed, making the numbers better for a few more hours.

My pager sounded, making me jump in the chair. I dropped my pencil as the second pager began, and when the third, fourth, and tenth started, I rose from my seat. My phone rang, and I checked the caller ID, groaning when I saw it was MedCom. "Whatcha got, Davey?" I asked when I heard his smooth voice on the other end of the line.

"I just got an update that the P1 I just paged is now a traumatic arrest," he said before hanging up on me, but I didn't fault his manners. With twenty-six counties, our Medical Communications center covered the largest area of any other in the country. They could hang up on me daily, and I would understand.

"The seventy-nine-year-old is in arrest," I said, walking into the bay as I read the pager. She was another person that fell from a standing position and was on blood thinners. Likely, she had a head bleed, and the damage was too severe to survive. I once heard a doctor say that the secret to a long life was not to fall. I came to learn the truth of his words over the course of my career. Blood thinners, rugs, and cats do not mix with the elderly; it is a sad truth. It is also a sad truth that elderly women are more prone to dying from falls than their male counterparts.

I took my spot at the computer, ready to scribe the events of the trauma on paper and electronically. I arrived her in the department as a Jane Doe to have her orders and patient labels ready when she arrived as it would save precious seconds when every second counted.

The team filtered in, signing my trauma sheet and taking their places. The bay filled quickly, leaving little to no room to move about. "Anyone not doing hands-on care, get behind the line," I said without looking up. I felt the air in the room shift as onlookers sighed and stepped outside of the room.

"I liked it better when she wasn't paying attention," someone grumbled, causing me to whip my head around and look for the offending party. If I found them, they'd be tossed out of my emergency department, but the patient saved them.

EMS arrived within the estimated time set forth on the pager, slapping the button by the door that started the big timer on the wall before crossing the line. "Seventy-nine-year-old female, fall from standing. On Coumadin for A-fib. Intubated on scene for GCS of three and apnea. Lowest BP 80/50 highest heart rate 136. We lost a pulse about fifteen minutes ago, and the last epinephrine was about three minutes ago. On three: one, two." The patient moved to the stretcher, and a nurse continued CPR while EMS detached their monitors to leave.

"Epi 1 milligram," the trauma attending said from his position at the foot of the bed.

"Pupils six and fixed," a resident shouted.

"Epi is in," the bedside nurse said, tossing the empty vial on the floor in the corner to be accounted for later.

"One amp of bicarb," the attending ordered.

"Bicarb in."

"Pulse check."

Everyone in the room stopped moving, silencing the rush of clothes while one resident checked for a carotid pulse and another felt the femoral artery for a few seconds.

"No pulse."

"Resume compressions."

CPR continued on the patient for a few more rounds. The room was absent the banter that usually accompanied a trauma. Most stood silently watching as there was nothing more that could be done. Chest tubes and rapid infusers wouldn't help this woman. Maybe neurosurgery could relieve the pressure in her brain, but that required her to have a pulse, and the next check found her again pulseless.

"Any suggestions?" the attending asked, looking around the room. When no one said anything, he added. "Time of death thirteen oh six. Thanks, everyone. Good job."

The room emptied, leaving a few nurses and a clinical associate to deal with what was left after seventy-nine years of life. I swept the surfaces of trash and turned the cardiac monitors off, letting the sense of emptiness roll through me and fade away.

How many times had this scene played out during my career? Thousands definitely, tens of thousands possibly. We scurried around the room, trying to make things presentable for the family who would want to see their loved one as soon as possible. She had a large head laceration, and dried blood was everywhere. Several nurses worked on the body while I cleaned up the trash left behind from the act of trying to save her life. It's messy business, all of it.

We talked and laughed about the rest of our day as we worked, wishing for a lunch break or, at a minimum, coffee. Does this make us callous? No. Death hung over us every day, and we were just trying to survive with some semblance of sanity until it was our time to go. Did it make us assholes? Maybe. We cared. Sometimes we care too much, but you have to find a way to let it go. I knew that better than most.

Once the woman was clean and presentable, I walked to the chaplain's consult room and ushered the family to see her. Lowered lighting and neatly folded blankets draped the woman, making her look as good as we could under the circumstances.

"What happened?" the woman's son asked.

"She came in after a reported fall," I started, only to be interrupted mid explanation.

"I know she fell. Why the hell did she die? It was just a fall. She falls all the time, and even this terrible hospital should've been able to handle that," he growled, crossing his arms angrily.

"She suffered a cardiac arrest before arriving in the Emergency Department, sir," I tried again. "More than likely, she had bleeding on the brain. We did everything possible, but I can get the doctor if you'd like more information. The team is very sorry for your loss."

"How long did you try?" he said, wrapping my arm in a bruising grip as I turned to grab the attending. "She lived alone, you know, and had a good life. She was healthy. You people fucked something up, and I'm going to find out what and sue you." I met his eyes cooly before staring at where his hand gripped my upper arm. He dropped it, crossing his arms and scowling at me.

When I was a new nurse, patients and families were different. They were appreciative of the care you gave and the lengths you went to make them comfortable or to try and save their lives. Now, your best was never enough. As technology evolved, they became more demanding of a perfect outcome. Still, some things can't be changed regardless of technology, and just because you can do a thing doesn't mean you should. We saved people that would then languish in a slow hell of feeding tubes, diapers, and nursing homes. It wasn't fair. But it also wasn't our choice.

Could we have eventually revived the angry man's mother? Maybe. With enough drugs, we might have gotten her heart to beat, but for what? So that she could be on life support until she died again in a few hours when her brain squeezed through the small hole at the base of her skull? We followed the guidelines when it came to CPR and the efforts to revive a patient. We'd actually extended the recommended time for CPR in this particular woman's case since she arrested before she came to us, and we weren't sure if they'd tried everything before placing her into our hands. We had tried, but it would never be enough for the people who loved her.

"Again, I'm sorry for your loss. I can get the chaplain and the attending physician if you'd like," I said, stepping from him and backing to the door.

"I don't want the doctor; I want my lawyer!" the man shouted, tracking my movements. In my days as an ED nurse, I had been punched, slapped, bitten, spit on, kicked, cursed at, and threatened. Was it right? Of course not. It just was, though. Abuse of healthcare workers rises each year, and nurses are trained to suck it up and take it. It isn't right. Yes, there are laws against it. Some of these crimes had even been made into felony assaults, but nurses are discouraged from seeking justice and judges slow to grant it.

I slipped from the room, meeting the eyes of the attending where he sat at his desk. I nodded my head toward the room, indicating he was being requested. "The son's very upset. He's asking for a lawyer and wants to know what happened, so you're up, Doc.

He groaned, looking at the ceiling. "Conroy," he tried.

"This is why you make the big bucks, but I'll let Parker know. I doubt he'll say anything to you anyway. When push comes to shove, they never do," I sighed, walking towards Parker's office to let her know what was going on. I'd never known a doctor to get assaulted, or a nurse manager, for that matter, let alone a director.

I filled Parker in, skating out of her office as quickly as I could. I slipped out the back door and down the atrium steps to Starbucks, feeling like a specter as I went. My good night's sleep had worn off, and I missed the chemical haze I'd worked so hard to obtain the day before.

Back at my desk, I found the department had blown up, and the three nurse shortage was affecting flow. The waiting room backed up, and the tracking board showed we were nearing a category three.

ED categories are rather like hurricanes. A Cat One meant that we were jamming up a little, and the wind was blowing hard enough to slow your movements. A Cat Two meant the waters were rising, and swimming against the current would be impossible without a little help from above. At a Cat Three, you were well and truly in trouble. It was an all hands on deck situation that required divine intervention and more people than were available to unclog the system's toilets. Next came diversion and all the devious fuckery that came with it. Yellow diversion meant that ambulances should divert to other hospitals capable of managing the level of patients they carried. Red Diversion is like a Category Five hurricane- it may not be survivable. The hospital is so overwhelmed that normal operations are impossible. It means there are no beds in the ED and no monitored beds or unmonitored beds anywhere in the hospital. You have to understand how hospitals work because most will park a bed in front of any available outlet and call it a day if they have to. I'd been a nurse for sixteen years and never seen Red Diversion or a mass casualty alert and hoped I never did. The massive tent we blew up in the parking lot to practice mass casualty drills was fantastic, though, and I wouldn't mind that part.

I rounded through the department, doing what I could to help, but ambulances kept rolling in, tying me to my desk. The ERT nurses came and went, helping where I couldn't, and by early afternoon, we blew through Category Three and straight into yellow diversion.

I was cleaning up from the most recent stroke when the pagers sounded for the first of what would be many traumas to follow. The Trauma Gods were angry and making their displeasure known. I glanced at the pager, groaning at what it warned. My stomach dropped, and a cold sweat formed under my arms, weakening my knees.

"Traumatic arrest," I said over the general noise of the department, the words sounding shaky even to me. "Five minutes out. Fifty-five-year-old male, BCC," I finished. A BCC was a bicycle collision with a car usually, and they never went well either. Knowing that the pharmacist was in the CT scanner with the stroke and an ERT nurse, I headed to grab the tray from the medicine room.

I pulled the cellophane-covered tray off the Accudose machine, noting that someone was still logged into it. Blindly, I picked a patient and hit the override button that allowed me to pull medicine that was not prescribed for them, pulling out a Klonopin. I logged out of the Accudose and pushed through the door and into the hallway, scurrying into Trauma One with a pounding heart.

As everyone rushed to set up for the fast-approaching trainwreck, I turned my back as if to ready something from the tray and opened the Klonopin, chewing it quickly. I tolerated the sourness of the powdered pill on my tongue as I willed it to work fast.

Way too soon, the ambulance arrived, spilling extra people behind it. Merc did CPR while I stood on my toes to see what was happening. The man was grey, his body contorted in ways that it should never be. His clothing was torn and the arms showing through looked like so much hamburger. His jaw was slack, and his empty stare pointed at the ceiling. His face looked...wrong, and I knew his injuries were not survivable. Blood ran from his nose, and bits of something was stuck in his hair.

"If you do not have a role in this trauma, step behind the line," I growled, feeling lightheaded from the adrenaline. From where I stood, the body on the stretcher reminded me of Keith, and I almost fainted. I had to clutch the edge of the counter and breathe hard to remain standing. Sweat beaded on my lip, and I felt the color drain from my face. The dark, blood-matted, slightly curly hair was streaked with gray, just as Keith's had been, and I couldn't look beyond it. My vision narrowed, and I fought to keep my eyes on the trauma sheet I was responsible for.

"Fifty-four-year-old male was intoxicated, argued with the neighbor who took a bat to him. Then he jumped on his bicycle and got hit by a slow-moving car. GCS on the scene was a three. We lost a pulse about ten minutes ago. Had two doses of epi in the truck. On three: one, two." The man was moved, and I finally caught a glimpse of his face. Even bruised and bloodied, he looked nothing like Keith. My heart slowed a few beats, but not many and it still beat way too hard.

"Epi, 1 milligram," Daniel demanded, expecting to be heard as he walked through the door late and having missed the paramedic's story. "Set up for intubation," he added, catching my eye and frowning at what he saw.

"Epi's in," Pam said from the bedside after I passed the drug to her.

"His jaw's clenched; hand me a paralytic," the resident from the head of the bed stated.

"100 milligrams of succinylcholine," Dan added, glancing my way again.

I handed the medicine to Pam, who gave it.

"Sux in," she said for my benefit. It was important not to miss anything on the trauma sheet and also for the person handing out drugs to know what's been given.

"One amp of Bicarb."

I handed the bicarb over, watching the monitor.

"End-tidal jumped to 50; we might have ROSC," I said.

Treating cardiac arrest evolves with time. We'd developed technology that measured carbon dioxide as it was released from the lungs. A sudden increase in the number signaled the return of spontaneous circulation or ROSC. Hopefully, it wasn't wrong.

"Pulse check."

"We have a pulse."

"Pack him up and get to scan," the trauma attending of the day said.

"Fifty of Fentanyl for the scanner, but hold off on any more sedation until we see if there's a bleed. Neurosurgery will want to assess him off sedation, if possible."

I pulled the Fentanyl up, handing the syringe to Pam.

"Fentanyl in," she said, pulling the monitor onto the stretcher for transport.

"I can take him," one of the ERT nurses materialized from behind the line just as the pagers sounded again.

"Thanks, he's going to SICU bed one, and it's ready," someone said from the door.

"Got it."

In a flurry of activity, the patient was taken from the room.

He'd go upstairs or to the operating room, whichever he needed first. His chances weren't great, but they weren't zero either. The one thing that kept me going all of these years was the fact that I'd seen some crazy shit. I'd seen cardiac arrest patients discharged from the hospital a week later, and it kept me sane. It didn't happen often, but it did happen. Somehow those rare moments had staved off the inevitable and allowed me to stay in my job longer than most ED nurses do.

Until Keith.

"36-year-old male, MCC at highway speeds. Car hydroplaned and crossed the median. He never saw it coming. Knocked him into the guardrail. No pressure and pulse is thready. Lots of deformities to the head, face, and neck. Helmet cracked in the back down the middle. We brought it. Lowest measurable BP 60 over palp, large bore IV infusing, intubated on scene with an 8-oh ET tube, highest heart rate 140's with peripheral pulses not palpable."Elle. Get the fuck out of here. Move on three: one, two. Elle, I mean it. Out."

"PTA Sixteen gauge in the left AC. Labs drawn."

"Sixteen in the right and warm normal saline up at wide open, the first unit of blood's up on the level one infuser."

"We have bilateral hemotympany, obvious skull and cervical spine deformities, and positive step-offs. White matter visible. Obvious deformities to bilateral femurs. Elle, get out of here."

But I can make the Level One sing. No one makes it sing like me, and I had refused to leave. My husband's best chance was for me to stay in the room and do my job. I was at the top of my game, and despite living every ED nurse's worst nightmare, I would make this work. The Trauma Gods owed me. For every life I had saved, could they not grant me the life of the only person that mattered? I watched every atrocity done to my husband, hoping beyond hope that he'd be one of the miracles, only he wasn't. He had taken a motorcycle to a car fight, and that never works out. I knew that.

"Lost a pulse, starting CPR."

"1 milligram of epi in."

"Get the rib spreaders."

"The heart isn't filling with internal massage. Probably ruptured something. He's been down for almost an hour."

"Call it."

"NO!"

"Time of death sixteen-oh-eight."

"Elle..."

"Elle?"

"I'm coming," I whispered, feeling the weight settle in my chest, but my mind began to lift as the Klonopin kicked in. I blinked slowly, enjoying being disconnected. Why would I want to be connected anymore? I turned to leave the ghosts of the trauma bay behind, knowing that your ghosts follow you regardless of where you try to put them.

The stretcher returning blocked my exit.

"Just a head bleed and a few skull and facial fractures. It might be enough to knock some sense into him, but I doubt it. Got bunches of fractures elsewhere, but he'll live. The lab called on the way to SICU and said his blood alcohol was 0.43," the ERT nurse, Nate, said as he drove the empty stretcher into the room.

"Damn," I said. Shaking my head. It amazed me that you couldn't kill some people with a shotgun while others seemed so fragile. It didn't seem fair, but then nothing did lately.

"Listen, Conroy. I was here that day," he started, not alluding to a specific day because I knew what he meant.

"I know, Nate. I remember. I can't seem to forget," I sighed, picking up the half-empty tray of drugs to return to the medicine room.

"Look, I can't imagine what you're going through, but I've wanted to say this for a while. You know we tried. We tried absolutely every fucking thing. Had he not made it in, you would've always wondered if there was anything we could've done. This is a great ED, and we have a fantastic team. You'd have believed that we could've saved him. Being here was a blessing and a curse for you because now you know, and I hope that brings you some peace," he paused, looking away for a minute, leaving me to believe he was done, but then he continued. "My dad died in this room, too. I wasn't here, and I wondered maybe if I had been, things might have been different.

"We think we're the best, and maybe we are, but some things can't be changed. You might think it won't get better, but it will. Right now, it's real, and it's raw, but I swear it gets better. We'd love to have you on the ERT team when you're ready to move on," he added as he parked the dirty stretcher in the middle of the detritus of medical war. "I know you want out of here, and that's probably for the best. When the battleax lets your transfer, come to our team, Elle; we take care of our own."

"Thanks, Nate. I understand what you're saying, and it means a lot," I said, meaning it for a change. I remembered when his dad died. He'd been hit by a car in a crosswalk at the university, and we had also tried every fucking thing, as Nate put it. He came to me later and grilled me for an hour about the actions we had taken in an attempt to save his father's life. I understood it then, and I understood it now. He was right. I would've always wondered. It was a blessing and a curse that I knew the answer, and sometimes I was glad Keith had survived long enough to land in my trauma bay, but most days, I wished he hadn't.

"Hey, a few of us are going to Crockett's after work tonight," he started. "If you want to join us, we can talk more about the job. You'd be a great fit. Rachel is going too," he added, sensing my immediate refusal.

"You know what? Okay. Sounds good. I'll meet you there." I walked away feeling lighter.

The feeling didn't last, and after the third P2, I had changed my mind, wanting only to eat and go to bed, but as I passed the bar on my way home and caught a whiff of hot sauce in the air, I pulled into the parking lot.

The ED had ended up on yellow diversion for the rest of the shift, but that didn't change the fact that we got two more strokes and three more traumas. There were thirty-two people in the waiting room, and several had been there for six hours or more. It chafed to leave such a mess, but only time would fix it. The ED would empty overnight only to start the cycle again the next day like it always did.

I sat in my car, digging through my pockets to dump out trauma sheers and rolls of tape. My heartbeat was erratic, and I knew what I really needed was sleep, but hot wings called to me. My mind was still too clear, and the events of the day had deadened the brief feeling of relief the Klonopin gave. I felt the glass vials as I dug through the trash and unfurled my hand to see what I'd forgotten to waste today. I stared at the vials for a long time. I was off tomorrow, and with a bit of help, I could sleep all day. Maybe I'd even wake up in a better frame of mind. Taking my sheers, I popped the rubber stopper and tilted the Fentanyl so that it landed under my tongue. I held it there until I felt it start to hit.

It started in my middle, like shooting a few fireball whiskeys in a row. I got warm and then felt light. My heart tripped a few times before steadying into a calmer beat. I sighed, leaning my head against my headrest. The initial rush passed, and I evened out into a much better mental state. There was a vial of Versed, too, a potent Benzodiazepine that would last a little longer than the Fentanyl. I'd never had it and wondered if it might be too much. In larger doses, it made you forget what was going on around you and maybe forgetting this day would be good for me. I popped the stopper and only used half, shoving the rubber back into the mouth of the vial as I waited for it to kick in.

My world went sideways, and my vision dimmed before righting itself, settling into something quiet and filled with peace. The slow smile that creased my face felt amazing, and each breath was like the first; it meant something. For the first time in a while, I felt alive. Opening the door, I eased from the truck and slipped like mercury up the stairs and into the door of the bar.

"Elle!" Rachel said, causing my head to do a slow turn and trace it to the source. "We saved you a seat."

"Awesome," I said slowly, smiling as I walked across the floor, careful of where I put my feet. They felt leaden, like the heaviness that generally lived in my heart had settled into them.

The waitress appeared at my elbow with a Grey Goose on the rocks before I could ask, and I slid into the seat, taking it up. "I come here sometimes," I laughed.

"Man, I wish they knew our order; we had to wait ten minutes," Nate said, gripping Rachel's hand in his. I hadn't known they were a couple, but they made a cute one.

"Wings, Ellie?" the waitress asked from the edge of the table.

"Yeah, thanks. Some chips and salsa too, please," I added, taking another sip of my drink.

"Today sucked," Rachel laughed. "The whole place was a dumpster fire."

"I know the ED was," I agreed, acknowledging that my world view of the dumpster fire was limited to one area.

We talked about our day, ate wings, and sipped drinks. I felt light and happy in the moment for the first time in ages. Crockett's filled, and we had to talk louder to be heard. Nate and Rachel were good company but other people filtered in too, stopping to say hello. It seemed everyone was trying to unwind from a tough day, and various colors of scrubs were the dress code for the evening.

I sipped my third Grey Goose, listening to Nate and Rachel talk about one of the cardiac arrests they'd worked earlier, and felt myself growing distant. My head spun pleasantly, and I laughed at something she said a little too loudly.

"Are you okay?" she asked, her eyes sweeping over me in a rapid assessment.

The thing about experienced nurses is that they can never shut it off. They walk through the world doing quick assessments and visual exams on everyone around them. Face a little pale? They are going to notice. Eyes a little jaundiced? They're going to see that too. You can't hide much from them, and what you can hide, they will find some other way. It's the nature of the beast they carry on their shoulders.

"I'm good. I don't think I ate today. I'll be right as rain at the bottom of this wing basket," I chuckled. "If I clocked out 'no lunch' every time I didn't get lunch, I'd make a lot more money, but Parker would lose her shit." I dove into another wing, loving the sting of the hot sauce on my tongue.

"I hear you," Nate added, shoving his burger down his throat, but Rachel's eyes narrowed.

I concentrated on eating wings and listening to the excited chatter from around the bar. I sipped my water, leaving the vodka on the table for a bit.

"Elle. Uh, hey." I looked up from my wings to see Tim Franks standing at my shoulder. "Can I talk to you a second?" he asked.

"No," I said, picking up another wing and ignoring him. Another resident stood near him and had engaged Rachel and Nate in conversation about one of the traumas from earlier. I couldn't remember his name, but I'd seen him around the ED.

"Come on, Conroy. I'm sorry; I've been an ass. I just wanted to apologize," he added. "Sometimes I'm too big for my britches," he laughed, leaning his elbows on the table.

Nate laughed loudly at something the other doctor said, and the noise in the bar amped up as their conversation continued.

I looked away from Tim, scanning the bar to see that it was now standing room only. Movement from the corner of my eye drew my attention back to him. He stared at me, resting his chin on his hand and waiting for me to answer. I blinked slowly, breathing in the scent of hot wings and beer that surrounded me. My breaths were slow and easy, and I got distracted by the feeling of my lungs expanding my ribcage.

"I hear you, Tim. Thanks for the apology; I appreciate it." I picked up my vodka and took a sip before grabbing another wing.

"No hard feelings?" he asked, holding out his hand.

I smiled, shaking my head. "No hard feelings," I answered, shaking his hand.

He walked away with his friend, and I returned to Nate and Rachel's conversation, though I couldn't help but notice that Tim kept his eyes on our table. He probably hoped he'd get lucky again, but that wasn't happening. The entire ordeal with him had been a mistake I wasn't repeating.

I sipped my drink, feeling the pull of the vodka. It was time to go home, but the food wasn't helping the heaviness the way it should have. I narrowed my eyes, struggling to follow the conversation at the table. My mouth felt dry, and my vodka sat empty, so I picked up my water and chugged it, feeling some leak around my lips. My lips went numb, and I struggled to gather my thoughts.

"Are you okay, Elle?" Nate asked, tilting his head at me in concern.

"Yeah," I said, the word sounding breathy and quiet. "God, I'm a lightweight," I laughed, easing to my feet. My vision narrowed, and I saw black at the edges. "I'm going to hit the bathroom and get an uber," I finished, knowing I couldn't drive. The problem was that I wasn't a lightweight. I'd only had three Grey Gooses, and lately, I could drink twice that and barely feel buzzed. Something was wrong. I checked the table and counted straws.

Maybe it was the Versed. God, how many milligrams had I taken? Or the Klonopin. I wondered, knowing I was a mess, and that I shouldn't have to ask myself these questions. I wobbled away from the table to the well-meaning jeers of the other nurses scattered through the bar. Shaking my head, I laughed along with them, flipping them the bird as I stumbled away.

My chest felt heavy, and I had to force each breath. My legs were leaden, and my arm was so heavy I couldn't grab the edge of the pool table to catch myself as I started to fall. I felt a hand on my elbow, steadying me.

"Hey, Conroy, you're not looking so good." I looked into Tim's face, unable to answer him. Another hand slipped under the opposite elbow, and I slowly turned my head to see the other resident whose name I couldn't remember. I struggled to speak as I felt my body get heavier.

"What?" I croaked, unable to finish my thought.

My body was guided down Crockett's back stairs, and I could do nothing to stop it. My mind wasn't working, but it worked well enough to know that the residents at each elbow had given me something. They used the distraction of noise and conversation to slip something into my vodka or water. I tried to pull away but couldn't. I felt like they'd given me a paralytic. However, as my diaphragm was still working well enough to breathe, so I knew it was something else.

"Did you think you could get away with it, Elle?" Tim asked, and the other one chuckled in my ear, running his fingers down my cheek. "You don't get to embarrass me like that and walk away scot-free. That's not how it works. So you're going to get a lesson in humility that's long overdue, in my opinion."

I sagged under my weight, feeling my heart stutter and pause, only to pick up its ragged rhythm again. Blood rushed to my head as it started to beat again, and the pressure in my neck was unbearable. I moaned, forcing another breath into my lungs. Whatever they'd given me was too much. My head lolled forward, and Tim tripped under my dead weight.

"Fuck man," I heard the other man say. "You fucking overdosed her. That shit isn't going to be much fun," he laughed, hauling me forward so that Tim could catch his balance.

"Shut up. It'll be plenty of fun. For us anyway. Besides, I've used this dose before, and it doesn't usually hit this hard. Bitch is a lightweight," Tim answered.

"If you say so," the other resident said.

I forced my head up and saw that I was being dragged to Tim's townhouse. I tried to pull away, but my muscles refused to work. My vision narrowed further, and I knew this was a tight spot I might not get out of. I heard rapid footsteps and felt the crash of a large body into us, and I couldn't so much as raise my arm to break my fall onto the pavement and into darkness.

Chapter 12

Daniel saw Elle being dragged by Tim Franks and Jordan Crites through the parking lot of Crockett's. It was one thing to watch her make bad choices sober but another to see her stumbling between them like she was too drunk to make a choice. Her head hung so low that her hair dragged the ground in front of her, and she was stepping on it without noticing. He got out of his car and sprinted toward them.

"Elle!" he yelled as he ran to catch them, but she didn't respond.

"Fuck you, Ross. Mind your own goddamned business," Franks said, trying to increase his pace but unable to because Elle had become unwieldy.

"Elle is my fucking business, asshole," Daniel yelled, crashing into Franks and sending Elle flying.

Horrified, he realized too late that Elle wasn't just drunk; she was unconscious. She fell to the ground with a sharp thud, not even trying to break her fall.

"What the fuck did you give her, Franks?" Daniel said, slamming his fist into the other man's face.

"Fucking nothing!" Franks lied.

Daniel pounded into Tim's face, splitting knuckles and cheekbones. "What did you give her? She can hold her liquor, and twenty minutes isn't enough to get her this drunk," he asked again. "And understand," he rasped between punches, "that I will have your license for this shit. You're done. Finished. Maybe you can go somewhere else and finish your residency, but as of now, you are fired. The paperwork is just a formality. You too, Crites. You better speak the fuck up before I have charges filed," Daniel yelled, watching as the other man tried to back away from the scene.

Footsteps pounded, and Daniel saw two of the ERT nurses from work leaning over Elle, feeling for a pulse. "She's not breathing," Nate said, dropping his mouth over Elle's and giving her a breath. "But she has a good pulse. Crites, this isn't you. What the fuck, man?"

"Valium," Jordan spit. "He gave her Valium."

"Shut the fuck up, Jordan. You're in this too!" Tim screamed at his friend, covering his face in cast-off venom.

"How fucking much?" Daniel screamed, watching helplessly as Nate pressed his mouth to Elle's again. Her chest rose and fell, and her color evened out.

"The whole vial."

"That's fifty fucking milligrams, Crites. Jesus. You could've killed her. She's a hundred fucking pounds," Rachel screamed into Jordan's face. "You're fucking done. I can't

154

believe this shit."

Daniel pulled his fist back one more time, the last punch knocking Tim Franks out. Then he rushed to Elle's side, feeling for a pulse and sighing when it leaped under his fingers.

"How much did she drink?" he asked Rachel.

"Three vodkas and ate some wings. She'd been off the whole night though, kinda spacey," she answered, and Daniel's heart sank. Elle had been off a lot lately, and he feared there was more than grief behind it.

"Dr. Ross, I have Narcan and Flumazenil in my car. Take over, and I'll grab it." Nate left Elle and sprinted across the gravel lot.

"I'll call an ambulance," Rachel said, rising to her feet and reaching into her back pocket.

"Rachel," Daniel paused his breaths to look up at her. "Don't. Please. She is so private, and she'll be horrified. Let's give her a chance; she's breathing now. I think her airway was just obstructed.

"Dr. Ross," Rachel started.

"Please, Rachel. As a personal favor. I'll take care of her."

Rachel nodded, looking uncertain. Jordan Crites looked on, the terrified look on his face not changing, and Tim Franks lay knocked out in the gravel. If they hadn't been behind some bushes in a dark section of the lot, someone else would've called EMS and the police already, but they'd gotten lucky.

Nate returned in a spray of gravel as he slid to the ground beside Elle. "My sister is a druggie," he started, swiftly tying a tourniquet on Elle's arm. "I'm not supposed to have this shit, but she's OD'd too many times for me not to." He slipped the IV needle into Elle's vein quickly, screwing a cap to the end and flushing it with saline. "I keep a bag in my car, and I've used it more times than I care to admit. Just keep this between us, please. I would lose my job if my boss found out."

"I think we are all crossing a line, Nate," Rachel said, pulling up drugs into a syringe. "Right, Dr. Ross?" she asked, leveling him with a glare.

"This goes no further. Dr. Crites and Dr. Franks are going to quietly resign, and if they breathe a word of this, they'll never be licensed to practice. Do you hear me?" Daniel asked, waiting for Crites to nod in acceptance. "Drag your friend out of here and keep your mouth shut. Are we clear?"

Tim was dragged into a nearby car, and Jordan gunned it out of the parking lot while Rachel finished drawing up drugs. "0.4 milligrams of Narcan and 0.2 milligrams of Flumazenil, Dr. Ross?" she asked, watching him for his response.

And this is where it got tricky, and Daniel knew it. "I think it's safe to say that we are all on a first-name basis now, Rachel," he sighed, weighing his options. Flumazenil reverses Benzodiazepines like Valium, but the problem is that if the person is addicted or takes one of those meds frequently, reversing the effects can cause a seizure. Elle had been off lately. It was more than possible she'd been taking something regularly, but she was pale and lifeless in the dim light of a faraway street lamp. Her chest barely rose and fell, and he was under no illusion that she'd come around without help. Fifty milligrams of Valium was more than twice the recommended dose for a woman her size. "Fuck," he said. "Yes. Give them both."

Rachel pushed the Narcan first, followed by the Flumazenil, while Daniel held his breath and prayed he hadn't made things worse. Within seconds Elle took a heaving breath, then rolled onto her side and vomited. She gave a drawn-out moan and gulped for air like she was starved for it before rolling onto her back and opening her eyes.

"I have a liter of fluid strung up if you want it, Dan," Nate said, his voice so soft Dan had to strain to hear it.

"Yeah, thanks." Nate attached the IV fluids, holding the bag high as Daniel scooped Elle into his arms and carried her to his car. "I'll take her from here. I can't thank you enough." Daniel slid Elle into the backseat, hanging the IV bag from the clothes hook on the roof. "Put your number in my phone, and I'll let you know how she does."

"Thanks," Rachel said, handing Daniel the remaining drugs. "Just in case you need another dose. Get her out of here." She took Daniel's phone, typing in her contact information before handing it back.

"Thanks." Daniel fell into the seat, started the car, and left the parking lot without hesitation. Elle hadn't moved, but he could see the gentle rise and fall of her chest in the rearview mirror.

Keeping his car below the speed limit, he eased out of Star City so as not to catch the eye of the local police that usually laid in wait, but once he crossed the bridge and veered onto Route 7, he gave his Audi S4 her head, taking the narrow road with its wicked S-turns to Elle's house as fast as the car would handle, needing to get her someplace safer than his backseat.

He was out of the car and had the backdoor open with Elle in his arms before the vehicle finished rocking on its axels. Rushing through the unlocked front door, he kicked it closed behind him. As much as Daniel currently appreciated Elle's penchant for keeping her doors unlocked, he hated that she did so now that she lived alone. Still, old habits died hard, and few in the outskirts of the town regularly locked their doors.

Elle groaned in his arms. "What?" she tried, failing to get the rest of the words out.

Daniel carefully stripped her of her fouled clothes in the bedroom and ran a bath as hot as it would go. "It's okay, baby. I've got you." He settled Elle into the tub, careful to keep her arm straight so the IV fluid could finish infusing. He wished he had another bag, but one would have to be enough.

He left her long enough to turn the heat in the house up to eighty degrees, knowing that Elle was always cold and that the overdose would make that worse. Back in the bathroom, he kneeled by the tub, taking a minute to wash the dirt and debris off her skin. Her vacant eyes were open and staring now, but she said nothing.

When the fluid finished, he went to her cabinets to find a bandaid and took the IV out.

"What happened?" she whispered, not looking at Daniel.

"Tim Franks slipped fifty milligrams of Valium into your vodka, Elle. Jordan Crites said he was pissed off about you embarrassing him and wanted to humiliate you."

"They were going to rape me?" she asked, punching Daniel in the gut.

He sighed, scrubbing his hands down his face. "Jordan wouldn't admit it, and I knocked Tim unconscious, but that's my guess."

"I don't remember anything," she said, her voice raw and her dark eyes flat.

"You may not. You may not remember this either. Valium at any dose can cause amnesia. At that dose, I would be surprised if you remember today at all. I'm sorry, Elle." Daniel sighed, sitting back on his heels. "I'm so sorry."

"You didn't do anything, Daniel." Elle's eyes drooped closed, and he pulled the plug on the tub, wrapping her in a towel and lifting her out.

"But I did, didn't I?" he whispered, watching as she shook her head in denial. Daniel knew better. Maybe it was what he hadn't done, but the end result was the same.

"Let's get you into bed. You need to sleep this off. We'll talk in the morning."

Daniel dressed Elle in warm pajamas and placed her in bed, covering her to her chin. Then he took the comfortable rocking chair by the window that she read in and watched her chest rise and fall long into the night.

Chapter 13

Awareness came slowly, more slowly than usual. I felt it slide into my mind from the corners, bleeding across my brain in slow moving streams. My eyes were heavy, and opening them was a struggle. I couldn't find my last memory, and I shuffled through them like cards, hoping they would settle into something that made sense. Finally, a card slipped into place, and I remembered driving to work yesterday but nothing more. Had it been yesterday?

What had I done?

I was in bed alone, judging by the chill of the covers around me. It felt like ten days had passed since that last memory. Had I driven to work at all, or was that a dream? I groaned, reaching for my phone, hoping it knew what the day was. As a nurse, it isn't unusual for me not to know. I knew my schedule and lived by that: dates were irrelevant. But this was different. I felt like I was missing something big.

On the periphery of my vision, I saw the slumped figure of Daniel sleeping in my chair, and my arm froze in mid-reach. I sat up, feeling the slow spin of my head as my headache increased. Light from unclosed drapes highlighted the gray at his temples, making him look years older while lines etched his face, telling a story I'd clearly forgotten. His eyebrows were pinched in worry. Shadows of a long night hung under his eyes, and my worry dug deeper into the darkness left behind from...something.

Hoping to let him sleep, I eased out of bed, swaying on my feet when I tried to stand.

"Elle?" Daniel's hand went to my elbow, steadying me. Had I blanked out? How had he gotten to me so quickly? "Are you okay?" he asked. "You've been standing there just staring."

"I'm okay," I said, ignoring his statement. I took a few steps with him at my arm. "I'm okay," I repeated. "Will you make coffee?" I asked, looking at my feet. As much as I needed to know what happened, I needed a minute to get myself together more.

Daniel placed a kiss on my head before letting go of my elbow and watching me walk the rest of the way to the bathroom alone. "I'll be in the kitchen," he said as I closed the door behind me.

My bathroom yielded no clues. My laundry basket was empty, and clean towels hung on my towel rack. Even the trash was empty. The only clue to be found was the lack of dust on the edge of my oversized tub.

When the house was built, I'd insisted on the big thing, thinking how nice it would be to soak after a long shift. The problem was that it took so much water to fill as to be impractical to use regularly, so it tended to sport a fine layer of dust from disuse. Not today.

I peeled off my pajamas, turning the shower on super-hot. As I did, I noticed the bandaid in the crook of my arm and the small bruise that signaled either a shot or the removal of an IV. My trepidation grew as I noticed that my hands and knees were scraped, but the harder I chased the memories, the faster they ran from me.

Fuck.

Sighing, I washed quickly. I felt between my legs, searching for the telltale soreness sex sometimes leaves, and decided that at least that hadn't happened. I thought anyway. I didn't know, and I didn't understand why. I refused to look at my behavior over the last two weeks, denying it predicated why my memory was faulty. After toweling off, I dressed comfortably and went to find coffee and Daniel, knowing he held the answers.

"Hey," I said, shuffling into the kitchen following the smell of coffee and bacon.

"How do you feel?" he asked instead of a greeting.

"Better. I have a headache," I said, sighing. "What happened? Was I supposed to work today? My memory is kinda fuzzy." I tried for something light, but it didn't come out that way.

"No, you're off," he said, pulling the pan off the stove and turning to face me. "What's the last thing you remember?" he asked, not answering my question. Tension raised his shoulders and rode every line of his body.

I poured a cup of coffee, breathing the scent of it into my lungs, noticing the slight pain in my chest that it brought. "I think I drove to work and that maybe it was yesterday, but honestly, the last day I remember was the day Tim cornered me in CT scan. What was that, Wednesday?" I hated that my voice shook and felt a single tear fall.

"That was Tuesday. Today is Thursday, Elle. After work yesterday, you went to Crockett's and met a couple of the ERT nurses. Tim Franks put 50 milligrams of Valium in one of your drinks. You ended up having three, and the vodka and the Valium were too much. You almost died," he started. "That nurse, Nate, saved your life. He had some reversal agents in his car; you had stopped breathing," he finished, scrubbing his hands down his face and taking a shuddering breath.

"Tim?" I stammered, clutching at flashes of something.

"And Jordan Crites," he interrupted. His chest rose and fell heavily.

"Why?" I asked, knowing the answer.

"Tim planned on raping you, humiliating you," he said, tilting his head to the ceiling and showing the strong curve of his jaw. "At least that's what Crites says. Tim was a P2 last night and had his jaw wired shut soon after. Both have officially resigned for personal reasons." Daniel blinked at the ceiling rapidly before leveling me with his green gaze. "I found them dragging you through the parking lot, Elle. You were unconscious, and they didn't even notice that you were nearly dead. Nate and Rachel helped me, but we didn't call the police, and they aren't going to say anything."

I slumped into the barstool at the island facing the stove, staring into my coffee. "Thank you," I said, clutching at the cup like a lifeline. "I don't remember any of it."

"The Valium alone was double what you could've handled. Add the three vodka drinks, and it was a significant overdose. I'm just glad Nate was there."

"I'm glad you were there," I said, meaning it. "I'm not ready to die," I added, not meaning to. The thing Daniel didn't know was that it was more than just vodka and Valium that had me messed up. Things could've gone sideways very quickly.

"I'm worried about you, Elle," he said, walking to the island and reaching across it to cup my chin.

I nodded my head in acknowledgment, not denying that he had a valid reason to worry. Daniel would be horrified if he knew the truth. "I'm trying," I whispered, but even I didn't believe it.

"I know," he said, letting the lie stand between us. He turned from me and put the pan back on the stove, adding eggs to the bacon and flipping them expertly.

Daniel moved about my kitchen with a familiarity that reminded me of what he meant to me and my life. He'd been here hundreds of times for parties or coffee. For every occasion and none at all, he'd been there for me. He'd saved the life I was throwing away, only he didn't understand the depth of the hole I'd dug myself. I was that train wreck you couldn't look away from, and he was a bright spot of hope that I didn't deserve.

A plate slid in front of me, and I picked up the fork, taking a bite of eggs that tasted like ashes on my tongue. "This is amazing," I lied again, eating by muscle memory alone. I felt hollow. I'd felt empty since Keith died, but this new feeling was something else. Empty is a state of being that suggests a space can be refilled. Hollow is something entirely different. Hollow suggests that the center has been scooped out and that no amount of shoving things in there will ever fill it.

Daniel's smile chased the lines of worry away and made the lie worth it. He really was a beautiful man. Tall, muscled, and barefoot in my kitchen, he made it brighter than it had ever been. But sometimes we are beyond the place where beauty reaches.

"Do you want more toast? Jelly?" he asked.

"No, I'm good. Thanks. Were you supposed to work today?" I asked, changing the subject.

"Yeah, but I have a ton of vacation time so I took the day

off." He sat his plate opposite mine and picked up his coffee. I noted the knuckles on his right hand were abraded and that tiny flakes of skin hung off of them at the edges.

Daniel had been a fighter in college. While an undergrad, he boxed for the university and had an undefeated record as a middleweight. He could've gone pro but went to medical school instead, choosing to mend lives instead of rending them. He kept himself in incredible shape and still boxed for fun at the local gym. That Tim was a P2 instead of a P1 or dead showed Daniel's restraint, and I wished I shared a small portion of it.

"It was worth it," he added, seeing where my gaze had settled. "Elle, I don't care about Tim Franks. I don't care about any of it. All I care about is you. Please come back to me. Whatever you'll give me, I'll take. I miss my friend. If that's all you want, I'll take it." He sat his cup down, grabbing my hand and holding it tightly in his larger one.

"Daniel," I groaned, closing my eyes and letting the tears that had sat on the edge of them fall. "You know how I feel about you," I started.

"Please, Elle. I'm watching you float away. I can see it. You aren't moving forward but drifting back. You have such a beautiful soul, but it's almost gone, and a ghost has taken your place, baby. Please come back. Come back for me. Come back for us. Come back for any reason if you can't come back for yourself." Daniel's shoulders slumped, and he ignored the plate in front of him.

"Daniel, you told me yourself that I wasn't ready for that." I gripped his hand, hating the pain this was causing him.

"I was a fool," he said, not looking at me.

"No, you weren't. You were right." I took a shuddering breath, walking around the island to place my arms loosely around his broad back in an attempt to comfort him. I rested my chin on his hard muscles, saying, "Do you remember the time all of us went to the beach?" I asked, smiling fondly at the memories.

The ED old guard took vacation time and left nothing but interns and new grads to run the department. We called it a team-building exercise, and somehow all the vacation requests had been approved. It was one of the best times of my life, and hearing the stories of the dumpster fire we left behind made it even better.

Daniel's shoulders moved with a weak chuckle letting me know he did, indeed, remember.

"We had the best time. The twenty of us single-handedly tore Myrtle Beach apart. Not only were they unprepared to handle the type of fun that many seasoned, depraved emergency service professionals needed to unwind, but they were also unable to handle the fallout." I smiled fondly, remembering the dares, the double dares, and the attempts to drink one another under the table. We'd taken our own hangover supplies, and empty bags of IV fluids hung from floor lamps daily.

"Correct," he said, letting some of the levity of the memory reach his voice.

"Keith told me then that he knew he'd been my second choice. He knew, Daniel." Always down for a good time, Keith had gone with us, even though no other spouses had. It wasn't designed to be a couples trip, but he'd wanted to go anyway. I'd always been affectionate with Daniel. Even as just friends, we'd been close and without the boundaries some friends maintain. Keith saw that. Daniel had given me piggyback rides down the beach, buried me in the sand when I passed out drunk, and swam with me in the ocean. We'd gotten into water gun fights and an epic drinking contest that ended up with liters of fluids hanging down to both arms. Keith had seen firsthand what was between Daniel and me. Maybe he'd understood, and maybe he hadn't. I'd been loyal and faithful to Keith our entire marriage, devoting myself only to him, but that didn't mean he missed that I still loved Daniel too. "I loved Keith, but I loved you too, and he was right. He was my second choice, but he was still my choice. I can't just forget that and move on like it didn't matter. It was ten years of my life, Daniel. He was such a good man, and he deserves better than to be forgotten like it meant nothing. I've got to find my footing before I leave the past behind."

"I know, Elle. Please just don't shut me out. We've been

something to each other for too long. Don't let his death change that. Don't let it make us strangers. That's all I ask, please," he said, finally picking up his fork to eat.

I moved back to my seat after refreshing my coffee and Daniel's. When he finished, we cleaned the kitchen together, enjoying the companionable silence that had taken root. Once the last dish was drying, Daniel turned, flashing me with his bright smile. "What do you want to do today?" he asked. "It's going to be really nice, and you know that it won't last.

I chuckled out loud. This was one of the few areas that can experience all four seasons in one day and vacillate between them hourly. A fall day can start with snow, get to seventy-five degrees, and finish with the chilly rain and fog of spring. Fall meant those seventy-degree days were fast coming to an end. There were brightly covered leaves starting on the trees, and we'd be fools not to take advantage of the beauty available to us.

"I don't know, Dan. I should probably rest up," I said, sighing at the thought of being alone with all the bullshit running through my head. My body lagged, though, swimming through water to even take a breath.

"You can rest on the front of the boat. Put on a bathing suit; we're going to the lake. I'm not taking no for an answer, and I'm not leaving you alone. What if the Valium has residual effects? Nope. You're under a doctor's care today. Sorry, friend. I'll pack a cooler."

Daniel made money; there was no denying that. He worked hard for it, picking up extra shifts and socking it away like a frenzied squirrel. He splurged on a few things, but not many. He had a nice Audi sports sedan that he'd driven for years, a smaller house on the lake with a modest boathouse, and his boat. Daniel loved the water. He gravitated to it, pulled by the magnetism of the clear, blue depths, he flocked to it like a seabird needing to rest. He wasn't from the mountains either and had only stayed after medical school for one reason: me.

I'd grown up in the South Carolina low country and had ended up here because I'd wanted a change. After graduating from nursing school, I'd applied to jobs all over the country, taking the one that called me first. I'd grown up on the bays, lakes, salt marshes, and oceans of the southeast coast and had hated being landlocked. But the mountains made up for some of that. Their beauty was stark, wild, and uninhibited. I'd also loved the fact that there were seasons: four of them, to be exact. I'd never experienced that before, and it had been a pro, not a con when I chose to move.

Daniel came from Florida's wrong side, the darker, wilder area where Georgia meets it on the bay. He'd grown up sun-streaked and wild in that uncultivated environment. Being in the mountains had tamed him some, or maybe suppressed was a better word. Dimmed. Extinguished. We'd always talked of going back and finding some little hospital in the south that treated sunburns and jellyfish stings. With our experience, we'd be a dream team in a place like that. But dreams change as you age. Whether you let them go, they die, or you fail, they change. I shivered, remembering the plans we'd made.

I dragged my thoughts back to the lake. The one true splurge Daniel made was his boat. Sleek, fast, and loud, everyone on the lake knew which one was his. "Okay," I said, letting a smile ghost my lips, and I went to change.

Though there would be a chill in the air this morning, it would be hot on the water by noon. I dressed in layers, tying a sweatshirt around my waist. My clothes were hanging off of me, and I felt dangerously thin. Daniel would notice; he always did. Then again, he'd dressed me last night and said nothing about the ribs protruding or the sharp angles of my hip bones. Sighing, I pulled my long, black hair into a ponytail and dragged on a visor to shield my pale skin from the sun.

I slid onto the warm, leather seats of Daniel's Audi. The vehicle smelled so strongly of him that I held my breath, not wanting the scent to seep into my soul like I knew it would. It was the scent of summer and home, of fresh-cut grass with a hint of dirt, but under that was the smell of cleaner, and I wondered if I'd wrecked his interior last night. I tried to be embarrassed but didn't have the strength for it.

I couldn't believe that Tim Franks had fucking overdosed

me on Valium. He'd intended to rape and humiliate me. Despite a shower, coffee, and breakfast, I remembered nothing. There was not one memory from yesterday. I couldn't recall anything, had the shift been busy? Had I been able to do my job without my hands shaking? No clue. I remembered nothing. I didn't remember meeting Nate and Rachel or even making that plan. It was a complete blank.

I knew why he did it. I'd seen the look on his face after I'd refused to let him fuck me against the wall of the CT scanner. I'd known that storm cloud of hate that swirled on his face would require a reckoning. I'd never dreamed he would go to the lengths he did to get back at me.

I couldn't say I was sad that he was gone. I also wasn't upset that Daniel had beat the crap out of him. My only regret would have been if Daniel had killed him because Daniel would've gone to jail defending honor I didn't have.

He slid into the driver's seat, smiling at me and reaching for my hand. I gave it willingly. "Thanks for coming. You need some vitamin D and hydrotherapy; doctor's orders. "

"You know I'm shit for following doctor's orders, Daniel," I chuckled, closing my eyes and letting the sun warm the cold places through the windshield.

"That's not entirely true. Sometimes you follow them. I mean, if you agree with them and think they are appropriate, you're all over it. Fastest nurse in the department." He cast me a shit-eating grin and winked, looking like the boy he used to be.

"Fuck you," I growled, turning my head back to the sun and closing my eyes. The trickle of a smile that curved my lips gave me away, and Daniel chuckled, throwing the Audi in gear.

He zipped through town, avoiding the interstate and taking the backroads to his house while I sat and enjoyed the ride. I watched the fall splendor glide by, taking in the scenery you miss while driving. I hadn't been to Daniel's house in over a year when he'd thrown a Friendsgiving party, and Keith and I had gone. We'd had a great time, but the night ended early when Keith had to leave for a business emergency, asking Daniel to drive me home.

I felt shadows cross my face and opened my eyes to see the brightly colored leaves of Daniel's long drive blocking the sun. I'd fallen asleep, curling into the warmed leather seat toward him. Sitting up, I stretched, looking side to side at the narrow drive leading to his house. Without the sun on my face, I was chilled, and I pulled my arms tighter to my chest. Pressing the button on the Audi's roof, he slid into the garage as the door opened.

"Do you want to run inside for anything while I get the boat ready? The door is open." Daniel pulled the cooler from his car's trunk before shutting the lid and heading down the steps to the boathouse.

"Don't you need to change?" I asked, looking hesitantly at

his front door.

"I've got clothes down here," he answered, pausing on the steps to look at me.

"I'm good then," I answered, following him down.

Daniel's house was gorgeous, and I didn't need another hit of that particular drug. It was decorated exactly the same way I would have done it and had always fit me like a well-worn shoe. I could feel him settling into my system, and I didn't hate it. But under the circumstances, it was more than I could handle.

He pushed through the door to the boathouse, setting the cooler down and heading toward the large bathroom that contained a closet filled with bathing suits, swim trunks, and towels. It was nothing for people to show up en masse at his place on sunny days, and Daniel was always ready to take friends out on his pride and joy.

I sat on the couch of the main room, facing the unlit gas fireplace and staring into the dark shards of broken glass that lay beneath the logs. I knew they glittered beautifully when the logs were lit, and the irony wasn't lost on me. Rising, I went to the fridge, pulling out two beers and opening them. I handed one to Daniel as he walked from the bathroom in swim trunks and a hoodie. He took it, narrowing his eyes at me as I slipped by him to freshen up before getting on the boat.

In the bathroom, I drank the beer and emptied my bladder,

noting in the mirror that the dark circles under my eyes seemed to have taken up permanent residence. I heard the boat start in the slip, and its throaty idle vibrated the floor under my bare feet. After one more glance in the mirror, I went into the kitchen, tossed my empty, and grabbed a bottle of water before walking back out and taking the stairs to the boat slip.

"Ready?" he asked, giving me a real smile that chased the rest of the worry his face held and reminding me again of the boy he'd been.

"Yep," I said, stepping into the boat and immediately loving the sway of it under my feet. Daniel was right, it had been far too long.

As he suggested, I made my way to the nose of the boat, picking a seat that wouldn't interfere with his view. The sun made the hoodie around my waist superfluous, and I took it off, tossing it to Daniel to stow in a safe place. Stretching my legs, I let the late morning sun warm me as he backed the boat from its dock.

He liked to listen to loud, bass-filled pop music while driving, but I loved the silence broken by the deep growl of the boat's inboards. He left the music off as we idled away from the dock before picking up speed once away from the house. Wind whipped my hair from its long tail, and I gloried in the feeling of being on the water again. Maybe this was what I needed. Perhaps some hydrotherapy would indeed make me whole again.

Daniel did quick laps around the lake, showing off the boat's agility with quick turns and vicious slowdowns that brought water over the back, spraying onto me.

"Daniel Allen Ross!" I yelled the third time he nearly soaked me.

He laughed, whipping the boat around and heading toward the mouth of the Cheat River where the bank was sandy. He ran the nose aground, turning the motor off so that the noise of the surrounding woods prevailed. Since it was a weekday, the short stretch of beach was deserted despite the good weather, and I closed my eyes, soaking in the peace. Daniel hadn't moved, and the water slapping against the sides of the boat and the rocking it caused lulled me.

Subtle motion pulled me momentarily back to awareness, and I heard the casting of a reel from the rear of the boat. How many hours had we spent doing just this same thing? So many. I let the sun warm my face as I dozed until it became hot enough that I was forced to move, stretching profanely as I rose.

"Ready for some lunch?" Daniel asked, laying his rod down.

"I could eat." I smiled up at the sun and pulled my cover-up off, and jumped off the nose onto the sand, wading out into the lake.

Daniel watched me for a beat before grabbing the cooler

and joining me. He sat on the sand, spreading out a blanket and setting our sandwiches, chips, and fresh bottles of beer. I waded towards the shore to join him. Taking my beer, I watched as he sipped his as he looked across the lake.

"Man, this place is nice. I feel like I haven't had the boat out nearly enough this year," he added, setting his beer down and grabbing his sandwich. "We should go to Coach's for dinner on the way home," he added, missing the reflexive jerk I couldn't suppress at the word.

I knew the reason Daniel hadn't had the boat out was Keith's death, ergo, me. Keith died before summer really kicked off, and my life had been in stasis since. As many of his friends would show up for a day on the lake with Daniel, he often waited to see if Keith and I would join them, and I'd isolated myself since he died. In years past, it was nothing for us to take the boat out for morning coffee. Why sit at a counter when you can watch the sunrise from the backwaters of Cheat Lake? Even though Keith and I shared so many memories on the lake, it felt like a blank slate. On the slim stretch of sand along the dark waters of the lake, I was free of the ghost that haunted me everywhere else, making me realize just how heavy that shadow had been to carry.

"Coach's would be nice," I managed, picking at chips but ignoring my sandwich. "We could share a seafood boil."

"Share? Not happening. Get your own," he laughed,

finishing his beer and grabbing another from the cooler.

"I feel like I'm horrible company," I added, breathing in the scent of changing leaves and lakewater.

"Are you kidding?" he laughed, tipping his head back so that the sun caught the angles of this face. His lips tilted up, and I knew something was coming. "You're beautiful, female, in a bathing suit, and silent. I mean, what could be better?"

I picked up a rock and threw it at him, laughing as he dodged to the side.

"Fuck you," I growled, smiling anyway. "You're incorrigible."

"Just saying," he caught my eye, holding it as he shook his head.

We laid in the sun for a while before pushing the boat from the shore and jumping in and taking off. I drove some, pulling Daniel as he skied. It was one of his favorite things, and he didn't let just anyone drive his baby. The morning's silence gave way to the heavy beat of the music he played as he jumped wakes and twisted in the air. Daniel was an expert skier and loved doing tricks most envious college boys couldn't. I laughed at his antics as we did lap after lap before he fell into the water for the last time, and we motored to the backwater for a few minutes to see if any boats were there.

On the weekends, the backwater, a small cove off the lake, filled with boats that moored together to form a large party barge. People jumped from boat to boat, drinking, dancing, and doing whatever it was they wanted in the seclusion of the trees. It was an instance where age didn't matter, and you might find a pontoon of grandmothers tied up to a ski boat filled with college kids. The point was to have fun and enjoy the summer days, and that's what the backwater accomplished.

We ducked under the low bridge, idling through the no-wake zone, finding only a few bass boats and their fisherman. The tall rock that people jumped off of was abandoned, and the rope swings empty, showing me that summer really was over. Undeterred, we floated by ourselves, watching the anglers bring in a few bass as we sat side by side, enjoying the day. When the sun dipped lower, Daniel started the boat, and we slipped back into the lake proper, heading toward Coach's.

Coach's Crab Shack was one of the few restaurants on the lake that offered boat docking and tolerated sweaty partiers in bathing suits. Daniel idled the boat into a guest slip, and I reached forward, tying it off to disembark. Our flip-flops slapped deck boards quietly as we walked the stairs to outdoor seating, catching the wait staff's eyes as we sank into a spot along the rail.

Without looking at the menu, we ordered seafood boils, vodka, and beer. The restaurant filled with those finishing their workday as we waited, looking out over the calm surface of the water. We didn't say anything, just watched the sun begin its final descent into night.

Dinner was delicious as always, and we talked comfortably about anything that wouldn't trigger something deeper. Daniel was a skilled conversationalist and steered adeptly around any topic that might mar the perfection of the day. I sipped my Grey Goose and watched him devour his giant pot of seafood after eating as much of mine as I could.

"You're too skinny," he grumbled around a bite of shrimp.

"I didn't know that was a thing," I said, smiling as he slurped buttery noodles.

"It's a thing."

"If I eat more, I'll burst," I said, watching the way his lips curled around a corn cobette. God, was he sexy. I felt my smile slip at the thought.

"I mean, don't let it make you frown, Ellie. I was just saying you shouldn't lose any more weight. Gotta fatten you up for winter."

"You're right. It's almost ice-cream season anyway."

"You're weird. Ice-cream season is summertime," he said, launching into one of our oldest debates.

"No, weirdo. Ice-cream season is wintertime," I encouraged. "No one cares if you pack on a few extra winter pounds. Winter is comfort food season. Ergo, winter is ice-cream season." I huffed, knowing what came next.

"Bullshit. Summertime is ice-cream season. Who the hell

wants to eat frozen ice cream in the winter when it's cold. Hot days beg for ice cream."

"The pounds," I start.

"Melt off in the sun. They don't even count as calories. As a nurse, you know this. Ice cream has no calories if consumed on a hot day. Duh, Elle. Get your head out of your ass." He set his fork down, grabbing his beer as he scowled at me.

The smile that curved my lips was natural, and I felt it reach my eyes. Damn, Daniel was good at this.

"So you say. You went to a Caribbean medical school for two years," I taunted, beginning yet another old argument.

"That shit was hard!" he said, tossing his napkin on the table in mock horror. "There is no difference between an accredited medical school in the states and one in the Caribbean except for the good weather," he huffed, crossing his arms and grinning widely at me.

I'd always teased Daniel that Caribbean medical schools weren't as stringent and that he had printed his credits off the internet after surfing all day. He'd only transferred to WVU on the hunt for a prestigious match in the emergency department, and his ploy had worked.

"I'm just saying," I added, mirroring his earlier words. I laughed when he threw his napkin at me and waved for the check.

The sky was painted pink and blue by the setting sun when

182

Daniel nosed the boat toward his house. Although it was still daylight, tall trees surrounding the lake blocked the remaining light, bringing the feel of early dusk. Daniel pulled the throttle all the way back, bringing the nose out of the water and making the boat fly. We skimmed across the smooth surface, leaving a deep wake behind. Within minutes, his house was in sight, and he slowed the boat to idle into the dock under his boathouse. We hopped out, and I tied it off. Daniel pressed a button, raising the boat out of the water on a lift. He sprayed it down with clean water while I picked up the cooler, took it into the boathouse, and tidied up our mess.

I was tired and relaxed from a day on the water and couldn't remember the last time I'd felt such peace. I was emptying the melted ice from the cooler when Daniel came in, ruffling my hair and kissing the top of my head. "You're welcome to stay the night. You can have my bed, and I'll take the guest room. You could sleep for a week in there with the blackout curtains and soundproofing."

It was a tempting offer. "I should probably go home," I tried.

"Okay, I'm coming with you. Let me pack some clothes."

"Daniel," I started.

"I'm not leaving you alone, Elle. Not yet."

I sighed, looking through the picture window to the darkened lake beyond. I'd steeled myself to start dealing with

Keith's estate finally. I was going to drag out the paperwork and find a copy of his will. I hadn't dealt with any of that yet and knew I needed to. He had a will filed at the courthouse, but I was the one that needed to get the ball rolling.

Keith had accounts at the local bank and bills that needed to be paid. His investment firm was handling things on their end, but I needed to get my shit together. "Okay," I said. "I'll stay, but tomorrow I'm going to start wading through his estate."

"And, I'll help with that too," Daniel said, opening the door for me.

We walked up the stairs to the main house, and I trudged across the front patio, dumping our wet things by the door. It wasn't that I didn't want help; I probably needed it. But Keith's affairs seemed so personal that I hated the idea of anyone helping and had refused all offers to do so. Keith had a brother in California that had called, offering assistance after the funeral. I'd said no to him too. Of course, his investment firm had also offered lawyers and their time, but I hadn't been ready. I was Keith's executor, and nothing would happen until I started the process. It had been over two months, and I hadn't done a thing except run from it all.

"Daniel," I tried for the second time.

"Elle, I can help. I want to help, and this isn't something you should do alone. At least let me shuffle around and fold your laundry while you work so that I'll be there if you need anything.

"Okay," I said, giving in to the idea of not being alone all the time.

"Popcorn and a movie?" he asked as we walked through the door.

"Monty Python?" I answered, laughing as he groaned. I loved Monty Python and frequently quoted it, and Daniel called me a nerd after forcing himself to sit through the movies. Secretly, I knew he loved it by the way he laughed the entire time.

"God, those movies are so dumb," he said.

"Uh-huh. Sure they are. Those are my demands." I headed for the stairs so I could shower off the lake water.

"Fuck. Fine. Monty Python and popcorn. Borrow some sweats, if you want, but you might have something of yours leftover if you dig through my drawers." He disappeared through the kitchen, and I heard cabinet doors opening.

Daniel's bathroom was huge and modern. He didn't have a tub, just an oversized shower with two heads and lines of pulsing massagers down the walls. I dug through his drawers while the water warmed, pulling out one of his old tee shirts and a pair of my sweats from when I'd been here last summer. Keith and I had stayed the night after drinking too much on the lake, and we did that often enough that I had something on hand to wear now.

The smell of popcorn wafted to me as I hurriedly rinsed off and dressed, not taking the time to enjoy the perks of his shower. Downstairs, Daniel was already settled on the couch in his media room with a bowl of popcorn and an open bottle of wine with two glasses.

"What wine goes best with popcorn?" I asked, knowing the answer.

"Riesling, duh," he answered instantly while perusing his Roku TV for a movie. "Come sit." He uncurled his legs, making room next to him. I sat, waiting for the movie to start. After three sips of wine and a bite or two of popcorn, I fell asleep before it could even get to the good parts.

Chapter 14

It took me a while to realize I wasn't at home, and the room's absolute blackness let me know that I was at Daniel's and not in my bed. Where I'd tried to make my room blackout dark, he had succeeded. Because sometimes he worked night shift, Daniel took the amount of light his windows allowed in seriously and had installed not only blackout drapes but applied a blackout film to the glass. Where I hadn't wanted to give up the view of the outside to achieve darkness in my space, he hadn't cared. The result was that his room had the pitch black at midnight on a moonless night effect that I hadn't managed.

I'd slept like a baby, and not even a clock illuminated the space to let me know what time it was. Groaning, I rolled over, reaching to his nightstand to check for my phone. I'd fallen asleep early, and Daniel must've carried me to his bed. It couldn't have been eight o'clock when I'd dropped like a stone. My phone told me it was eight-thirty in the morning, meaning I'd slept for over twelve hours.

After rolling in his soft sheets for a minute, I got up and headed for the smell of coffee. I found Daniel in the kitchen making waffles and bacon. Sunlight filtered through the sliding door leading to his deck overlooking the lake, making my eyes squint at the brightness of it all. It looked like a heavy frost settled onto last year's fallen leaves along the path to the shoreline, where chairs and a grill sat waiting for a cookout.

"How'd you sleep?" he asked, handing me a steaming black coffee.

"Uh, great. I don't remember the opening credits," I said, stifling a yawn behind my hand.

"You snored through them," he answered, dodging the dishtowel I threw at his head.

"Sorry. I must've been tired."

"Don't apologize for taking care of yourself. You needed the rest."

He was being nice, and I knew it. The circles I'd been sporting under my eyes for weeks looked much better when I glanced in the mirror this morning, but Daniel would never mention that. I sat at his island in silence as he flipped the waffle maker over and pulled a fresh-made waffle out. He dusted it with confectioner's sugar and passed it and the syrup to me before starting his own waffle. A plate of bacon followed, and he stole a piece, munching while he waited for his waffle to cook.

It was nice being taken care of. As a nurse, it seemed I was always caring for others, and Keith hadn't been the pampering type. He doted on me, sure, but making my favorites for breakfast was not something he'd have ever done. He would've bundled me into the car and taken me out to eat instead. I ate the waffle, loving the hint of vanilla under the maple syrup.

The waffle maker chimed, and Daniel pulled it out, offering it to me. "Do you want another?" he asked.

"Hardly, big guy. Fatten me up over time, not one meal," I chuckled, seeing his lips tip into a smile.

"Am I that obvious?" he asked, dousing the waffle in syrup before diving in for a bite.

"Yes," I answered. "Not that I mind the sentiment. I appreciate everything you're doing, Daniel." I shoved another bite of waffle into my mouth before smothering a piece of bacon with syrup and adding it to the mix.

"I like taking care of you, Ellie. Always have. You're not going to change me. I'm too old to learn new tricks."

I snorted, almost losing my waffle through my nose. "Hardly. We're not old; we are seasoned."

"Right," he added, shaking his head.

We finished breakfast in silence, and when I was done, I started working on the mess he'd made. I sipped coffee and loaded the dishwasher while he scanned the newspaper's headlines. The entire scene was just a little too comfortable, so I stopped looking too closely at it. I wasn't ready to move on from Keith, but if I was, this is what I'd be doing; I couldn't lie to myself about that, but it upset me on a fundamental level because I felt like I was cheating. The sex hadn't felt like as much of a betrayal as this peaceful moment in Daniel's kitchen.

"I should go," I said as I finished wiping the counter. "I work tomorrow and really do need to start going through things," I added when I saw Daniel's frown.

"And I told you I'm coming with you. I'm ready when you are, unless you are walking to your house," he said, chuckling. "I know how much you love to walk."

"I walk like a hundred miles a day at work," I growled, knowing he was right.

"And I know how much you love that, too."

"Fine," I said, shaking my head. Daniel had made up his mind about something and was following through with rigid determination like he always did.

The Audi should've been warm in Daniel's garage, but it still held the chill of the morning. It had dipped below freezing the night before, and the cold after the warmth of Daniel's house was bone-deep. After months of relative warmth, the air felt colder and sank in deeper than it should. Daniel turned the engine over, and I hit the seat warmer button as he backed out of the garage. Days like this made me glad for the fireplace in my living room, and I planned to light a fire as soon as I got there. I didn't care how warm I made the house; it was still cold during the winter, as if the feeling itself couldn't be changed.

Keith and I had always argued about where to set the

thermostat. To him, seventy was seventy, but to me, winter seventy hit different, and I preferred to set the thermostat higher. It was a constant battle of wills where the winner beat the other with stealth and quickness. Sometimes he wouldn't notice it was set on eighty for days, and sometimes I would miss that he'd turned it down to sixty-eight. It had become a joke between us over the years, and he lamented where I would want the setting when I hit menopause. Daniel jacked the heat up as high as it would go, and between it and the seat warmers, I was toasty as we rode through town.

I didn't miss that he avoided the interstate, and I knew why. I hadn't been past the scene where the accident happened since Keith died. Someday, I planned to plant a roadside cross there, but I couldn't make myself even head in that direction, so that plan had to wait.

Outside of my house, I had bent to pick my dirty clothes bag off the floorboard when I heard the side door to the garage open.

"Wait," I tried, rushing forward, but I was too late.

"My God, Elle," Daniel said as he took in the motorcycle parts strewn across the empty bay where my truck might sit were it empty. He scrubbed his hands down his face, not looking at me as he scooped me into his arms. "Jesus, Ellie. Why? Why would you do this?" he asked, pushing back from me. Deep lines of concern etched across his forehead, and I felt the dismay coming from him.

"I don't know, Daniel. I just needed to." I tucked my arms to my chest, trying to block the comfort he offered as he reached for me, pulling me to him. He just hugged me tighter and refused to let me go as he rocked me gently from side to side.

"I'm boxing it all up, Elle. No more of this, okay? How long were you going to torture yourself?"

"I don't know, Daniel. He loved that bike," I said into his chest, not even sure he could hear me.

"Yeah, but he loved you too. Would he want this? Would he want any of this for you? He would tell you to stop. He would have told you to stop on day one, and you know it. Keith was practical, if nothing else," Daniel said as he unwrapped his arms.

"Daniel," I started.

"No, Elle. I'm getting rid of the motorcycle. You can do what you want with the Mercedes, but the bike goes." Daniel pulled away, moving toward the corner of the garage where the boxes the bike had been brought to me in were waiting.

There hadn't been many pieces large enough to be carried alone, and the entire wreckage fit into ten-ish medium-sized boxes. I knew Daniel meant well, but it hurt to see him picking up the remains of Keith's life to haul away like trash. I turned my back, closing the door to the house behind me.

Scents assailed me as I entered, and despite the living I'd done in it, after being closed up for a day, it smelled even more strongly like Keith, and I stopped myself from hating it.

I needed to go through his things and take what I didn't want to keep to Good Will, but it seemed too daunting a task. Instead, I pulled out the files relating to his finances and piled them on the formal dining table we had so rarely used. Before setting myself to the task of finding insurance policies and investment account information, I took the time to start a fire, hoping to chase some of the chill I felt in my soul away.

I was sitting at the table in front of piles of papers when I heard Daniel open the door and come into the kitchen. After some quiet rustling, I smelled coffee and smiled in appreciation. He brought a cup around the corner, holding it in front of him like a peace offering. "Forgive me?" he asked, giving me a boyish smile.

"There's nothing to forgive because you aren't wrong," I added, accepting the cup from him. Sighing, I tipped my head back as if it were too heavy to hold upright.

I'd arranged everything in neat stacks with bills and loans on one side of the table and investments and bank statements on the other. Keith had money in places I hadn't known about, and he'd paid bills I didn't know existed. Due to the nature of his job, he had his fingers in so many pies that it was hard to track. His investment account balances, life insurance, and retirement were more than enough to pay off any outstanding debt.

It would take time to sort through it all, but it appeared that I would be well off when the dust settled. The first thing I needed to do was take his will to the probate court and file it. I'd had a copy of his death certificate for weeks and hadn't even opened it. It sat on the end of the table furthest from me, and I pointedly ignored it. Instead, I made a list of his debts and bills and what assets I knew. Keith's firm had forwarded a list of his accounts and instructions on accessing them; I just hadn't done it.

I opened bills, making notes to cancel his cell phone and credit cards. I laid everything out, feeling like I was making headway on the task of finalizing things. It felt like the end, and my heart beat heavily in my chest as if it were weighed down.

Daniel muddled through the house, folding laundry and straightening things, and his presence was comforting, if I was honest. He was right that we'd always been something to each other and now was not the time to change that. I smelled food cooking and knew he was working on lunch.

The last bill in the stack came from a bank I wasn't familiar with, and I opened it, tossing the envelope aside. It looked like a mortgage statement, but it was in Keith's name and not mine or ours, adding to the confusion. I'd owned the property the house was built on before I'd met him, and the loan for the house had been in my name only. I hadn't met Keith until a few months after I'd moved into it, and we'd never changed the deed to add his name. He had a few rental properties in town when we met but had recently sold them to a big company looking to put up high-rise student housing.

The statement didn't list an address, and I added it to the stack of debts, planning to call the bank and get more info. Keith had probably changed his mind and kept one of his more lucrative rentals and not mentioned it. A flash of irritation went through my mind, but I pushed it aside. Keith was the money man. He was fantastic at financial planning and investing, so it was natural to let him handle that part of our lives. He'd invested our money well enough that we had planned on retiring early and could have done so.

With the preliminary work of settling his estate finished, I rose, stretching my stiff back with a groan. I followed the smell of food and coffee into the kitchen, finding Daniel on his back under my sink. His tee-shirt had ridden up, exposing the silky blond hair trailing under the waist of his jeans. I smiled with a shake of my head as I kicked his foot.

"What'cha doing?" I asked. Glancing at the cleaners scattered about around him.

"Did you know your sink was leaking?" he asked, his arm turning something underneath of it.

"Uh, no?" I answered. Leaning down, I peeked at what he was working on, finding him turning a wrench.

"A fitting on your faucet was loose. It leaked a little onto the cabinet floor, so you might want to let it dry before putting that stuff back in there. It might warp a little," he added, crawling out from underneath the sink.

"Thanks," I laughed. "I didn't know."

"Lunch is ready. It isn't much." He popped to his feet, sidestepping to the cabinet where I kept plates, pulling them down.

He'd made fettuccini noodles tossed with oil and a bit of herbs and scattered it with shrimp I'd had in the freezer. The scent of garlic drifted from the pan, and my mouth watered. "Just threw it together, did you?" I asked, grabbing a plate and piling it high.

"I mean, yeah," he said, bumping me on the shoulder.

Daniel had always loved cooking and had taken some culinary classes during his undergrad years. He took every opportunity to throw together the most amazing meals, and half the time, I thought he had parties just to have an excuse to cook. He was good at it, and the ease at which he moved around my kitchen showed that. I hadn't been grocery shopping in weeks, but he still managed to make a gourmet meal.

"Thanks, Daniel. This is amazing." I took another bite of pasta, letting out a long groan as the flavors melted on my tongue.

I caught him watching me through half-closed eyes.

"Thanks," he said. "Glad you let me hang around today. I need to go soon; I've got to go in at eleven."

"Tonight?" I asked, surprised.

"Yeah."

"I thought you were off today?" I asked, scrunching my brows at him.

"I am off today, but I am not off tonight," he groaned.

"Daniel Allen. You should be home in bed," I said, glaring at him over the island.

"I'm going," he said. "I'd rather spend the day with you and work tired than nap all day. I've missed you." He gave an unapologetic shrug of his shoulders and dug into his meal without another word.

I smiled, glad he'd stayed. Going through Keith's papers had taken a lot, and if I'd been in the house alone, it would have been so much worse. Daniel's presence had made it bearable. "Thanks, Daniel," I said, reaching for his hand.

"Always, Ellie. Always." He straightened, loading his plate into the dishwasher. "I'll see you in the morning. Come in early, and we'll have Starbucks and pretend we aren't at work."

"Good plan," I chuckled, finishing my plate and handing it to Daniel, who stacked it.

"Okay, sunshine. I'm off for a nap. See you in the morning." He swept me into a quick hug, kissed the top of my head, and was gone, leaving behind only emptiness.

Sighing, I closed the door behind him before walking into the formal dining room. One look at the stacks of papers told me I was done with them for the day. For someone not having to work in a few hours, it was early. I was still feeling sluggish but wasn't up to sitting in the house, so I changed, throwing on jeans and a light sweater to chase away the chill. In typical Appalachian fashion, the temperature was expected to barely hit fifty.

I headed for the front door, planning a trip to the grocery store, but I stopped, going to the garage instead.

True to his word, Daniel had picked up the pieces of Keith's motorcycle, and they were gone. How he'd gotten them into his Audi, I didn't know, but there was no trace of the bike scattered on the floor of my garage. The empty space had been swept clean and was now ready to be used by my truck. Winter was coming, and I knew I would never have done it myself. As nice as it would be to park out of the elements, I felt the tears start. Feeling like I had betrayed Keith somehow, I sat on the step and cried.

An hour later, I found myself at the Mason Jar. I'd gone to get groceries, and instead of heading home, I'd turned left, taking the backroads to the bar. It was cold enough that I didn't have to worry about the milk spoiling, and I nursed the Grey Goose that sat at my right while I devoured the wings under my nose.

Jill served drinks, occasionally looking my way to ensure I didn't need anything. People moved around me, and I listened to the ebb and flow of their conversations. I sat in a bubble that people were unwilling to break, and I wasn't upset about it. Just because I hadn't wanted to be alone at home didn't mean I wasn't okay with being left alone in a bar. It was quiet, but as it was Friday, the place would fill up before the night was over, so I didn't plan on lingering. I finished my drink, pushing the bones from my wings away as I lifted my finger for another.

It slid in front of me, and I didn't look up, choosing instead to sip the vodka from the skinny straw. I heard the smack of balls as someone shot the break on the pool table. A song cued up the digital jukebox, and the noise level rose as the minutes passed. I stretched to my full height in my seat, feeling my back crack as I rose from the slouch I'd settled into. I had to work tomorrow and planned on leaving so I wouldn't be tired.

"Hey."

I blinked myself to awareness from the sea of thoughts I'd been drifting on to find Charlie standing at my shoulder.

"Would you like another?" he asked, sliding onto the stool next to mine.

"You know what?" I started, stifling a yawn. "I don't think so. Thanks, maybe the next time. I think I was almost asleep in this one." I yawned again, rising to my feet with a shake of my head. "I work tomorrow and I should just get some sleep."

"Okay, Elle. Next time, I'll hold you to it." He smiled as he watched me leave, and I waved back.

In the parking lot, I put the truck in gear and steered toward home, and after putting the groceries away, I poured myself another drink. On the way to a hot shower and bed, I walked by the formal dining room, pausing to stare at the papers on the table. Instead of continuing, I stepped in and picked up the paper for the mortgage loan. I'd take it with me in the morning and call the bank to get the address of the rental property Keith must have kept.

With that thought in mind, I finished my drink, prepped for my   day,   and   went   to   bed.

Chapter 15

Daniel sat at the desk outside the trauma bays, resting his head in his hands. He'd only slept a few hours, and the shift had sucked. But it had been worth it to him to see Elle resting on the front of the boat and the genuine smiles she'd given throughout the day. It had been a long time. Elle might not remember, but Daniel did. Her smiles had been few and far between the last few years. Daniel didn't know why, but he'd seen the change in his friend and wondered. Loss can do crazy things to people. It can make you see things that weren't there or blatantly ignore others that were.

The pager hadn't quit all night. Like Daniel, most people in the healthcare trenches were superstitious. Find the one who isn't and revisit the issue when they get some experience under their belt. Daniel blamed the change in barometric pressure for the current amount of bullshit he had to put up with during the long hours of the night.

A man had come in high on meth and brandished a broom like a weapon. He'd claimed he'd stolen it from his wife and was trying to ride it away from her. Police had found him trying to kick start the broom and fly away. Upon further investigation, they'd found out that he'd killed her. It had taken so many sedatives to knock him out that Daniel had been forced to intubate him and send him to the ICU until he came off his high and realized what he'd done. He'd wake up with his hands cuffed to the bed rail, guards sitting by his side, and his wife in the morgue.

Some commonality of this theme played over and over on the worst of nights. The I-79 corridor wasn't just known as a hotspot for accidents. It was also a well-known drug trafficking route from Detroit to points south, and that poison spread along the back roads and tributaries into the small towns beyond. As one of the states with the highest incidences of drug addiction, Daniel was surprised the crime rates weren't higher than they were. But the man in ICU aside, murder rates were relatively low.

It wasn't only the number of traumas the ED had seen overnight that made Daniel's heart heavy, it was also the details of them. They'd seen a twelve-month-old non-accidental trauma, a fourteen-year-old rule out sexual abuse, and a ninety-three-year-old whose daughter had stepped over where she'd fallen because she couldn't be bothered. It was nights like this that made Daniel question his life choices. Humanity could be remarkable in good ways and bad, but he hadn't seen the good side of it in more shifts than he could remember.

He didn't know how the nurses did it. Daniel could escape to the relative peace of the desk and write orders, but the rest of the staff had no such luxury. Nurses and techs were left with the lion's share of the burden these traumas left behind, and he couldn't imagine that any of them went about life unscathed when he certainly had not. Not only were nurses responsible for patient care, but they were also charged with keeping a strict eye on the residents and their orders. They argued and harangued his staff into putting clear, concise, and correct orders in to be followed, and they were rarely wrong.

A nurse never would've given 50 milligrams of valium to a woman weighing what Elle weighed. They would have known better. A shudder went through him at the thought of what could've happened if he hadn't been at Crockett's and seen her being dragged through the parking lot. She'd have died if her friends hadn't been there with an overdose kit. It was too much for him.

The pager sounded again, and he almost smiled at the myriad groans that went up from behind computer screens across the department. Glancing down, he read the screen. A garden variety P1 was coming. Someone had zigged when they should've zagged and would land themselves in his ED collared and on a backboard. If the person was lucky, their bad luck would end there, and the damage they did to themselves after wrecking their car could be fixed. If they were unlucky, they would die from their injuries, and another name would be added to the running list Daniel kept in his head of the ones that couldn't be saved.

Sighing, he rose, looking to see which nurses were putting on lead and blood proof gowns. It was a good crew. Maybe not as good as Elle, but they were seasoned and knew their jobs. Grabbing his gear off the wall, he went and readied for the next disaster.

Three hours later, he sat at his desk, staring into the cup of dark sludge his peers called coffee. The day shift had made it before they left, and its freshness expired hours ago. He drank it anyway. He couldn't remember the last time a shift was worse than this one, and the only good thing about it was that it was almost over. Elle would be here soon, and they'd have coffee before her shift started and his ended. Daniel needed to talk to her and had put off doing so for longer than he should.

Before Keith's death, Daniel had decided to make some changes in his life that he'd put on hold as Elle grieved, but it was getting close to crunch time. He'd loved her for so long that he couldn't imagine life without her, but he needed to leave. At least he'd thought so until Keith died, giving Daniel the one opportunity he thought he'd lost. And now he had decisions to make.

Chapter 16

Daniel looked terrible as he clutched his coffee, breathing in the strong scent of the Americano he'd ordered. "Last night was the worst, Elle. I don't think I've ever had a night like that," he said, sipping from his white and green cup.

"That's saying a lot," I answered, feeling sympathetic. When an experienced ED doctor like Daniel said it was a bad night: it was a bad night. I felt terrible even though I was happy I hadn't had to work it. "Do you want to talk about it?" I asked, wondering what kind of dumpster fire could put the look of defeat I saw on his face. It went far beyond physical exhaustion, and I could see he was emotionally done for the day.

The thing about Daniel was that he would bounce back and be ready to do it all again tomorrow. It was one of the things I admired most about him. He was resilient when others wilted and strong when they faltered. I wished I could be more like him on most days, but on others, I thought that maybe he needed to guard himself a little better from the hazards we faced daily. He was ever optimistic that tomorrow was going to be better when I'd stopped believing that fairy tale a long time ago.

"I'm good," he answered. "Thanks," he added, already looking brighter. "How'd you sleep?"

"Okay," I lied, remembering each hour I looked at the clock and bemoaned the time. I sipped my Starbucks, avoiding the subject. "I went to the Mason Jar and grabbed wings; they kept me up all night," I chuckled. "I should've stuck with bottom of the jar sauce, but no, I had to get hot instead. I'm still burping up hot wings."

Daniel smiled, shaking his head. "I was hoping you'd stay home and get some rest."

"I know. I intended to, but my fridge was empty, and who wants to cook the food they just bought from the store? No one, that's who. I let the Jar do the cooking." I reached for his hand, seeing the worry through his smile. "I didn't stay long. I'd have slept better if I had made better life choices. I learned a long time ago not to eat hot wings before bed." I made my tone serious so that he would know I was joking.

He smiled, shaking his head. "Okay, okay; I just want to make sure you're taking care of yourself." He took a deep breath and looked to the side before looking at me again, his expression grim.

"What?" I asked, seeing words on the tip of his tongue and his reluctance to let them fly.

"Nothing, Elle. I'm good. I just need to go home and pretend last night didn't happen."

I burst out laughing. "My God, Daniel, if I had a dollar for every time I felt the same way, I'd be treating those jellyfish stings we always dreamed of."

His face fell, and my eyebrows sank as I looked at him in confusion. He might not want to talk about last night, but he wanted to talk about something. Reaching forward, I covered his hand with mine. "Are you okay?" I asked, leaning forward and lowering my voice. "You know I'm here for you."

He took another breath and held on to it. "I know. It's good," he added. "Just a long night."

"Okay." It wasn't okay because I knew that he wanted to say something that he didn't want to say. But I'd done this a lot lately myself and didn't feel like throwing stones lest I hit my own glass house. Sighing, I glanced at the clock over Daniel's shoulder. "It's almost time," I said more to myself than him.

I felt the weight of the upcoming shift over my shoulders. The heaviness of it flipped a switch that made my heart thud and my breathing come more quickly. I hated this feeling- hated this job. Regardless of what Parker said, I didn't think it would get better. I was getting closer to the day when I could transfer out of the ED, and I couldn't screw that up, though. "I've got to get clocked in so Parker can't write me up, Daniel. Get some sleep; things will look better tonight. I'll see you at shift change."

I jumped up, giving him a quick hug that I felt him sink into before racing to the clock. With one minute to spare, I swiped my badge and jogged up the stairs in the atrium.

"Conroy!" Parker yelled as I walked into the department, and I couldn't help but wonder why the hell she was working on a weekend. The one perk to weekends is that there is no management there to manage you. I mean, that's why weekenders worked weekends. It kept them under the radar. I'd intentionally signed up for as many weekend days as I could, knowing that Parker wouldn't be there to fuck with me, yet there she was, fucking with me.

"What's up?" I asked, not pausing on my way to the assignment sheet.

"Get in here," she barked, and my steps faltered. I detoured into her office and stood in the doorway just far enough to make it look like I was doing as she asked. "Sit down and close the door," she added, looking up from the file she was reading. Her reading glasses perched on the end of her nose, adding to her no-nonsense attitude, making me comply.

Sighing, I pulled the door closed and sat in the chair furthest from her desk. I said nothing as I waited for her to launch into whatever tirade she had planned for me.

"You are best friends with Dr. Ross, are you not?" she started, surprising me with the direction of the question.

"I am," I answered simply.

"Do you care to tell me what happened this week that brought Dr. Franks into the ED as a priority two or why he and Dr. Crites resigned their residencies?"

"No," I answered without adding any detail.

"No, you don't know, or no, you're not answering?" she asked, leveling me with a glare. Used to be, those glares got me, but I just couldn't rally myself to care. I mean, maybe I could goad her into firing me. Maybe that's what I needed. As much as I wanted to keep my seniority and my retirement, maybe I needed a swift kick to get me moving.

"Either or, Parker. Pick one. What happened between Drs. Ross, Crites, and Franks happened when they weren't on duty. Therefore, it is none of this institution's business. I'm assuming it was personal," I answered, and I meant it.

"See, that's where you're wrong. Those doctors have a responsibility to uphold the reputation of the institution they work for. If they get caught up in illegal activities, their license could be forfeit. Now, the only reason I can see Daniel Ross getting so mad that he broke a man's jaw in three places and caused him to have a plate in it is you. So, what I want to know is what happened?"

"Do you even know that's what happened?" I asked, watching her face.

"That's the rumor. There were people at the bar who said you were there. I've known Ross to be level-headed and calm. I can't believe he would beat a man as badly as Franks was beaten if it wasn't for you."

"Maybe he didn't hit him at all," I said, quirking my

eyebrows and giving a little shake to my head. "Rumors are just that sometimes- rumors. I didn't see anything out of the ordinary," I added because it was true. At the time Daniel was beating the shit out of Dr. Franks, I wasn't breathing. I don't remember a thing from the entire day other than what Daniel told me, and I certainly wasn't telling Parker any of that. I'd thought that my memory might come back, but it hadn't, and I wasn't sure I wanted it to. I knew that the people directly involved in the situation would keep their mouths shut because there was too much to lose, so I wasn't worried there was evidence that Daniel did anything wrong.

"And you're sticking with that story?" Parker asked, shifting her weight in her chair and crossing her leg over her knee.

"It's the truth, so yeah."

Parker stared me down, and I met her eyes unflinching. I could take a polygraph on this event and pass because I genuinely had no clue what happened.

"Dismissed," she said with a sigh, turning away from me like a disappointed parent as I rose to my feet.

I left her office without another word, listening to the sound of her getting to her feet and shutting off the light. She'd probably come in just to catch me off guard. She'd go home now and enjoy a lovely weekend away from the short-staffed shit show we likely faced; it's just the way it was.

I dropped my bag in the breakroom and looked at the assignment sheet. I'd been assigned to the non-e side. It had been scratched through, and I was now in the bay. I had no doubt this was Parker's doing, and I wanted to march back into her office and throat punch her, but there was a difference between getting fired and being charged with assault, so I kept my mouth shut and went to check my rooms.

If I hadn't already known the night was a disaster, I would've clued in quickly. The floors of my rooms were trashed. There were no stretchers, and the large monitors on the wall were missing the little companion monitor used to transport patients. Hopefully, this meant that they were being moved upstairs, and I wouldn't have to deal with them. I went to track down the nurse to get report only to find out she was in CT scan.

Pam was in charge, and I let her know that I was going off the floor to track down the night shift nurse and replace them. Her smile was forced and her eyes a little wild; I didn't blame her. The department was wrecked, and being in charge of that is a handful. An overhead page went out for housekeeping, and I heard Pam on the phone with the house supervisor asking for help as I walked toward the scanner. Every room I passed was destroyed. Trash littered the floors, and empty, bloody stretchers waited to be cleaned. If a trauma came in now, we'd struggle to find a place for it.

I walked the short distance to the CT scanners, checking the control rooms until I found a lone nurse and a haggard trauma resident in the last one.

"Car wreck," she said when I walked in. "Negative fast exam has a room in SICU. Twelve maybe? Six? I don't fucking know. I called report to someone." She handed me the patient's trauma sheet and walked out.

"Have a good one," I said after her, smiling a little. This part of my job was still good. The back and forth between most staff hadn't changed. They'd already forgotten I'd suffered a personal trauma and didn't treat me any different than they ever had, and I appreciated that.

My eyes swept over the monitor at the end of the table, ensuring the patient's vital signs were stable. The room was quiet except for the soft beeps the equipment made. The trauma resident had fallen asleep, her head resting on her hand as her closed eyes faced the real-time images that popped up on the screen. Oddly, there was peace in the darkened room. The CT techs didn't like outside noise or drama in their control rooms, and unless it was a shit show, others honored that about them.

"We're done," the tech said, rising from his seat and throwing on a pair of gloves to help move the patient to the stretcher.

I glanced at the resident, noting that she hadn't moved. Technically, they were required to travel with the patient, but I didn't have to heart to wake her, so we moved the patient by ourselves. "Did you see anything I need to worry about?" I asked the tech. They weren't supposed to answer that question, but I trusted their reads.

"Nah, you're good."

I grabbed the elevator, wheeling the patient in. He had his eyes closed, remnants of blood trails drying down his face. I caught the glint of staples under his hair. His leg was splinted, and he'd get a trip to the operating room for that if nothing more.

The elevator doors jerked open, and the trauma resident jumped in, giving me side-eye as the doors started to close again. I shrugged my shoulders, smiling at her back as the elevator rose. She didn't change my destination from the SICU to the OR, so I knew the tech's read was correct, and there was nothing big, bad, or ugly that would cause the patient to go there immediately.

I rolled through the doors of the Surgical Intensive Care, noting that it also looked like a bomb had gone off. The ED and the SICU were tied so closely that I knew it actually had. Most of the adult traumas Daniel mentioned would have landed here, and as the unit wasn't large enough to begin with, it had been a hard night for them.

"Where am I going, Linda?" I asked the clerk.

"Four," she answered, not looking up from the mass of

papers littering her desk.

Chuckling, I wove around the desk, beds, and computers scattered haphazardly about. The unit was kidney-shaped and open concept. Glass doors separated the patients from the centralized desks, allowing staff to have eyes on the patients at all times. The patients on this unit were sick, like sick as fuck sick. As small as the unit is, anyone not actively dying was quickly shipped to other units, leaving only the worst of the worst to linger. The man on the stretcher I pushed would be here a few hours or possibly until after his surgery at the longest. If he had wrecked during the day shift, he'd have gone to one of the trauma step downs that functioned like any other hospital's ICU.

As big as the hospital is, it's never big enough, and it's a constant shell game to keep the wheels turning. I didn't envy the nursing house supervisor that managed the beds in this place at all. I might want out of the ED, but that is one job I wouldn't take if offered. No doubt they drank their weight at the end of each day.

A group of nurses and associates met me in SICU four, waiting to take the patient off my hands. They'd get him cleaned up and shipped out probably before I could get back to the ED; that's just how efficient they were. The SICU was the one unit that didn't complain overmuch about naked, bloody patients arriving after a one sentence report from an ED nurse that never saw the patient. They got it. It didn't mean they didn't talk shit about FERNs, but it was halfhearted shit at best.

After dropping the man off, I walked into the department to find an eerie calm that had spread like fog, dampening everything around it. Housekeepers in the dirty rooms swept away the mess of the night as nurses and techs restocked supplies silently.

Sometimes, the strain of the shift before carries over, causing a pause to the ever-present stream of conversation and noise. The pagers were silent, and the department held its collective breath, waiting to see how the day would go. But you can only stay hyper-alert for so long, and soon the sprinkling of voices sounded, and the day resumed as usual.

It was one of those rare mornings that reminded me of years past when we weren't constantly hammered. The department emptied out as patients either got beds or were discharged. Groups formed, and conversations got louder around the scattered nurse's stations. Someone made a Starbucks run, and someone else bought dozens of hot cookies from a delivery place in town, and a party atmosphere replaced the silent anticipation.

I sat with Pam, Kat, and a newer nurse Michael at the central nurses' station, listening to a story Rachel told about a code blue on one of the floors and laughing my ass off as she mimed each step to what sounded like a train wreck. It felt good; it felt familiar. I hadn't taken any Klonopin this morning. I'd ignored the Fentanyl left on the counter in one of my rooms, returning it to the accudose machine, and was feeling more like myself than I had in ages. There was a sliver of hope in my soul that maybe I could make it. Maybe, I could move past recent events and find the spark in my job again.

Days like these were so rare that we weren't even a little ashamed to be eating hot cookies and drinking coffee in the open.

Let someone catch us; we didn't care. We'd earned this moment through the blood, sweat, and tears of a thousand others. You couldn't take peace like this lightly as it kept you sane when the shit hit the fan.

Rachel said the whole place had quieted down and that the other ERT nurses were enjoying a break too. Then, she told stories about the crazy shit the ERT team saw, making the rest of us laugh until tears flowed.

It was hours later when the first pager sounded, making the department sigh. Like all good moments, we knew it couldn't last, and we paused our laughter, waiting for the other pagers to sound.

"P1 ten minutes out, Elle," Pam said, dropping the pager on the counter with a clatter and a groan. "Fifty-nine-year-old male GSW to the head."

"I mean, his wife told him to shut up; he probably

should've listened," Rachel joked, rising to make sure my room was ready. It struck me how well-adjusted she seemed, and I wondered how their team handled it. If anyone saw more death than an ED nurse, it was the ERT team. Yet, they seemed to love their jobs, and the position turned over so rarely that it was a testament to their longevity.

I rose from my chair, feeling the stiffness in my bones from sitting too long. The bad thing about having a peaceful beginning to your shift is that if it gets crazy, it's harder to gear up than to gear down. Around me, people started moving, their sighs and groans adding to mine.

I grabbed lead, covering it with a fluid impervious gown. The blood cooler arrived, and Rachel and I chanted the donor numbers on each bag like a prayer, hoping they wouldn't be needed. P1 gunshot traumas could be anything from a shot to the shoulder to a shot to the head. If the bullet entered the body above the knee to above the elbow, it met the criteria to be a P1. It also didn't matter if it was a BB or a .40 caliber; it was all the same to MedCom.

It could be a self-inflicted nightmare or a hunting accident; neither was uncommon in this region. Archery deer season was in, not firearm, and it wasn't suicide season either, so it was hard to say. Most suicides occur in April, May, and June, with April having the highest numbers. You would think it would be the dark of winter when the days are short and the nights are cold, but people hold on until the spring. Maybe it was something about new growth in nature that made them hopeless instead of hopeful, but the statistics bear this out. Suicide is also more common on the night shift between midnight and four a.m. Obviously, desperate people can reach the end of their tolerance for life at other times; it just isn't as common.

We waited in the room, Rachel by my side, and the rest of the staff scattered about. I couldn't remember the last time she'd put on lead and come into one of my traumas. Whether it was the events of the other night or boredom, I couldn't say, but I appreciated her presence. A crowd had gathered behind the line but thinned as the pagers sounded again. And again. Our break had been far too short, and the atmosphere changed yet again.

Lifenet strode through the door, beginning to unpack their patient before the stretcher stopped rolling. "Fifty-nine-year-old male, self-inflicted GSW to the head. .45 caliber projectile through and through. GCS one, one, one. Intubated on scene, no protectives. Lowest BP 70/palp, highest heart rate 165. Move on three: one, two."

The patient was carefully moved, his head wrapped in blood-soaked dressings supported by the ED resident at the top of the bed. One swollen eye was visible through the dressings, but the other was covered. Blood ran in dried trails down his exposed skin and puddled on the sheets below. It was starting to congeal, and one of his hands was buried in it.

"Two units up on the level one," the attending said from his spot on the foot of the bed.

The Level One hummed in readiness, and as I was nearest, I turned, spiking the first bag.

"BP 82/46, heart rate 147."

"16 gauge in the left AC."

"Gray matter visible at the left temple."

"85.6kg."

"Repeat pressure 94/60. Wound is still bleeding extensively."

"Two more units."

"Fast exam is negative."

"Roll on three: one, two."

"Back exam negative."

It happened smoothly, each part of the machine running flawlessly. I ran the Level One, concentrating on switching bags so that no air got into the line. The doctors hadn't put in a trauma rated central line, so the blood ran a bit slower. This man needed a CT scan, and any delay in getting him there would be a detriment. To what? Possible organ donation.

There's a misconception that if you shoot yourself in the head, you will die instantly. While it's possible that you won't survive more than a few seconds, it's also possible that you will. If you miss the brain stem, the exit hole created by the shot might actually let you live longer than you planned. The cracks in the skull allow the brain to swell without cutting off flow to the brain stem, and as all life functions are carried out there, you may survive.

A GCS of three meant that this patient wasn't responding, moving, or opening his eyes to any stimulus. The lack of protective reflexes meant that he was brain dead or headed in that direction. His life was over, even if his brain stem didn't know it yet. The team would do everything in their power to keep him that way until decisions about organ donation could be made. Fortunately, that wasn't a conversation that I had to have.

"BP 110/67. Heart rate 120."

"Get to scan."

"I'll take him, Elle," Rachel said, laying the travel monitor on the stretcher and rolling out the door.

"I'll call report," I said, wading through the trash on the floor and skirting the pools of blood.

"SICU nine," Pam said, laying the trauma sheet on the stretcher as it passed.

The man who thought his life should end today was in my bay for six minutes and forty-seven seconds before he was wheeled away. Sighing, I grabbed a trash can, swiping trash off of the counters into it. The pharmacist grabbed meds, and housekeeping rushed in. Within minutes the room was ready.

Another trauma was being worked in my other room, so I hurried to set up for the next page that might roll through.

"Mon County is bringing in a respiratory distress that needs tubed," Pam said, sliding in front of the computer to check the patient in.

EMS rolled through the door before I could move the stretcher into place and lock it.

"Sixteen-year-old history of asthma," the medic started. I looked around, not seeing a resident or attending. Pam and I were the only ones in the room, and I held up my hand, stopping his report with one look.

"Hang on."

"He needs tubed."

"Are you gonna do it? I've got to get an attending," I said, yelling out the door for someone. Anyone.

"No, I'm not."

"Then hold your horses."

"History of asthma. Got into something he may be allergic to; parents weren't sure. Didn't respond to Albuterol. Couldn't get an IV."

I rolled my eyes. They really wanted this kid off their cart, so they could get out the door. His partner came around the side of the stretcher, helping him to pull the patient over without waiting. Sighing, I put the kid on the monitors, checked his vital signs, and grabbed a quick weight as I walked to get the things I needed to start an IV, but Pam ran out to deal with something, leaving me alone to finish checking him in.

At first, the kid looked okay, and I stopped popping my head out and asking for help. He was tachycardic with a heart rate of one-twenty, though, and that gave me pause. The tachycardia with an oxygen level of ninety-three percent and a respiratory rate of twenty-six had me yelling out the door again, asking for a doctor.

I had his IV started, and a liter of fluid hanging, but the doctors were overwhelmed with traumas and hadn't made it to the room yet. I hadn't made it to those other rooms either and hoped that someone was picking up my slack.

The cool thing about kids is their remarkable ability to compensate physiologically- until they don't. I called the respiratory therapist. The bad feeling got stronger as I watched his breathing become more labored, and I stuck my head out of the room, looking around wildly.

Ambulance crews with empty stretchers lined the main hallway, and I knew we'd gotten an influx of patients. With one last look at the monitor, I walked quickly to the closest room, looking for help.

There is no running in a hospital. Well, there probably is, but it's not done by the professionals working there. There's a swift walk and a joggish walk, but no running. Running instills panic. When a Code Blue or cardiac arrest is called, there are already people with that patient. Those people do what needs to be done until the code team arrives, and let me tell you, the code team doesn't run. I've seen Nate, Rachel, and the other ERT nurses leave the ED at a brisk walk, but I've never seen them run.

I found no doctors in the second room. The high alert beeping of the monitor in my room made me turn back. And I ran. It wasn't far, but I ran anyway. When I got back into the room, the sixteen-year-old was a dusky blue, and his oxygen levels had dropped into the seventies. Respiratory hadn't arrived, so I grabbed the Ambu bag and pressed the Code button on the wall. The kid's heart rate had jumped to one-sixty, and he was struggling to get air into his lungs, even though I was forcing it with the bag.

"Hey Ellie, did you know your code button is on?" Pam said, sticking her head in the door. "Holy fuck," she added when she saw me bagging the kid alone in the room. I'm not sure I'd ever had to press the code blue button before. It's possible no one even knew what the noise meant. I couldn't remember being in a situation and not being able to get help when I needed it. "I need a fucking attending in here. This shit is real," she yelled down the hallway before walking to the crash cart and opening it up.

The kid was hard to bag, and I knew that his airways were so constricted that my interventions weren't working. The room filled with people. I continued to bag so that respiratory could set up the ventilator. Someone took over bagging, and I moved over to draw up drugs that might open up his lungs. I drew up magnesium and steroids, passing them off to be given, and his oxygen levels began to rise.

"20 milligrams etomidate and 70 milligrams of Sux," the attending said from the head of the bed.

I drew the drugs up, handing them over.

"7.5 ET tube, 22 at the lip," he said, raising up and attaching the Ambu bag to the tube as respiratory secured it.

"Continuous albuterol. Get Xray in here."

The kid reached for his tube and was restrained by staff near the bed.

"50 milligrams of Fentanyl, 2 of versed, and set up a Fentanyl drip."

I handed over the drugs before heading to get the drip from the Accudose. I bumped into the pharmacist as I left the room.

"Hey, whatcha need? We were intubating bed seven. Sorry, Elle."

"No worries. The kid in Trauma One needs a Fentanyl drip. I can set up the pump if you grab it." I turned on my heel, taking the pump on the counter and programming it to speed the process.

Within fifteen minutes, the room calmed. The Pediatric Intensive Care was notified, and a bed was assigned.

The pagers went off again, and I cringed as my heart pounded in my ears.

"Let Kayla take the kid up and get ready for another trauma. P1 ten minutes out," Pam said, shaking her head. "Gotta love a fall day."

She was right. With winter threatening the Mountain State, people were out en masse wringing every last drop of fun from what must have been a pretty day beyond the windowless walls of the ED. ATV accidents, car accidents, a boating accident, and falls rolled in one after another until there was nowhere to go with them. Add to that the chest pains and other garden variety complaints, and the ED was quickly overwhelmed.

Patients spilled into the hallways, and like a flash flood, we ran through categories of alerts like paper towels. I couldn't get one patient out before the next one came, and there was no help to be had. I saw all three ERT nurses power walking through the department, which meant that we were on a minimum of a Cat three to possibly yellow diversion.

The P1 came and went, taking the last SICU bed. A P2 followed, only to be tossed into the hallway to accommodate a cardiac arrest that was unable to be saved. The body was moved into the decontamination room to make room for a stroke rushed to interventional radiology for clot removal. My rooms turned over so fast that I wasn't always sure what patient was where.

I came back from CT scan with a P2 to find another stroke had taken her room. Checking the board, I saw the trauma had a ready step-down bed, so I wheeled her up without calling report.

The one good thing about being on a Cat three or diversion was that we could give bedside report and not wait around. The floor nurse would be unhappy, and she could send all the emails she wanted to Parker, but my actions were not only sanctioned, they were also encouraged.

I gave report to the pissed-off nurse and wheeled the dirty stretcher through the hallways to the elevator. Taking a moment, I rested my head on the elevator wall. My spirit was worn paper-thin, and I felt broken in ways I hadn't at the start of the day.

Back in the department, the chaos was overwhelming. The pagers sounded again, and bodies shifted quickly from room to room, preparing for the next thing. EMS was arguing with Pam at the charge nurse's desk. The drivers were trying to drop off a woman with vaginal bleeding. We couldn't refuse, but they should have gone across the street to the other hospital if we were on diversion.

Then the crew flipped out when Pam sent them to triage. Ambulance crews always expected a room immediately, and so did the patients. They would call for an ambulance on purpose for their toe pain, thinking it would get them out of waiting, but they were wrong.

The overhead pager sounded, and a voice announced that the ED was now on red diversion and my hear stopped. I looked around, and things moved in slow motion. There were people everywhere. EMS crews with full stretchers lined the hallways looking for a room, but patients were already lined up as far as I could see. A nurse cried in front of a computer, furiously trying to chart something. Phones rang without being answered. The pagers sounded again, and before that alert finished, the next one began. A house supervisor sat at the charge nurse's desk, trying in vain to unclog the department's arteries, but it was too late. It was always too late.

My breath caught, and my throat tightened. I felt lightheaded and dizzy as I pushed the stretcher into the empty room only to find it not empty. Another patient had been put into my trauma bay, and I didn't even know why. The room was empty of staff, and the too pale arm of the woman lay limp off the side of the stretcher, and the side rails were down. Funny how that's the thing that caught my attention. You never leave the side rails down. The woman was clearly dead. I'd been gone for ten minutes, and a woman had died in my room, and I didn't know why. Trash and empty vials littered the counter, telling me that someone had worked the room, but they were gone now. I walked to the bed, raising the side rails on autopilot, then turned around and walked out.

I kept walking.

I slipped through the ambulance bay doors, knowing that if I didn't catch my breath, I was going to pass out. I was hyperventilating, and I knew it. The pagers sounded again, and my hands started to shake. I'd had nothing but cookies and Starbucks, and that was hours ago. I hadn't peed since I left my house. I leaned against the brick wall, tilting my head so that the sun hit my face as I tried to find some semblance of peace. Only there was nothing but shattered glass in the void left by my soul.

I waited as long as I could before walking back through the doors. The body was gone from my room, and one nurse waited with a few medical students for the next disaster to blow through the doors.

"What's coming?" I asked.

"What's coming, Doc-Cin?"

"Someone took a motorcycle to a car fight."

"That never works." I laughed.

I'd laughed. The Elle before Keith's death had chuckled. Yes, it was a coping mechanism and probably a terrible one. The Elle left behind after Keith felt another piece slip away.

"Motorcycle collision. P1 traumatic arrest," a medical student answered.

"Elle, get the fuck out of here."

"Elle, get out. Please," someone else in the room said

because not everyone had forgotten.

And I left.

I am no hero.

Somedays, there are no heroes.

I left them to fight for that man's life alone because I couldn't do it. Not this time.

I slunk into the supply room and used my trauma sheers to pop the top off of a vial of Fentanyl left in my pocket from one shitshow or another and slid the entire contents under my tongue with a shaking hand. I was tired of fighting. I had tried, and I had failed.

Chapter 17

.

In the other room that belonged to me, I found a nurse I thought I recognized from one of the ICUs, maybe even a step-down. She wore a lead apron, and her eyes snapped to mine when I walked in. She looked more than a little shell-shocked, and I wondered where the poor thing had been pulled from. During Red Diversion, the house supervisors can drag people from other units to help. This poor kid had probably never seen beyond the locked double doors leading into the joint, and now someone wanted her to handle a patient or three.

"What'cha got, kiddo?" I asked, stepping into the room. I could see that neurology was there, but the lead apron confused me.

"Stroke page?" she answered with a question. "I think?"

"Okay. What needs to be done?"

"I got an IV," she said proudly, and I was proud too. For a stroke page, that's half the battle.

"Okay, good." I started packing the patient up, tossing monitors and cords onto the stretcher.

"Hey, uh, Elle?" Carpenter, one of the neuro residents, got my attention. "Can you, uh, check the patient in? We didn't know how to do that. Jessica over there can take them to scan with us," he finished.

I looked over the room again, noting that Jessica was the only nurse. The attending and residents had probably done most of the tasks needed before the scan, like putting the patient on the monitor and grabbing a manual blood pressure. Jessica wouldn't have known all the steps to a stroke page, leaving them on their own.

"Papers are on the computer," Jessica said as she followed behind the resident pushing the stretcher, which was technically her job, still wearing her lead apron. That shit is heavy, and I wanted to tell her she didn't need it, but she looked happy, proud even. I didn't want to ruin it for her.

Jessica would tell her friends and family about that one day she got pulled to the ED to help in a crisis for the rest of her life. Maybe her experience would be pleasant, and I damn sure wasn't going to ruin it for her. Maybe she felt like a hero, and it would extend her career a few more years. Maybe it would motivate her. Maybe not. I smiled a little as she left, even though the neuro resident caught my eye and rolled his.

How dare he, I thought as I watched him walk away. She did a lot more than most people would've in the same situation. She was trying, and I appreciated her for it. She'd looked uncertain but wasn't crying. I'd seen new ED nurses cry daily for weeks and felt like maybe this kid might make it.

I sat at the computer and had the patient checked in within

seconds so that the CT techs could actually do the scan. Then I put the blood Jessica had left in syringes on the counter into tubes, labeling and sending them. I caught up on the stuff the tech would've done if there had been one available before walking over to the scanner and popping my head into the control room. "Any intervention?" I asked.

"Nah, her last seen normal was last night," the resident said.

"No LVO?" I asked, wondering if there was a large vessel occlusion that interventional radiology could remove.

"Not that I saw," came the reply.

"Thanks, team, you're the best." I left them to bring the stroke back, peeking around the corner into the P1 in my other room.

It didn't look good.

I turned and walked away.

The Fentanyl had soothed the rawness deep inside of me, giving me a false sense of well-being. I knew that. I knew it wasn't real, but I didn't question it. Instead, I went into another room and started an IV and drew labs for the nurse trying to do it all by herself.

When I stopped back by my room, the traumatic arrest was gone, meaning they'd gotten a pulse and had likely rushed him to the OR. What would his outcome be, who could say? But he had a chance, something Keith never did. I started scooping trash from the floors and counters, my eyes snagging on the blood puddling and congealing on the floor and pieces of cut clothing in the corner. I threw towels over it all, bundling the clotted mess together and dumping it all in the trash. The tray of drugs abandoned on the counter caught my eye. I looked and saw two vials of Fentanyl and one vial of Versed. I shoved them in my pocket and continued cleaning up the other side of the room.

Pam popped her head into the room, finding me far away from the drug tray. She looked like I felt, which was done and over it. "There's a possible fucking aortic dissection in the goddamned waiting room," she said, cluing me into exactly how many bottles of wine she'd drink tonight. Pam was one of the few nurses I knew that didn't swear like a sailor- except for when she did.

And when she did, it was bad.

I sighed, looking around. My supplies were gone. Empty blood bags were thrown into the corner, and the Level-One was missing. If this was an actual aortic dissection, I would need it. Housekeeping ran in and ran a mop over the worst of the blood as I continued to shove trash into bags. "Bring'em back," I said, knowing that was the only choice. The patient was wheeled into the room before I could finish speaking.

Housekeeping flew in the door with a clean stretcher, and I helped the patient from the waiting room get onto it, even as the scent of drying blood clogged my throat.

It always amazed me that the vaginal bleeders came in by ambulance and the aortic dissections walked through the triage doors after driving themselves to the hospital like a goddamned boss.

And this woman was definitely dissecting. Her voice was breathy, and her breathing labored, but the true sign that this was the real deal was the blueish-purple line that crossed her chest right above her breasts. She was blue from her hair to that line, while she was cherry red below it.

"Fuck," I said, not meaning to. Pam put the patient on the monitor while I slammed two large-bore IVs into her upper arms and hung manual pump blood tubing.

I called the blood bank asking for an emergency cooler as the ED attending walked into the room, hurrying his pace when he saw the woman's color.

"Set up for intubation and get Cardio-Thoracic Surgery down here now," he said.

The cooler arrived, and Pam and I checked off all four bags, chanting the comforting rhythm of donor numbers and expiration dates. If the patient hadn't completely dissected, it was only a matter of time, but her blood pressure was low, telling me she was leaking blood somewhere.

Where's the Level-One?" the doctor asked.

"With the last trauma. The other one never came back from

the OR," I said. "I can squeeze this in almost as fast," I added.

And I did. The manual pump on the blood tubing worked great, and I had a ton of experience squeezing it. The room filled as the surgeons crowded in, reviewing X-rays and ultrasound images. Within minutes, she was taken by the surgeons to the OR, leaving me alone with another mess.

And it was seven-oh-five.

Where was the night shift?

Feeling stripped, I left the room and didn't look back.

I was done. Daniel was working again, and I could only manage a nod as I walked past him, my steps heavy. It was apparent he didn't like what he saw, but there was nothing to be done about it. The peace I'd found with him on the lake evaporated when the pager sounded the first time hours ago.

"Elle? You good?" he asked, knowing the truth if not my answer.

"Yeah. Hell of a day. I'm going to bed," I lied, not stopping on my way out the doors.

I sat in my truck for a long time, unable to start it and drive away. My arms were heavy from squeezing multiple coolers of blood into the dissection as quickly as I could, and my body felt like it had died hours ago. I still hadn't peed.

Finally, I started the truck, letting the throaty hum of the diesel engine soothe my damaged edges. I thought for three seconds about stopping for a drink, but I worked two more days and didn't want to take chances that I would be late and get written up. I could get a drink at home.

I parked outside of my garage, unable to bring myself to drive into the spot where Keith's bike had lain. I dumped the contents of my pockets on the counters, noting the crumpled mortgage statement and the bank number I'd meant to call. I could've done it in the morning but had forgotten; now it would have to wait until Monday.

I poured myself a shot of Grey Goose and chased it with two more. The Fentanyl was wearing off, but the tail end of the smoothness it embued remained. Add the warmth of the vodka sitting in my stomach, and I felt no pain in minutes. I took a deep breath and then another as I leaned against the counter.

My arms were speckled with the blood of other people. It dotted my scrubs from top to bottom. The fine dots looked like arterial spray, and I wondered how and when it had happened. Not that it was the first time and not that it mattered, I just wondered. My body was exhausted from wearing lead most of the day, and I should've been clean.

Stripping my scrubs, I dropped them in the washer and added a disinfectant before turning it on and walking naked to the shower. I drifted in and out of awareness, trying not to think about the day but unable to do anything else. Bloody images ran through my mind on repeat, and I couldn't stop them. When the water ran cold, I dried off and stumbled into bed.

Alarms dinged, and pagers sounded as I walked through the ED doors the next day. The tracking board was full of patients waiting for rooms, but the waiting room was blessedly empty. There was a chance we'd get caught up if people went to church or slept in and gave us a chance.

I dropped a Starbucks off at Daniels spot, searching for but not finding him among the rush of staff. I'd known I was in charge today when I left last night, and if my position were any more stable, I would've called off. I couldn't afford to draw Parker's ire as I inched closer to being able to put in for a transfer. It had taken half a Klonopin and a shot of vodka to get me up and out the door, though. The shot had kicked in, and I felt light on my feet.

My breathing was slow and deep, and my heartbeat steady in my chest. The pagers hadn't triggered my fight or flight reflex, and I hoped that was a good sign. After a few more weeks of ineffectual coping, I was out of here and on to someplace else. I might not be a hero, but by God, I was a survivor.

I got report from the night shift charge nurse and watched her walk away before digging into the staffing sheets and reviewing the tracking board. Some of the people on the board had been there overnight, and a few were leftover from the day before. As no one was in the waiting room, we were on Cat two instead of something higher. Administrators hated to go on diversion since it messed with the beans they counted. Diversion required more phone calls than seemed reasonable, and I couldn't imagine what the Red Diversion phone call yesterday sounded like. Funny that none of the management had to come into the ED proper for it.

Rachel rounded by me, checking on the ED first thing in the morning as she usually did. She once told me that her day was dependent on how the ED functioned and that she liked to know first thing in the morning if she was getting dry humped or not. I'd laughed at the time, but she wasn't wrong. Her steps were a little heavier, and I knew that the team had gotten their asses kicked the same as us the day before.

"Hey, girl. Hey," I drawled, flashing her a smile. "Nice ass," I added, trying to replace her grim look with a smile. If they ever took the ability to sexually harass my coworkers on a low-key level, I was retiring. It's the one healthy coping mechanism I had left, and I knew it. Fortunately, I was not alone in this.

She sighed, tipping her head back. "Yesterday blew foot-long, wrinkled, elder nuts."

"It did. This place is terrible, and I can't wait to get the hell out of here," I said, lowering my voice. "That's if Parker lets me transfer next time."

"Fuck that old bitch," she huffed, lowering her voice to match mine. "Listen. You need to come to the supplemental pool. Come into the ICU cluster and travel the units like a superstar on a farewell tour, then leave this place, this profession, this state and go someplace better." Her words were bitter and filled with venom, making me wonder.

"I mean it, Elle. Our manager would snatch you up in a second, and she is nothing like Parker. Our management runs a tight ship, but it's fair, and no one plays favorites. You'd orient and be on your own in no time. Plus, SP pays a little more since you float. Hell, go to the step-downs if you don't want to do ICU. You're so used to insanity that your days would be half as hard as the easiest one in the ED. This place isn't good for you; it isn't good for anyone long term."

"Oh, I know. God, do I know," I said, rubbing my hands down my face." Tipping my head back, I stared at the overhead lights until my eyes watered.

"When you can transfer, let me know, and I'll see if they can get you in a position. It's a good gig, Elle. It is."

"What kind of position do they want to get me into?" I joked half-heartedly as I nodded my head, taking her words into consideration. She wasn't wrong about any of it.

"Just think about it."

"I will."

The morning wasn't bad, and we were able to decompress to the point that we dropped the category status and went on green. I hounded the staff, and the minute they had a ready room, making them get their patients into it. It might be nice to hold on to an admission so that you didn't get a new patient, but after yesterday, I couldn't afford to let them. If the day was a repeat of that, then we needed all the room we could get.

A steady stream of non-critical patients flowed in and out, keeping us busy but not overwhelming us. Our turnaround times, meaning the time it took us to either admit or discharge the patient, were fast, and people moved efficiently through tasks and kept up with orders. I roamed the ED, helping where I could and checking in the few ambulances that rolled through the doors.

The emergent side of the ED was empty, and I double-checked rooms for readiness. The night shift would've had a hell of a time. Not only did we leave them covered with patients, on diversion, and with no beds upstairs, we also left them with no supplies, expecting they'd fix it. And they had. Most of the rooms were set up, and ready to go, with only a few were missing anything.

I set up arterial lines and chest tubes so that they'd be ready when needed. Both Level-One machines were back, cleaned, and ready to go. I should nominate the night shift staff for an Instant Applause award, but the reviewers would probably say they were just doing their jobs. The thing is, there's a difference between doing your job and doing your job in the middle of a tornado spawned by a hurricane that followed a tsunami. Most people didn't understand that. If you worked in trauma, you did.

The pager sounded for the first time well after eleven, pulling me from the calm place I'd found at the bottom of my mind. "P2. Eighty-eight-year-old male. MVC," I said, checking the board to see who had what assignments again. "Chelsea, you're up."

She groaned, and I wanted to slap her. She hadn't been here yesterday and didn't deserve to groan. But she got up immediately, going to her room and making sure it was ready causing me to mentally take my slap back. The pager sounded again, and I checked it. "P2. Seventy-six-year-old female. MVC. Jordan, this one's yours. Five minutes out," I said, rising from my seat.

"Thanks for the warning MedCom."

"Grandma and Grandpa just got out of church and ran afoul of the Trauma Gods."

"Grampa was a cradle robber."

"Hey, nothing wrong with a little May-December lovin'."

I listened to the banter, smiling a little as I grabbed trauma sheets and gave one to Susan and took the other for myself. People gathered in the rooms and the back and forth between staff.

"If you won't have hands on the patient, get behind the lines."

"Damnit, Conroy. It's Sunday. Can't you let us crowd over

241

the traumas and fuck things up one day a week?"

"No."

"Come on."

"No."

"You look pretty today."

"Fuck you. Get out," I laughed, knowing it wasn't serious and that we were all just joking around. I listened to the amused snorts and the shuffling of feet as people stepped behind the line.

Shaking my head, I sat at the computer, pulling the check-in screen up and yelling at people to sign my trauma sheet while we waited. The pagers didn't go off again, which was good. Often, we got multiple traumas from the same accident, but it seemed we might've avoided that today.

EMS rolled through the door, unpacking the monitors as they spoke. "Eighty-eight-year-old male, restrained driver. Low-speed collision into the back of a pickup. Moderate damage. Airbag deployment. On Eliquis for A-fib. Lowest BP 146/80. Highest heart rate 121. On three: one, two."

I wrote everything they said, watching to make sure they followed the steps and didn't forget anything. The patient was hard of hearing, and it was almost comical the way he misunderstood everything they said. He seemed fine, and I was glad for that. Blood thinners are a necessary evil, but to the elderly, they are a double-edged sword. Without them, atrial fibrillation can cause strokes, but with them, traumas can be made worse from excessive bleeding. Grandpa seemed fine, and I laid the trauma sheet on the stretcher as Chelsea rolled by me on her way to scan.

I popped into the other room where Grandma was, and things seemed okay there too. She had a broken arm and a cut on her head but otherwise looked okay.

I checked a few chest pains and dizziness into the non-e side of the department before the pagers sounded again.

"Stroke page. Last seen normal two hours ago. Ten minutes out. We'll go to trauma five."

Another chest pain rolled through the door with EMS, who said they had a STEMI, and just like that, the day changed. It wasn't as bad as the day before, but it wasn't slow either. There was a used P1 from another hospital that should've been paged as a P2 and a few other traumas, but nothing crazy.

Sometime in the afternoon, I grabbed an Americano and some egg bites from Starbucks, trying to remember the last time I was actually hungry. I made myself pee a few times to make it up to my kidneys that I hadn't peed at all the day before. I even drank a cup of water that I had meant to take to the stroke page but forgot to.

In the evening, I popped the other half of the Klonopin, not willing to lose the soft, fuzzy feeling it cradled me in. Before long, the night shift rolled through the door, and I barely remembered the day. What I did know is that people were still smiling; we'd seen a shit ton of patients and hadn't gone on category status. I thanked everyone for their efforts and left as soon as I could. One more day, and I'd be off for three, and that sounded like a fantastic thing to me. Every day was one day closer to joining the other dinosaurs in pre-op. In the ED, I was one of the old folks, but in pre-op? I'd be the baby. I was looking forward to it.

As much as Rachel's offer to get me a job in the supplemental pool tempted me, I wanted out of bedside nursing, and pre-op sounded like a winner. It wasn't jellyfish stings and sunburns, but it was close, and it would allow me to keep my seniority and build my retirement.

Proud of myself, I drove by Crockett's again, promising myself I'd stop there after work tomorrow for a drink or four. At home, I poured a double and took it into the shower, sipping it as I let the water run over my body. One more day, then I was free for a while.

Chapter 18

I had trouble getting up. I still managed to clock in with thirty seconds to spare but without makeup to hide the dark circles under my eyes. The third day in a row was always the roughest for me. The fourth wasn't bad or the fifth, but the sixth would kick my ass again. It was like every three days, my body demanded I hold up and think about my life choices. People think, hey, you're a nurse. What a great schedule because you have four days off, but little do they know that you might work six or seven days in a row to get two days off, depending on how the week is split or how your schedule runs. I've seldom had four days off, and when you work twelve and a half hour shifts, it doesn't matter anyway because you spend your first day off dead to the world.

Daniel was on his last night shift and switched to day shift Tuesday. Meaning he'd only have a day to make the turn-around. He came by looking exhausted and gave me a long hug.

"Our next day off, we are sitting by the fire and watching a movie. Or golf. I need to catch up on naps, and so do you," he said, his sleepy voice sounding cute and a little sexy.

"Deal," I laughed. "Today is it for me. I'm off tomorrow, but you work."

"I'm off Wednesday," he said.

"Me too."

"Movie night," he said, slumping against me and fake snoring.

"Okay, okay. Get me an Americano, and I'm there."

"Oh, Elle. No. That demand came from Conroy, charge nurse extraordinaire, not Ellie, my friend."

"Nevermind, Daniel," I said, ruffling his hair. "Go home and go to bed. See you Wednesday."

"See you Wednesday."

Ten minutes later he walked by, sliding an Americano into my hand and giving me a pointed peck on the cheek. "Now, I'm going home," he said as he stumbled out the door and into the dim fall sun.

Shaking my head but smiling, I looked at the tracking board, noting we were filling up. Mondays sucked because people waited to come in, especially if the weekend was nice, and it had been, even though I missed it because of work.

Most weekends, the hospital caught up on discharges so that on most Mondays, there are at least a few empty beds to admit patients. Still, if you consider that the OR's busiest day is Monday, and the ED's busiest day is also Monday, you have the makings of a perfect storm.

Six patients on the board were being held pending admission and had been in that particular purgatory for hours.

Consults were backing up, and the waiting room was already twelve deep.

Sighing, I sipped my Americano and stared at the computer screen like I could change it.

"How's it looking?" Parker said as she loomed over my shoulder like the vulture she is.

"Like shit," I answered, not bothering to look at her or care about my language. Could she write me up for it? Maybe, but she wouldn't. Bad language is inherent to emergency departments everywhere, and that wasn't a hill she'd die on.

Nodding, she leaned closer, pointing out a few room changes she wanted to be made before heading into her office. "Call me before they push the button for diversion," she added over her shoulder.

"Okay," I answered, wondering why it mattered. It's not like she could do anything. Sometimes she'd come out of her office and wring her hands in front of the tracking board, but I doubted she had a pair of scrubs that weren't twenty years old, and I damn sure didn't think they still fit. She hadn't worked as a bedside RN since her daughter died, and no, I don't blame her for that. I wanted out too, only she was the one holding me prisoner, so I wasn't feeling generous where Parker was concerned.

The pager sounded, causing my heart to rip through my chest and lodge in my throat. I felt faint and saw dark spots in the periphery of my vision. I swayed in my chair, cursing my inability to adapt. "P2 ten minutes out. Seventeen-year-old MVC."

Grabbing a trauma sheet, I passed it off to another nurse while I moved the patients that Parker wanted to be moved. In the meantime, two patients went upstairs, opening up a few more beds. The P2 rolled by on the way to scan, and I hoped that maybe the Trauma Gods would be kind to us on this fine Monday.

I dared leave the charge nurse spot to run to the breakroom and shovel in yogurt because I still felt lightheaded and unsteady. I wanted to blame it on not eating. I wanted it to be anything other than the post-traumatic stress disorder I knew it to be. Still, I had weeks before I could transfer and needed to find a way to deal with it. It's funny how educated, and knowledgeable people lie to themselves in an attempt to make a situation right.

The pager sounded again, and I cringed when I checked it, finishing the yogurt in two bites. Hustling into the department proper, I found the trauma docs already there and putting on lead.

"P1. Six minutes. Five-year-old versus a tractor." I grabbed lead and threw it on as I walked into the bay. Despite how it made me feel, I was still one of the best in the room and couldn't let this kid die because I was fucking shaking in my shoes. I took three deep breaths and then pushed the pain aside.

"P1. Thirty-six-year-old male. Motorcycle collision. Six minutes out."

I dragged myself to the present, feeling my respiratory rate spike. I focused on tractor accidents and toddlers, trying not to see Keith on the empty stretcher.

"Someone took a motorcycle to a car fight."

"That never works out."

Why anyone put their kid on a tractor and gave them a ride, I'll never understand, but it happens more than you would think.

Tractors are difficult to control in perfect conditions, and most older models lack power steering or reliable brakes. Add in the sloping hillsides of the Appalachians and a squirming kid, and you have a recipe for pain. I've seen more kids versus tractors than I ever wanted to, and I never wanted to to begin with.

Medivac came in the door at a brisk walk, beginning the process of unpacking the kid before they stopped rolling. My quick assessment of him was not favorable.

"Five-year-old ran over by a large farm tractor. He was playing in the yard and ran towards his dad, who could not stop in the wet grass. Crush injury. Intubated on scene for apnea and low oxygen saturations. 5-oh ET tube, fourteen at the lip. IO left leg and a twenty-four gauge in the left hand. Highest heart rate 175, lowest BP 60 palp. On three: one, two." We slid the kid over, and the dance began.

"Manual pressure 40s over something I can't hear. Heart rate 180."

"24.6kg."

"Eighteen gauge right AC," I added seconds later.

"Jesus, Elle. That's just mean."

"It won't be mean if we have to mass-transfuse this kid," I grumbled, adding 'asshole' under my breath. Peds trauma attendings rarely dropped central lines in kids, and the larger the IV, the better blood went through it.

"Petechiae to the face and eyes. Blood in the nares and right ear."

"Throw up Plasmalyte. Thirty migs per kg."

"Warmed fluids up."

"Flail chest on the right."

"Abrasions to the right chest wall and right upper arm."

"Fast exam positive."

"Put a catheter in and see if the urine's clear."

"Eight French foley placed. Urine is clear."

Seven people did ten tasks simultaneously, and it flowed as it should.

"BP 86/50, Heart rate 136."

"Fentanyl 25 mics."

"Fentanyl in."

"Chest tube on the right. Twenty-two French. Bloody return."

"Sats improved to 96%."

"Roll on three."

"Back's clear. No step-offs."

"Get to scan."

"Order blood and have them meet us in the OR."

I tossed the monitor on the bed and moved to take him out the door. On my way through, I glanced at the timer on the wall. Six minutes and forty-seven seconds. That was a damn good time, and I was proud of it.

"Hey, Elle. I'll take him." I looked from the timer and saw the pediatric transport team waiting in the hall.

I didn't want to give the kid up, but they were better equipped to take care of him, and as the charge nurse, I wasn't supposed to leave the department anyway. "Let me know what the scans look like," I asked, handing the Ambu bag over.

"You bet," she said, walking with the peds crew down the hall.

I dumped my lead on the hanger and went to the desk to find that the waiting room was now sixteen deep. A few more beds had opened up, and I walked around the department, asking staff to move their patients as quickly as possible. Back at the desk, I directed three ambulances and took reports on two transfers from other hospitals.

The pager was quiet, and we went through the morning with relative ease. During lunch, I handed my phone off to the flow coordinator, grabbed a sandwich, and went to call the bank about the mortgage.

It took me three tries and two automated systems to get through to a person. It took me three more attempts at an explanation to get to the right person, who then wouldn't talk to me until I faxed a copy of my marriage certificate and his death certificate along with a copy of my driver's license. Thankfully, it wasn't my first rodeo dealing wih a bank, and I'd brought that documentation and more because I'd known I would need it.

The work that death brings is exacting. You would think that the mortgage company would be happy that someone called. You'd think they'd be hopeful their bill would continue to be paid. Instead, I was met with questions, suspicion, and caution. I could've walked into the federal reserve and gotten away with millions more easily than it took to get information about a mortgage.

Finally, I got an address.

814 Summerville Lane in Deep Creek, Maryland, not downtown. I'd asked if the property was listed as a rental. They could only say that it was deemed a secondary residence according to the escrow account that paid the insurance and property taxes. You could list a residence as primary or secondary and still rent it, but they might not pay if there was a

claim on the insurance, the bank explained, leaving me confused.

Deep Creek was a local vacation hot spot. In the summer, the lake was a beacon for weary Baltimore-DC dwellers, and in the winter, world-class skiing brought people from far and wide. Had Keith bought an investment property without telling me? Had he quietly owned it before we met? I'd never heard of this house and wondered. Maybe he bought us a vacation home and meant it to be a surprise but died before he could tell me. He'd always said he wanted a place to get away to, and that was something he would do.

With the answer to the immediate question settled, I hurried back to the department to find the flow coordinator hanging her head at my spot, shaking it slowly back and forth. The place had blown up with EMS crews lined up from the doors to the desk, looking for placement.

"How do you do this?" she asked as the pagers sounded. "Never ask me to watch this place for you again. Ever." She put the portable phone on the counter and sprinted away.

One glance at the board showed me that a bus had dumped a bunch of people in the waiting room and that we were almost out of beds. Ignoring the EMS crews, I ran the category tool and groaned when I saw that we were at category two. Why was it every day?

I directed ambulances to rooms if indicated and triage if

not, earning the grumbles from crews who thought their patient's back pains were emergent. Within minutes we were at a category three, and a short time later, we were greenlighted for diversion. Fortunately, it was a peaceful kind of diversion because patients trickled in slowly after the initial surge. The lack of beds was the problem and not the continued influx of bodies. Once orders were completed, the only thing left to do was wait on discharges upstairs.

I was playing cards with Rachel when the pediatric trauma surgeon came up to us, eyeing our game with amusement. Some politician years ago had complained that all nurses did was play cards and the fallout from her statement was widespread and catastrophic to her career. We laughed about it, making a point to keep a deck at the nurses' station for times when it was slow.

"That kid is fine," he started. "A few broken ribs, that's all. His head was clean. The great thing about kids that young is that they are all cartilage. You can squish them, and they pop right back up. I just wanted to let you know he'd be okay. Thanks for the eighteen gauge; the PICU loves it," he finished before walking away.

Rachel was laughing out loud, and I felt my look of incredulity to my soul. What the fuck? They pop right back up? But a smile came to my face anyway because it was funny. It was fucked up but funny at the same time. There was something deeply wrong with all of us, so how could I judge him? I've seen a lot, but what had he seen? We couldn't go a week without a toddler some woman's boyfriend beat the crap out of. We couldn't go a month without a newborn that someone smacked off a wall because it was crying too loudly or a pre-schooler that the mother couldn't bother to put in a seatbelt. That was commonplace, and he had to see more than we did. I wouldn't judge him, not even a little bit.

The afternoon went to evening, and beds opened up. We got the admissions out of the department before the evening trauma rush began. I was glad that I worked twelve-hour shifts and didn't have to deal with the nine to five traffic because it sucked. Say what you will about it not being a big city, but if you sit in traffic that's lined up all the way through town, that's a traffic jam. It might not be an Atlanta-level traffic jam, but it's still a jam.

Then people got on the interstate and acted out their deepest NASCAR fantasies and ended up boarded and collared while looking up at me as I slammed the biggest gauge IV in them that I could. That's how it went. Add in that it was a sunny day, and folks would try to beat the earlier sunset home to squeak out a few minutes of daylight, and wrecks abounded.

So it was no surprise when the pager sounded two consecutive times in a row, and then after a beat, a third. It didn't matter that I knew it was coming; I still jumped. My heart pounded in my throat, and I felt my stomach drop.

Sighing, I looked down. "P2, pedestrian versus car five minutes out, P2 MVC, and P2 MVC also five minutes out. Using the overhead paging system, I announced the traumas department-wide so that nurses from the non-E side would know to come and help. Every trauma took three RNs at a minimum to run, or they should. Three traumas at one time required a minimum of nine RNs, and if one of those traumas was severe, more would be needed. I knew the ERT nurses would come down if they could, but sometimes they were tied up elsewhere. I needed to get my ducks in a row.

Grabbing trauma sheets, I shuffled away from the desk after hiding the fact that I popped the other half of my Klonopin with the movement. "Trauma rooms seven, four, and three," I added. I waited at the ambulance bay doors to direct the traumas and eyeball them to make sure they were appropriately paged and that no one was actively dying.

Once the ambulances were directed, I followed the last one, logging into the computer to arrive the patient as I wrote the woman's story.

"Twenty-one-year-old restrained driver of the car that hit the car that hit the kid in the crosswalk," he started. I paused my pen, rethinking what he said.

"Minor damage to the vehicle, no airbag deployment. Highest heart rate 76 and lowest BP 112/70. On three: one, two." I watched as they moved the patient over, noting that there seemed to be no damage to the person either.

Sometimes people just wanted to come in after an accident. Frequently they were hedging their bets for a lawsuit later. Often they were bored and had nothing better to do. Even the pedestrian hit in the crosswalk had looked fine when she rolled through the door. She hadn't had a mark on her. It was likely that these were college students with nothing better to do or with helicopter parents that had screamed at them on the phone to get checked out. I rolled my eyes inwardly, resuming writing on the trauma sheet.

I always said that the only way you'd get me through these doors was if I was unconscious or feet first. So, in other words, the only way they were dragging my ass in here on a stretcher was dead or mostly dead. I'd walk it off otherwise. My pager sounded, and I scanned it. One of the other traumas got downgraded to a trauma consult, confirming my suspicions that this accident was less serious than it had sounded. I finished writing and dropped the trauma sheet on the stretcher as it rolled by before checking on the other patients.

The pedestrian was sitting up and drinking water. The person from the other car was gone, likely in the scanner. I shook my head with a sigh. Maybe we could discharge them before the next round came in. It was a pipedream but a girl's gotta dream.

The pager sounded again, and the ERT nurses took care of

the stroke while I discharged the three traumas with prescriptions for Motrin. After that, the pagers sounded so often that I broke into a cold sweat that never stopped dripping down my back. I had to sneak into the bathroom and put the remainder of someone's Fentanyl under my tongue to get my hands to stop shaking because my heart was pounding so fast that I thought I was going to pass out.

I couldn't do this. Even if I could get over the actual job, I didn't think I could ever react normally to the sound of so many pagers. Each time it got worse until I found myself on the toilet holding the drug under my tongue until the black floaters blurring my vision went away. It was terrible.

They weren't even major traumas, but they were traumas, and I struggled to be both good and sane while working them. The cycle was endless, and madness chased me constantly. By the time I clocked out, I was done. In reality, I'd been done for weeks, but the last trauma page had sent me into an abnormal heart rhythm, and I'd had to sit down or risk passing out. The drugs helped, but it wasn't a long-term solution. I was trying; I wanted to try. It's not like I wanted to be like this.

I stopped at Crockett's and had three vodkas in the span of about ten minutes. I chased them with a burger and fries, knowing my stomach was empty. I'd texted Daniel to see if he wanted to come with me, but his night shifts had left him drained, and since he worked tomorrow, he was being a baby.

So after dinner, I drank two more vodkas and limped home.

I slept in the following day. My legs ached so badly overnight that I'd tossed and turned before dry swallowing the last of Keith's Percocet and praying for sleep. When sleep came, it was fitful, and I'd dreamed of the pagers.

I sat drinking coffee, staring into the dark liquid as if it held the answers I wanted. My body hurt. Three days in a row, and none of them easy, had done me in. I was tired, but more than that, I was weary. I might've also been slightly hungover.

I stared at the key rack for a long time before grabbing the keys to Keith's Mercedes, hoping the battery charger had worked. I'd dressed in jeans and a sweatshirt, and the fabric was soft against my skin compared to the rough-hewn scrubs from the day before, and like the arms of your first boyfriend, it was comforting. I threw my hair into a ponytail and grabbed a coffee to go before walking out to the garage. I stared at the Mercedes for a long time, and I felt the weight of the car in my soul that almost changed my mind.

I'd only driven his Mercedes once when he'd drank too much at the lake. It was a sexy car, both sleek and gorgeous; it had a sunroof and leather interior that cupped your skin like a lover. It wasn't a new model, but new enough to have all the bells and whistles. My hand shook when I opened the door.

Keith's sent assaulted me, causing my heart to skip several beats. I closed the door, backed away from the car, and went into the house. My hands shook as I poured myself a shot of courage and threw it back. I drank one more, hoping that the hair of the dog would smooth my jagged edges. I needed to do this; I knew that. Something was pulling at me to move. The only way forward was through the remnants of Keith's life, and now that I was trying to do it, the compulsion was relentless.

Grabbing a bottle of water from the fridge, I held the door open and stared into it before deciding to skip breakfast. My stomach was queasy enough from last night that I didn't want to tempt fate. I felt terrible, and I couldn't think of anything that would fill that hollow void. Instead, I went into the bathroom and took half of a Klonopin. I looked at a vial of discarded Fentanyl long and hard, but I was driving, and half of the Klonopin would be enough to calm my racing heart. I grabbed the vial anyway, shoving it in my pocket.

I waited until the Klonopin kicked in, sighing when my shoulders lifted. Soon, this would be behind me, and I wouldn't need the crutch I knew it to be. But, for now, it was a lifesaver. I rode the calm from the vodka and Klonopin before walking through the house and into the garage.

Ready this time, I opened the door to the Mercedes and let Keith's caress wash over me. I dropped into the seat, allowing myself to go limp under the barrage of memories and feelings. Keith had the soundtrack to Purple Rain in the CD player, and tears sprang to my eyes when it picked up where he'd left off as

I turned the key half over.

We'd come across the movie while we were dating. It was old by then but no less sensual. He'd claimed the soundtrack was the sexiest thing he'd ever heard, and we'd made love to it often in the beginning, but I hadn't heard it in years. Just for a minute, I gave in, letting it all wash over me. I lay my head back and smiled. Had I known it would be like this, I would've slept in the car until the rush faded and my mind moved on. As it was, everything came back like it happened yesterday. Feeling slow, almost heavy, I forced my hands on the wheel and started the engine. The Mercedes purred to life, and I opened the garage door, backing into bright fall sunshine.

There's something about the skies of fall. There's a crispness in the white clouds and a bluer tint to the atmosphere that doesn't seem natural. There's sky blue, and then there is fall sky blue. There was enough color on the trees to contrast with the absolute blue of the sky, and it made the view breathtaking. I opened the sunroof, letting the brisk air pull me from the emotional pit I'd fallen into. At the bottom of the long drive, I stopped and started to type the address the bank had given me into the car's navigational system. I got three numbers in, and it popped up. My eyebrows narrowed as I frowned at the car's screen before touching it to complete the choice. I began the hour-long drive with anxiety that didn't ease. My knuckles white on the wheel, I turned onto the interstate and set the cruise control.

I had easy access to two major interstates. Avenues North, South, East, and West can all be reached in minutes. But for those who avoid interstates, you could get anywhere that you wanted without them. I knew because I hadn't been on one since Keith's accident. I'd avoided them entirely, knowing I wasn't ready to see the place where he'd effectively died. So I slowed when I reached it for the first time, my mind churning in confusion.

Connections my mind didn't want to make flared as I passed the roadside memorial in the westbound lane as I headed east. Trepidation chewed through my Klonopin, and the beautiful blue sky did nothing to assuage it. I couldn't breathe and didn't understand why.

The miles went by in minutes, and in no time, I turned off the interstate and onto the winding road through Friendsville. I passed ramshackle houses and farmland. Soon, I was through the town, heading toward Deep Creek. Following the prompts, I turned off the main road and into a small housing development on the outskirts of Deep Creek proper. The houses were nice but nowhere near the level of a vacation home or an Airbnb investment property. The lake might only be a few minutes away, but this was clearly an established neighborhood.

I rolled to a stop outside of a cute yellow cottage that looked more beach than lake. Clean white shutters and trim accented the house, as did perfect flower beds and a freshly paved drive. A new honda sat there, and I stared at the house, willing it to tell me its secrets.

The front door opened, and a trim blond stepped out, her hand flying to her face when she saw the Mercedes. It began to shake as our eyes met. And I knew.

I knew that she wasn't a renter or a client for an Airbnb.

She began walking toward the car, and I caught a sheen of tears in her eyes. Then, I shattered like the pieces of Keith's bike that had once littered the floor of my garage.

Fishtailing the car, I flew back the way I came, unable to think. The only thing I could do was feel. I watched the woman run after me in the rearview, and I didn't stop. I couldn't.

On the outskirts of Friendsville, I pulled over and stumbled out of the car. On my hands and knees, I vomited bile onto the hardpacked ground. My shoulders heaved as my body tried and failed to find more to expel. I stayed like that for a long time with the lyrics of a Prince song running through the speakers. *'How can you just leave me standing? Alone in a world that's so cold?'*

I guess I knew the answer to that now.

I struggled to my feet and slumped into Keith's leather seats. I felt the pinch of something against my hip and pulled it out of my pocket. The vial of Fentanyl popped into my hand, and I shook uncontrollably while rifling through Keith's console. I found a pocket knife and a box of condoms. I popped the top on the vial using the pocket knife and dumped the entire contents under my tongue.

How can you just leave me standing?

Fuck it. I threw the box of condoms as far as I could into the trees, letting the empty vial of Fentanyl fly after.

Seconds later, the Fentanyl kicked in, and relief poured through me, taking away my thoughts of Keith, the woman, Prince, and condoms.

I was done- done with it all.

Swinging my legs around, I put my hands on the wheel, seeing nothing in front of me and hearing only Prince. *'Maybe I'm just too demanding.'*

I banged buttons on the console, screaming at the top of my lungs until the CD ejected, and I sent it flying out of the sunroof in the direction of the condoms.

How can you just leave me standing?

The tires spun as I took off, leaving it all behind.

I took the S-turns to the interstate with tears fogging my vision. The racking sobs had quieted, but I couldn't get the tears to stop flowing. They had a mind of their own and insisted on making their presence known, although I couldn't feel anything in my heart to cause them. Finally, I merged onto the interstate and set the cruise control so I could think.

Keith was my world, and I was a good wife to him. He'd

had it all. But to some men, everything isn't enough, is it? Maybe I'd done something. I didn't think I'd pushed him away, but maybe I had. I banged on the steering wheel, screaming as loud as I could as I blamed myself. I crossed the state line and sped up. Maryland police took the speed limit seriously, but once you crossed state lines, it was more of a suggestion than a hard-fast rule.

I reset the cruise, flying past Bruceton Mills and heading towards Coopers Rock. Traffic was light, and I was grateful. It was still early enough in the day that none of the major employers in town had disgorged their staff. All I wanted was a hot bath, a bottle of vodka, and my bed. I began the descent into Cheat Lake, my hands tight on the wheel at the thought of passing the roadside memorial I didn't place for a man I hadn't known. My breath caught, my heart stuttered, and a wave of dizziness passed through me, but I shook it off.

I was so close to home that I could taste the next shot of Grey Goose. I checked the speedometer, realizing I had sped up too much. I eased my foot off the gas at the final turn in the long hill. My eyes were glued to the white cross bearing down on me to my left, and the car didn't slow. The grade on this section of the hill was steep, and my truck had engine brakes that allowed it to maintain a set speed and not drift faster. The Mercedes Benz did not. I pulled the wheel to make the turn when I realized the cruise control was still on and not helping.

The rear end came around just as I tapped the brakes to negate the cruise, and the car didn't respond the way my truck would have.

Something caught, and I felt it begin to spin. I clipped the berm, and the car flipped and kept flipping. I watched the ground approach through the wide-open sunroof, and then everything slowed down. I tried to breathe through it. The airbags deployed, taking my breath, and still, I flipped. The seatbelt held tight, and I felt something pop.

The car repeatedly landed on the roof before stopping its countless rolls and sliding down the remainder of the hill to the bottom; the sound of metal on pavement was deafening, but the silence was worse. My vision narrowed, and my arms hung limply above my head. My breaths weren't coming at all now, and my head exploded with pain as blood rushed into it.

In my mind, I saw the faces of everyone I'd failed, including Daniel. All the children, all the teens, and all the adults that had died on my watch, their faces paraded behind my closed eyes. I relived their last moments as I had so many times before. And then, I let them go to where they should've been. I had a moment of clarity to mourn my life, just one. I listened in absolute silence as blood dripped down my arms and made small noises when it landed. My ears rang. I prayed Daniel would understand. I prayed he wouldn't end up like I had. I knew the pagers would be sounding soon and that his worst nightmare was about to greet him at the door. '*I never meant to cause you any sorrow. I never meant to cause you any pain.*' With those lyrics in my thoughts, I said goodbye and followed the souls of the lost.

Chapter 19

God, this job sucked, Daniel thought as he pulled the speculum from the woman's vagina. She was having a miscarriage and had come in thinking maybe something could be done to help her. It was her third one, and she knew better, but she'd come in anyway. She was about four weeks along, and he didn't want to sound like an ass and tell her that twenty-five years ago, she wouldn't have even known she was pregnant yet.

Early and very early pregnancy tests had made things difficult for women and ED doctors alike. Daniel felt terrible, and he knew that to the patient, it was a crushing blow. But he also knew that the reported rate of miscarriages was rising because of those very early pregnancy tests. Once upon a time, she never would have missed a period or known that she'd conceived. So he'd send her home with a prescription to get her HCG levels checked over the next two days and instructions to return if the bleeding got worse.

He went by another room, popping his head in the door and checking on the woman awaiting admission. She'd come in with a positive suitcase sign, meaning that she never intended to leave regardless that her complaint wasn't serious. Her large, polka-dotted suitcase rested against the wall as she busily scanned her phone. Meanwhile, the baby that the team just stopped doing CPR on lay cold and alone in the darkened room next to her.

God, this fucking job.

It took too much.

At his desk, he sipped Starbucks while he wrote discharge instructions for the miscarriage and signed the death certificate for the baby. There were newer nurses today and only a few of the more experienced ones. Luckily, the pagers had been mostly silent, and his day filled with vaginal exams, x-rays, and sutures, the non-accidental trauma aside.

The only thing Daniel hated more than night shift was the night shift turnaround to day shift. He knew he was a miserable bastard and made a conscious effort not to take it out on his staff and patients. He'd texted Elle and hadn't heard back, making his mood worse. She always answered unless she was asleep.

Maybe she was asleep.

The pager sounded, and he sighed, wishing he hadn't taunted the Trauma Gods by thinking about the pagers.

Pam was in charge, and she yelled across the department. He had his own pager, but he never looked at it. It was the charge nurse's job to keep him moving, and he let her do it. "P1. 36-year-old female. MVC. From scene. Three minutes out. Vitals unstable," she said, rising from her spot with a low groan. Pam was older than Daniel, and he wondered how she still did it. Most days, he felt like he was dying, but then again, maybe she did too. He knew Elle did, and he watched her suffer daily.

Daniel grabbed a lead apron and followed the trail of staff into the biggest resuscitation room, watching as nurses scurried to set up arterial lines and the Level-One. Had Elle been here, that shit would've been done at one minute after seven a.m. sharp. Nursing was an art that few practiced anymore, and despite recent events, Elle was still the best nurse he'd ever worked with.

Pam's phone rang as she sat down at the computer, ready to check the trauma in, and Daniel heard her gasp. "No," she said, her hand moving to her mouth. Her eyes snapped to his, and he knew something was wrong. "I understand," she said before hanging up and turning to the room. "Any medical or nursing students get the fuck out. This trauma is not for you," she started, her voice cracking before she steeled it again. "I mean it: get out." She leaned out the door, "Is the ERT here?" she yelled. "All of you, in here. Now. Chelsea and Michael- get out. Any resident less than a fourth year, get the fuck out."

"You can't do that," someone tried.

"I can, and I will. Get the fuck out now," Pam finished. Her face had gone deathly pale, and she handed the trauma sheet to an ERT nurse and donned lead. Pam was a damn good nurse, second only to Elle. Daniel felt the hair on his arms raise because he knew whatever was causing Pam to suit up was bad.

He looked across the team in the room and saw that only the best were gathered. "Daniel," Pam said, her voice gentler, and she was unable to hide the tremor as she spoke, "Please go. Please," she added. "MedCom called. It's Elle."

Daniel leaned against the steering handles on the stretcher as her words punched him in the gut. He took a shaking breath and gave himself precisely two seconds to let the pain roll through him before standing to his full height. "I'm not leaving, Pam. Get her stickers printed, and get the orders in the system so that there is no delay. Seven minutes to scan, right? We give our best to every patient that rolls through this door, but the best in this room right now is better than any of those times. If you live up to that, then so will I. So let's do this." Daniel met her stare with his own, and the room stayed silent as everyone thought about his words.

A hush settled over the people waiting behind the line. Everyone knew Elle. She made her mark good or bad on every person present. Med students might fear her, and some people might be intimidated by her, but everyone respected her. Eventually, Parker came flying around the corner, her eyes wide.

"Parker, no offense, but stay out of my room," Pam said when the woman crossed the line into the trauma bay. "This isn't the day for you to return to the bedside. Go play charge nurse if you want to do something." Pam didn't look up as she admonished the director that Elle hated with a passion.

Daniel watched the staff ready for the most important person in his life to roll through the door having the worst day of hers. She might think that day was when Keith died, but she'd be wrong. He'd been with her through that, and he damn sure wasn't walking away from her now.

He watched Parker leave, glad she didn't push the issue. Maybe she cared, but in reality, keeping Elle in the ED after she'd watched her husband die was a dick move. Everyone knew it. And here they were again in the same damn room, waiting on the same damn thing. It was torture, and it was the longest three minutes of his life. Elle was coming by ambulance, not Lifenet, and he was glad about that. It took forever to close both sides of the interstate so a helicopter could land, and with trauma, every second counts. He hoped Elle wasn't out of time. Daniel stared down at the patient ID band resting on the stretcher, tripping over the name on it.

Elle had always been Elle or Conroy. No one knew her by her married name, not even Daniel. Yet there it was in black and white: Elle Frazier. She should've always been Elle Ross, or maybe just Ross like he was to most people. Sighing, he readied himself for the worst trauma of his career.

Preston County EMS rolled through the door, making

everyone freeze. Daniel felt the blood drain from his face as he looked Elle over, not liking what he saw.

"Thirty-six-year-old-female. Single car rollover at highway speed or greater. She passed us a few miles before the accident, and we were doing seventy-five. She lost control on the last turn of Cheat Lake hill and overcorrected. We saw the whole thing. It took us a few minutes to get her out of the car. We scooped and ran," he finished, starting to move Elle to the stretcher. His voice shook as he spoke.

"Lowest BP and highest heart rate?" the trauma attending asked.

"Man, we are a BLS crew. We don't do this shit. Didn't want to leave her for the flyboys because they take too long, and we were right there. No one was even on the scene when we left with her. Her pulse was around 100, and I couldn't hear a blood pressure when I tried to take it. Let's move her," he added, looking pale and shaky himself.

Daniel understood. BLS crews could do basic care. They'd put her on a board for her back and stabilized her neck, but that was all. Then they'd undoubtedly driven like their ass was on fire, and he was okay with that. She was where she needed to be.

"On three," he said, cradling Elle by the collar around her cervical spine. "One, two." They moved Elle over, and the multiple simultaneous assessments began. He looked up and saw an ERT nurse standing on the chair so that her view of the room was unobstructed. She was scribing the trauma while the rest of the team danced the dance.

"Manual pressure 60 palp."

"Abrasions to her left arm. Deformities of her left wrist and fingers."

Elle moaned as the team moved around her. It was a long sound, low and pained. Daniel's eyes snagged on her blood-encrusted face, and his heart nearly stopped.

"Can we give some Versed and Fentanyl?" someone asked.

"4 milligrams Versed and 50 mics of Fentanyl. No nursing dose. Not with that BP."

"Sixteen gauge in the right AC," Pam said, ducking under the arm of the x-ray machine.

"Positive seat belt sign."

"Sats are eighty-eight."

"Versed and Fentanyl in."

"Facial burns to the forehead, nose, and cheeks. Laceration to the forehead. Laceration to the left upper arm. Laceration to the left shoulder."

"Laceration to the right knee. Bruising to the upper thighs."

"Two units on the Level-One."

"Laceration to the right hip."

"Heart rate 137"

"7.5 ET tube twenty-two at the lip," Daniel added after

he'd intubated Elle, forcing air into her lungs with the Ambu bag. "Positive color change on the easy cap. End Tidal CO2 47. Decreased breath sounds on the left," he finished, pulling his stethoscope away from Elle's now bared chest.

"Blood in the left ear and both nares."

"Pupils pinpoint and sluggish."

"Three percent bolus and start an infusion."

"Repeat pressure 70 palp."

"Positive fast exam."

"Initiate Mass transfusion."

"Three percent up."

"X-ray." No one moved or changed positions as the x-ray was taken and the films slid lower.

"Trauma triple lumen in the right femoral."

"Pelvis is unstable."

Daniel ducked intuitively as the arm of the portable x-ray retracted over Elle, and digital films were removed from the slots under the mattress.

"Sixteen French Foley, urine is clear."

"Eighteen French OG at fifty-five."

"ET tube is at the carina. OG verified. Left hemothorax."

"Repeat pressure 80 over 42. This one is reading on the monitor."

"Third unit of PRBCs in, fourth going up. Platelets in. Cryo up."

"Twenty-six French chest tube on the left. Positive blood."

"Sats are ninety-four."

"Let's get her off the board and go to scan."

"Arterial line left femoral. Pressure 94 over 56."

"Roll on three: one, two." Daniel supported Elle's neck, her bloodied hair trailing over his arms, and the team turned her to her side, keeping her neck and spine straight.

"Back clear, no step-offs."

"Back on three: one, two." Elle was rolled to her back. "Cervical spine clear, no step-offs," Daniel called out, replacing the collar around Elle's neck.

"OR or CT scan, Dr. Baer?" Daniel asked as the team began covering Elle in warmed blankets and packing up the monitors.

"Let's go to scan. I want to see what we've got. Pressure has stabilized. Keep the blood products running at a one-to-one ratio and bring the Level-One," the trauma surgeon answered.

Rachel came and took over the spot at the head of the bed. "She's mine now, Daniel. I've got her, I promise," she said, unlocking the bed and pushing the stretcher away from him. She bagged Elle expertly, driving one-handed and navigating the trash-strewn room as she headed down the hall.

Daniel choked out a sob and slid down the wall to the floor, his legs splaying in front of him. Elle looked horrible. She was pale. Her lips were white. She'd looked like she was already gone, but she was a fighter. She'd always been a fighter. She was the strongest person Daniel knew. He checked the clock on the wall. Six minutes and seven seconds. And that was unheard of. He'd never seen a P1 get the CT scan in that short amount of time.

He sighed from the floor, unable to get up. His head was spinning, and he felt pressure in his neck like the blood wasn't reaching his brain. He wanted to go to the scanner, but Rachel was right. Elle was in hands more capable than his now.

Daniel watched as nurses flit through the room, cleaning up and throwing towels onto the blood. But only nurses. And that was odd. His eyes narrowed as they watched him surreptitiously. A urine cup went in the trash and was replaced by another. A blood tube got tossed into the needle box on the wall, and another was labeled in its place.

And the royal blue wall went up.

Daniel watched it happen, saying nothing.

A few minutes later, Parker stuck her head in the door, finding Daniel still sitting on the floor and Pam finalizing trash pickup. "Make sure to send the tox screen and blood alcohol, Pam," she said.

"Okay, right here. There weren't orders for them," Pam said, scooping the tubes up.

"I'll send them," Parker added, grabbing the bags.

"She got Versed and Fentanyl before intubation," Daniel

said, meeting Pam's eyes. These nurses were good. They were damn good, he thought. They might fuck with each other daily, but they tolerated no one else doing the same. There'd been rumors going around about narcotic counts being off, but they'd stand by Elle anyway.

Finally, Daniel rose. He went to the computer to log in and check her lab results, noting that her hemoglobin was dangerously low and that her blood gas sucked. His hands shook, and all he could see was her mangled and bloodied body. There hadn't been a spot on her that was free of it.

They'd cut her clothes off, and she'd lain bared to all in the room. She would hate that. He remembered the awkward angle of her wrist and how blood had dried in trails down her arms. She had hung upside down. Limp. Dying. Alone.

He couldn't block it out. The pager sounded, and he jumped.

How had she done it? How had she put one foot in front of the other? How had she not cried and screamed during every trauma she'd been forced to work these last weeks?

He knew. At least he thought he did.

"Grade four spleen laceration; she might lose it," Rachel said, pushing the bloodied, empty stretcher by him. "Grade two liver laceration. Left radial-ulnar fracture. Left ribs are pretty much gone. Open book pelvic fracture with some vascular involvement. Subdural head bleed, but it's small. Back and neck were clean. It'll be a long road, but she'll make it." Rachel pushed the stretcher into the room; pooled blood outlined the spot where Elle once lay. "She's in the OR but is going to SICU ten."

"Thanks, Rachel. For everything," Daniel said, walking out.

When the dust settled, the House Supervisors called the night shift team, asking them to come in early. The department was wrecked after Elle's case, and nothing was getting done. Patients stacked up in the waiting room, and results went unchecked. Darkness in the form of thoughts and feelings draped the department, making it impossible to function.

Staff cried in alcoves or sobbed openly. From housekeeping to the unit clerks, no one was unaffected. Daniel took an Americano from his replacement and updated her on Elle. Last he checked, she was still in the operating room and not doing well. Her last documented blood pressures were too low and her heart rate too high. He hated that he knew what that meant. She was struggling, and he wished he could be oblivious to it like other loved ones.

Dismissed from duty, Daniel went to the SICU to wait in Elle's room. The charge nurse started to stop him, then closed her mouth and kept walking. Slumped in the chair in a corner, he waited.

Parker arrived a few hours later, waking him from a light

sleep in which he couldn't get away from Elle's bloodied face. "Her tox was negative. No alcohol either," she said. "Pam told me she pulled the urine before the sedation meds. I thought you'd want to know. There was nothing that would've caused the wreck," she added.

Daniel knew what had caused the wreck, but he didn't elaborate. He had also caught a whiff of alcohol when he'd leaned down to intubate Elle. Could it have been from the night before? Maybe. Maybe not. It wasn't strong, but it was strong enough that her blood alcohol level shouldn't be zero. Plus, she'd had Valium not that long ago, and that shit stuck around in your urine for a while. Regardless, his earlier suspicions were confirmed.

"Thanks, Parker. When this is over, you need to let her leave. It was never up to you where she transferred. I can't imagine coming to work tomorrow after what happened today, and Elle will survive. Keith didn't. She has nothing to prove to you."

Parker nodded her head and left him alone.

Hours later, the sound of the bed brakes releasing woke him. An OR team was in the room, taking the monitor and cables and piling them onto the bed. They left wordlessly, and Daniel sat up straighter, forcing himself awake. He rubbed his hands over his face, catching the five o'clock shadow that had grown while he waited.

It was almost midnight. Elle had been in surgery for over eight hours when finally the bed was pushed through the doors with her on it. She had color in her lips but was still deathly pale.

Her monitors beeped reassuringly, and a quick glance showed Daniel that her vital signs were stable. However, she was still covered in dried blood, and the sight of her bloodless feet sticking out from under the blankets gutted him.

"That was fucking terrible, Daniel. Not gonna lie," Dr. Baer said, sitting down next to him. "I don't ever want to do that shit again."

"But you will," Daniel said.

"Because we have to. You just never know when it's going to hit so close. Damn. She's a fighter. That bitch is tough as nails inside and out. It was touch and go for a while. I had to call in vascular surgery and interventional radiology, but she'll keep her spleen. They fixed her liver. Ortho plated her arm, a few ribs that weren't stable, and her pelvis. They also pinned her fingers. Neurosurgery signed off on the head bleed; no intervention there. I hate saying this, but she got lucky, Daniel. Jesus. I mean lucky for being unlucky. We always say that, but in her case, it really is true. Waiting on a helicopter would've killed her.

Those bastards saved her life, running with her like that.

"She's going to have a hell of a long recovery, but she'll

recover. I'm going to leave her tubed for a few days because of those ribs. Her lungs just aren't working well enough. Her chest was essentially crushed. In two to three months tops, she'll be right as rain. She'll need physical therapy but should be able to move on as if nothing happened," she closed her eyes for just a second before jumping up with a shake of her head. "Gotta go. There's a hot appendix waiting for me back in the OR," she said as she walked out the door, reminding Daniel why he went into emergency medicine and not surgery.

Elle lay peacefully, her left arm splinted and her right arm restrained so that she couldn't wake up and pull out her breathing tube. She was deathly still, and only the rise and fall of her chest and the colored numbers on the monitor let him know she was alive. But she was, and for that, he was grateful. He knew one thing for sure. He wouldn't ever leave her, not really, but when this was over, he would go. Maybe he needed to move on for both their sakes.

Chapter 20

Sunlight filtered into the room where I sat in a chair, looking at a brick wall through foggy glass. I felt the plastic tube down my throat and heard the quiet noise the ventilator made. I was intubated and sitting in a chair which could only mean one thing. I was in the SICU. Those crazy bitches got your dumb ass out of bed twice a day whether you wanted to get up or not-breathing tube and all. They were hardcore like that. Dialysis? In the chair. ECMO? In the chair, bitch. Broken from head to toe? You're getting the fuck up. No ifs ands or buts.

Hell, the cardiovascular ICU team walked their intubated patients on ECMO down the damn halls. No thanks. I wanted my intubated patients sedated. Have a nice nap; there will be no chairs for you today.

But why the hell was I intubated and in the SICU? My first thought was that maybe I overdosed. I chased that thought down a dead-end road, unable to catch it. I didn't think I'd overdosed. The last thing I remembered was driving. I chased a few more thoughts then gave up as claustrophobia set in.

I hated the feeling of the machine breathing for me and started fighting. I couldn't help it. I breathed in between when it wanted me to and tried to exhale against the pressure support. Alarms blared, and people came at a brisk walk into the room. It sucked.

"Calm down, Elle. We were just waiting for you to wake up to pull that tube, okay?" I looked through panicked eyes and saw Daniel beside me. "It's okay. You're okay. You're in the SICU. You had a car accident."

And then I remembered driving to Deep Creek Lake. I remembered the woman. After that, everything goes blank, but accident victims from severe wrecks seldom remember what happened, which was probably a blessing. My body ached, and each breath was pained. My left wrist was screaming, and there was an ache so deep inside of me as to seem impossible.

My eyes flashed to Daniel's again, and he smiled tightly. "You're okay, Elle," he said, using my name and not one of his many nicknames. That worried me more than anything else. "They'll pull the tube. Just give them a second."

I lay my head back, closing my eyes. It was hard, but I gave in to the steady rise and fall of the ventilator while the respiratory therapist made a few adjustments. She turned off the rate and pressure support, allowing me to breathe on my own through the tube as the team was notified and the nurse got ready.

I knew that they needed a few minutes to set up for reintubation should I fail to fly. I wanted to tell them not to waste their time, but as I had a plastic paper towel roll shoved down my windpipe, I had to skip it and focus on breathing.

Daniel's hand was warm in mine. I could feel the cold edges of my fingers against his warmer ones. His steady support made the situation tolerable. When this was over, I was buying him Starbucks for life.

Pressure was relieved in my throat as the cuff was deflated on the ET tube. Before I knew it, the tube was pulled, and I was coughing and hacking as the therapist sucked disgusting stuff from my mouth. "Don't try to say anything yet. Just focus on breathing: in through your nose and out through your mouth. I put a nasal canula on you. You have a chest tube that can hopefully come out in a few days. You might need the extra juice until then.

I nodded my head, closing my eyes as I leaned into the back of the chair. They took a big risk pulling that tube while I was up. They must've had faith in me. I was suddenly exhausted. The energy I felt upon waking leaked out or had been pulled from me with the tube.

"Rest a little, Elle," Daniel said as he pulled a chair beside me. I'll stay until they're sure you won't need reintubated. Just focus on breathing. I heard the chair squeak and felt his hand in mine as I drifted off to thoughts of why.

Chapter 21

When I awoke again, I was in bed. The blinds were open to the night sky, and I was alone. I shifted slightly, taking the pressure off my left hip. Loneliness echoed inside my head, and the sense of loss I felt seemed instinctual. I shifted again, unable to get comfortable.

"Hey, Elle. Can I get you anything?" A nurse who I thought was named Lindsay poked her head into the room. Lindsay worked the night shift, which is why I didn't know her very well. "Do you want some pain medicine?"

"I'll take some Motrin," I answered, thinking that would be enough to ease the dull ache in the center of my pelvis.

"I guess it's been enough to get an order for Motrin. You know they hate giving that if you had bleeding, but you should be good."

"How long has it been?" I asked, confused. They just pulled my ET tube; I couldn't believe I'd been intubated that long, and I still didn't understand why.

"You've been here ten days, Elle. I'm sorry. You know how it is; you lose time. We extubated you four days ago.

My heart sank, and I felt tears threaten. I didn't remember any of it. I remembered the chair and getting extubated. Maybe there were flashes of memories here and there, but nothing concrete, yet somehow, ten days had passed.

"How am I doing?" I asked, glossing over the traumatic amnesia.

"You're doing great. Really, really, good. You should've gone to step down two days ago, but Dr. Baer kept you here. You should go home in a few days unless you need rehab."

"I don't want rehab," I said, shifting in bed again.

"Elle. You had extensive injuries. Maybe we can get you up and moving, and maybe not. You haven't been doing much. You've given us a run for our money," she laughed, shaking her head. "Not that I expected anything different."

She ran through my injuries, and I got the feeling that she'd done it with me before. But whatever fog that had kept me from remembering things lifted, and finally, it stuck. I'd had a head bleed, so none of this was surprising. I learned that Daniel had stayed with me the entire time and had been helping care for me. I wasn't surprised by that either. Lindsay told me that he'd just left today and that I'd given him a run for his money too.

They say that nurses make terrible patients, and it seemed that I upheld that stereotype honorably. Staff came into my room to share stories and laugh at me throughout the rest of the night. And that's when I knew I'd turned a corner. You don't laugh at someone who might not make it; you save that for when they are healing. A few night shift nurses from the ED came up too, enjoying the break and laughter at my expense.

No one mentioned the accident or asked me what happened. They simply laughed because I'd called the ortho doctor a choad and had thrown him out of my room. They said that I hadn't liked the color of his scrubs and that it had set me off. I remembered nothing. Then there was the time I said thank you, sir, and asked for another when they pulled out my chest tube. That had them all going. I'd also apparently quoted Monty Python and insisted that I wasn't dead yet. In my defense, I was highly medicated at the time.

I asked to get up, and they brought me a walker, reminding me that my pelvis was broken. I eased out of bed, and with their help, I got into the chair and waited for shift change. I felt stronger than I remembered feeling, and I hoped it lasted.

It was mid-morning when Daniel came to see me. I had walked with physical therapy and was back in my chair, exhausted from that small effort, but he smiled when he saw me anyway. I'd been allowed to shower and was perfectly clean for the first time since the wreck. Despite the nurses' best efforts, I still pulled shards of glass from my hair as I sat on the shower chair, enjoying the hot water.

"Hey," Daniel said as he walked through the door. I was moving to step down today and was glad he'd come before I changed rooms. "You look good, he added, assessing me with a practiced eye as he pulled a chair next to mine.

"Thanks," I said. "I feel pretty good." I reached for his hand, and he gave it over, not meeting my eyes. He looked exhausted, and dark circles under his eyes accentuated the fine lines that seemed to have sprouted overnight. He hadn't shaved in a few days, and the facial hair gave him a hard edge not usually there.

He sighed, his shoulders slumping as he looked out the window at the brick wall. "Do you know what I remember about my residency, Elle?" he started. "You. That's all I remember because it's always been you. I should never have pushed you away. Let you push me away. I just didn't think we could make it right then and didn't want to be a statistic. We were so young and so damned driven. I thought there'd be time, and then you met Keith."

"Daniel," I started, but he interrupted before I could get any more out.

"No, Elle. Let me finish," he said, taking a breath. "God, you were so cute with your hair tied back in a ribbon and your bright smile. Look at you now, Elle. God, this place has changed you. But don't think it hasn't changed me too. This fucking job. It sucks the life out of you one minute at a time until there isn't anything left to take. No one should have to do this shit, but someone has to, right? That's the duality of it." He stopped, carding his fingers through his hair and tugging on it so it stood straight up, and I knew I wasn't going to like what was coming.

I thought back, remembering the day on the lake and how I felt something was looming. Daniel had wanted to tell me something for a long time, and I'd been too wrapped up in myself to push for answers.

"You're going to die here, Elle, and I'm going to die somewhere else because I can't do this anymore. I can't watch you speed up the process. I cleaned your house for you. And your truck. I threw it all away. All that shit you had stockpiled and stolen from the department, I tossed it all. I fucking love you. I always have, and I'll never stop, but I can't watch you destroy your life for a man that didn't deserve it."

"Wait," I interrupted.

"No, Elle. I've waited long enough. Where was Keith going when he wrecked? Where were you coming from when you almost died. His fucking cross that you didn't plant is twenty feet from where I would've planted yours. Where were you?" His voice rose, and his hand shook in mine. He was angry, and no doubt he deserved to be.

"I. He. He was going to work," I said, feeling hot tears pool in my eyes and slide down my face as I stared at Daniel unblinking.

"No, Elle, he was driving westbound on I-68. Westbound is toward town from the opposite direction of your house. He wrecked first thing in the morning. Where was he coming from? Don't answer that because I know, and so do you.

"Here's what you don't understand. You nurses sit at the desk and talk about everything. No subject is taboo, and we love that about you. But we hear everything. How many times did you complain to Kelsey or Rachel that Keith didn't come home or came home late? How many times did you mention that something didn't add up? That you were suspicious? How many times did you say there can't be that many emergencies in financial planning?

"I'm not saying that you should have jumped for joy when he died, but you damn sure shouldn't have tried to follow him to the grave, Elle. I can't do this; I can't. I love you more than anything. I breathe to see you smile," he paused, finally looking my way. Tears welled in his eyes, spilling over long lashes as he looked into my soul.

He took a deep breath, letting it out before starting again. "Before Keith died, I accepted a locum tenens position. I thought it was time to move on, but I delayed going because I didn't want to leave you until you were settled, but I have to go, Elle. I need to go. I need to do this for me, and I hope you understand that this isn't me leaving you. I'm always there, but I can't be here. And someday, if you want to find a way to us, you know where I'll be. I'm sorry, Elle. I love you so much, and I'll never stop, but I need to love myself a little more right now."

Then Daniel stood, leaving me to look up at him as tears rolled down my face and ragged sobs rocked my chest. He leaned forward, placing a soft kiss on my forehead. And then the last constant in my life walked out the door.

Chapter 22

I stood outside the doors of the emergency department, taking a deep breath. It had been thirteen weeks since my accident, and I still didn't remember what had happened. I didn't think I ever would, and I was okay with that. I had been through excruciating physical and psychological therapy to get ready for this day. I walked a little slower and had a limp that might never go away, but it wasn't pronounced and didn't slow me much.

Daniel had been right. He'd been more right than I ever dreamed. I'd had to unpack a lot of trauma to my headshrinker, and looking back, his leaving was the best thing for both of us. There is no way forward if your head is turned backward. The past may follow us forever, but it should always be behind you and not clouding the road forward. I knew that finally.

I heard the pagers start through the door, and I didn't cringe. I saw both sides of the coin now. My heart didn't drop, and my breathing didn't increase. This emergency department had saved my life and saved others' lives daily. Yes, people died. But a group of well-trained and experienced experts had come together and pulled a rabbit out of the hat, and my life had been spared. I was part of that. I valued my contribution to that team more than I focused on my personal loss.

When you work at the only level one trauma center in the region, you'll face your worse fears, and someone you love will come in and die. It's the way it was. As healthcare professionals, sometimes we win, and sometimes we lose. I accepted it.

I'd loved Keith, and he'd loved me. I knew that too. Maybe our relationship was strained, and maybe we'd have divorced someday, but I wouldn't doubt that he'd loved me. His affair didn't cheapen what we had, and I loved him enough to let him go and move on. No more lies, and no more looking back. The road ahead was uncertain, but I was excited to see where it went.

Intentionally or not, Keith had left me wealthy. If I lived frugally, I could retire on what he'd amassed, but there was a brand new Corvette at the Chevy dealership that had my name on it. I wanted that black beauty desperately, and I'd have it.

I'd be bored at home anyway. Parker had been right, too; trauma is in my blood. Live or die, life or death I would always be an emergency nurse. Maybe I didn't want the big ones every day anymore, but I would deal with them when they came. And you want me to. If it is your day to test fate, you want me there for you, and I would be body, mind, and soul.

The pagers sounded again, and I smiled as I pushed through

the doors.

"P1 coming, Elle. Parker said you were okay with being in the bays, so get your ass in there. Play time's over," the night shift charge nurse said, tossing me a phone and a lead apron. She strode through the door, making a mic drop motion, leaving the dumpster fire behind her like a good nurse should. "PS," she added, stopping to look over her shoulder. "Glad you're back." She gave me a big smile and a little wink as she walked away.

The ten-minute ETA on the P1 was more like five, but I had the arterial line, Level-One, and IV start supplies ready and waiting when the crew arrived. Everyone looked my way with cautious smiles and friendly waves. They were happy I was back, and I was too, if I was honest, and I'd promised myself no more lies.

Drugs and alcohol were the lies that got me through the worst time of my life. Only they hadn't. Not really. They allowed me to be functional in a dysfunctional environment, and I never would've gotten better seeing through the lens they provided. Thankfully, I hadn't been addicted and hadn't had a habit to kick physically. All my issues were mental, and I was dealing with them.

No more lies.

Trauma is like a rock thrown into still waters. The bigger the rock, the longer those ripples travel. But there is an end to them. When the ripples run out of energy, still waters return. I know that now. I'd survived not only personal trauma but the trauma every single day on my job caused. No more lies.

I loved it; I did. But no more shoving those images down to resurface at a later time. No matter what, I'd look at those ripples until they had no more energy, then I'd move on because as heroic as some of my actions are, I was right; I am no hero.

Yes, it was a tragedy, but every day was another day forward. As much as I loved Keith, I'd loved Daniel, who was right about that too. Maybe Keith had known, and that pushed him toward another woman. Although I wasn't ever going to doubt our relationship or look too closely at my role in its end. Still, I could admit that I'd always loved Daniel as more than a friend.

I was finding my way back to us. He was my something and my everything. When the last piece of the puzzle fell into place, I was finding him. But that wasn't right now. Now Someone had taken a car to a truck fight, and that didn't work out well for anyone. For once, that memory didn't haunt me.

Keith had taken a motorcycle to a car fight. It had been his choice, just as it had been mine to stay and fight for his life. Neither choice was wrong, but neither choice had worked out. I worked every day to move beyond that.

"Sixty-seven-year-old male in a multi-vehicle rollover. Got trapped under the box of a semi, then got kicked out and lost control. GCS is 8, and he was tubed on scene. Eight-oh twenty-three at the lip. Highest heart rate 133 and lowest BP 70s. Move on three: one, two," the paramedic said as we moved the man over, and the dance began for me. I loved dancing, and I loved *this* dance. Seven minutes to CT scan and rapid infusers save lives. They saved my life, and I could make that happen for this guy too. As a team, we can do things others can't, and maybe, just maybe, some days we are heroes.

"Fourteen gauge left AC," I said, hooking up the Level-One.

"God, you're a dick,"

"Am not." The smile that spread on my face was genuine, and I felt my eyes crinkle in the corners from the force of it.

"Abrasions to the left chest, positive seat belt sign."

"BP 68/40"

"Four units on the Level-One."

"First unit up."

"Deformity to the right lower leg."

"Positive fast."

"Art line ready."

"Arterial pressure 84/60," I reported after a glance at the monitor.

"God, we missed you."

"Second unit up in the Level-One. I missed you too, but time's ticking."

"Central line won't thread," one of the residents growled.

"Third unit up on the Level-One." I chuckled, knowing my line was better anyway.

"Elle already put a goddamned fourteen gauge in. We'll get a clean line in the OR."

"Fourteen gauge in the right AC," I chuckled.

"That's just ridiculous. Now you're showing off."

"Scan or OR?"

"OR. Spleen's toast."

And just like that, my patient rolled out the door. Rachel stood with her arms crossed, watching the trauma from the wall. She shook her head, smiling as she intercepted me and took over driving so I could get report on my other patient. Seven minutes and ten seconds. I was slow, but I'd also done a lot of it myself while people watched from the sidelines, and I was okay with that. I felt good. Not only did I feel good, I felt alive.

The day passed much the same way. Traumas came and went. Strokes got clot busters or interventional radiology and went on their way. Some people would live, and some people would die, but I gave it my all regardless. I said hello to all my new friends in the SICU on the multiple occasions that I took them patients, noting their smiles when they saw me. It probably wasn't often that they saw their success stories push a stretcher through the door. Maybe I made it worth it to them too, and maybe, just maybe, one of them felt like a hero because of me. It was a good day.

On the way to my truck, a trio of helicopters circled, waiting their turn to land and offload someone likely having the worst day of their life. Their lights blinked green and red in the dark, and the blue lettering was lit by a single clear light. I stopped, watching their progress. Lifenet was busy, and multiple bases were represented above me.

They really were beautiful. I watched the bird on the roof rise and dodge to the side so that the helicopter with the next sickest patient could land. The sound of the blades made my heart beat faster and not in a bad way.

Smiling, I finished the long walk to my truck.

The next few weeks passed quickly. Ice and snow made treacherous roadways worse, and even though winter was almost over, trauma season never ended. Soon it would be spring, and the shit would hit the fan in earnest.

It was a late winter's day when I walked into work to the sound of laughter and the feeling of peace. "Good night?" I asked.

"The best," someone answered. "We saw, like, twelve total patients."

The day shift groaned as one unit.

"That means we'll get our asses handed to us today. You spent all night taunting the Trauma Gods, didn't you?" I asked, smiling from behind my hand.

"We watched Netflix."

"And chilled."

Laughter erupted, and I shook my head because I was in charge, and I'd need to do some stretches. You might have a good four hours. Maybe even a good eight. But a good twenty-four was unheard of in a place like this, so the flood gates would open.

And open they did.

I laughed and smiled through the day, knowing something that the others didn't. It was so busy that Parker ordered pizza to appease the staff, even though no one had time to eat it. It was a nice thought, and management's go-to in that situation. I liked pizza, so I was okay with it. I was off for the next six days. Technically, anyway.

As the day went on, my smile grew larger and came more freely. I wrote for a half-dozen traumas and worked a half dozen more. I took a stroke to the CT scan with the ERT team and shot the breeze with the techs before returning to the department.

When the clock struck seven-oh-one, I raised my voice. "I love you all," I started. "These have been the best worst years of my life. I'm so grateful to have met each of you. You've made a lasting mark on me that can't be erased. But, as much as I love cake, I hate long goodbyes and farewell parties, so I'm going to keep it simple. I quit." I said, taking a long look around at the place that had been my life for longer than it should have. I didn't hate it anymore; it just was. Like everything else, it was good and bad. It was a part of me. Maybe it never should have been, but there is no changing the past. I'd certainly learned that.

Around me, people laughed, smiling at my joke. I used to say this all the time, and it had gotten to be a running theme. I'd say I quit until my next shift, only this time I meant it. There would be no more shifts for me, not here. I unclipped my badge, sitting it down with my phone and pager. As I walked by Parker's door, I stuck in my head. "I quit. You were right, but I quit anyway." And with that, I said goodbye to the last vestige of my past. I hadn't needed to prove anything, but I'd done it anyway. I'd done it for myself and for whatever the future brought me.

Chapter 23

"Sugar," I said, working on perfecting my tone. I'd lost my southern accent over the years I'd been gone, but it had come back quickly. "Y'all need to wear more sunscreen and maybe a hat, darlin'. Bless your heart. Here's some cream for that sunburn." I discharged my last patient for the shift from the tiny emergency room at the edge of the world.

I'd been on the job two weeks, establishing a place for myself. Initially, the staff kept me at arm's length, thinking I was a know-it-all hotshot from some fancy trauma center up north. Then the inevitable happened, and a bad trauma came in. Yes, The Medical University of South Carolina was right down the road, but the patient needed to be stabilized immediately before being flown there. They had the tools, but I had the experience, and together we saved that man's life. Since then, I've been one of them instead of an outsider.

I clocked out, sliding into the cool leather seats in my new redline corvette. It was the sexiest thing I'd ever seen with its blacked-out color scheme and small red accents scattered about the body. The days were getting longer, and the sun had barely set, leaving the sky with a hint of light. I turned the car north, driving past my rental and into town. I rolled slowly, enjoying the delicious purr of the engine and the way it felt under my seat.

I'd sold everything but my truck. It had been the one thing I'd been unwilling to let go of, so I kept the old beast for that one day a year this place got snow. I'd let go of everything else, starting over at a time in my life I never dreamed I would. I slid the sleek machine to a stop, closing the door quietly, before making my way across the sand.

A dim crescent moon highlighted a lone figure near the edge of the shore, and I made my way there. Daniel and I had always loved this spot. It had been one of our favorites. We'd swore that someday we would retire here and treat jellyfish stings and sunburns instead of heartwrenching traumas and high acuity disasters. It was a good way to go, and I certainly wasn't complaining.

I sat next to him, saying nothing. We watched the gentle rise and fall of the waves at low tide. Seagulls slept, bobbing on the water, and the only thing around us was darkness and a deep sense of peace.

"Took you long enough," he said eventually, breaking the silence.

I smiled, shaking my head. I had been ready weeks ago, but the sale of the house and all the stuff in it had taken longer than I planned, and I had wanted to start my job and get settled before I sought him out. He worked at the larger hospital a few miles up the Grand Strand, but I was still surprised I hadn't run into him. I was renting a motel room by the week, though, because I had other plans for my long-term living arrangements that I was committed to.

"What do you want to do tomorrow?" I asked, laying my head on his shoulder and twining my fingers with his.

He gripped my hand, and I didn't miss the slight tremor that ran through him as he answered, "Well, I thought maybe we could go to that miniature golf course that you like. You know, the one with the dinosaurs and the fog? We haven't been there in years."

"That's a good idea. Maybe hit the Rainbow Grille after?"

"Hot damn. Yes. I'd forgotten about that place. Have you found somewhere to stay?" he asked, finally looking my way. His face lit up when he took me in. "God, you look terrific, Elle. You look so good. Like a weight has been lifted off your shoulders." His green eyes danced in the light, and I thought the same about him. Sometimes change is bad, but sometimes change is good.

"I've been here a couple of weeks. I wanted to get the lay of the land. You know, get my sea legs. But I thought, maybe I could stay with you. I don't know, like forever." I smiled, trying to keep the pit in my stomach from growing.

It was a risk. It was a considerable risk, but I didn't care. I loved Daniel, always had, always would. No more lies.

He was worth whatever risk I had to take. We were better together. As friends and as family, it had always been Daniel and me.

Since he left, we'd talked on the phone a few times, but nothing much. He'd texted and told me he loved and missed me, but we'd kept it short. Still, I'd taken every one of his words to heart because he'd meant them. Daniel and I were celestial bodies on a crash course. There was no other ending to the story than for us to collide, finally joining our souls on the same path.

"Half of the closet is empty and waiting, and it has been for a long, long time," he laughed. "I thought you'd never get your head out of your ass," he said, putting his arm around me and pulling me to him. "God, Elle. I love you. I'm so glad you found me. I've missed you every day." His voice shook with emotion until it was a full-on sob. We held each other by the water, letting the sound wash us clean.

"I love you too, Daniel. It's something that's always been and always will be. I'd given up on myself, but you never did, and I know that. Thank you," I said.

Daniel may have been part of my past, but he was also part of tomorrow and the next thousand tomorrows that came after. I smiled at the thought, placed a kiss on the side of his cheek, and said, "Come on, Daniel. Let's go home." I pulled him to his feet, grabbed his hand, and together we walked into the night.

Acknowledgments:

I can't thank the pharmacists at work enough. Jeff, Amanda, and Cavan answered my crazy questions without blinking, helping me develop the perfect date rape combo for my imperfect situation. Thanks for not having me fit tested daily. Or arrested. I told you it was for a book.

As always, a huge shout out to my team for listening to me go on (and on) about this one. It was more challenging than the others, and talking about it helped me find the way forward. Taking something that we do every day and turning it into *Trauma* was hard. So many things about this book *could* be true. They aren't, but they could be. That made it mentally tough, and the team helped a ton.

And finally, to Heather. Thanks for reading the rough drafts, finding the extra words, and the Younglings hanging by their fingers...

About Sharilyn

Sharilyn spent most of her early years on the Grand Strand of SC, annoying local police officers and pretty much everyone else. She graduated from the University of South Carolina and now lives on a small farm outside of Morgantown, WV, with her family and various farm animals.

In her spare time, Sharilyn masquerades as one of the many superhero RNs working to make lives better. With over twenty-five years of experience, her knowledge of healthcare in general and trauma specifically is extensive and often finds its way into her writing.

Sharilyn writes Urban Fantasy, Fairy Tales, Omegaverse romance, and women's fiction. Each title in her Omegaverse series, Omegas of The New South, spent weeks on Amazon's best sellers list, and her Healer series has a following that borders on cultish. (She adores you, you crazy Lara Hennessey fans!)

She loves showing Quarter horses, trail riding, reading, and being annoyed by her kids. If she is missing, check for her horse trailer. If it is missing, no worries, she'll be back. Probably.

More by Sharilyn Skye:

Healer Series: Series Complete
Cerridwen's Tears
Healer
House of Fire
The Scarlet Heron
The Flame Keeper
Goddess Bound

The Eight Series:
Airmed
Ravena
Teagan

The Omegas of The New South:
The Omega Rule
The Omega Challenge
An Alpha's Grace
An Omega's Choice: Predators and Prey
An Alpha's Ruin

Goddess Rising Series: Lara Hennessey returns
Goddess Rising: Spring 2022

Trauma

Follow Sharilyn on Facebook, Instagram, Twitter, Goodreads, and her plain old website.
www.sharilynskye.com

Made in the USA
Monee, IL
27 May 2022

97111806R00185